A Perfect Match

THE CRICKET CLUB
BOOK 1

MARGAUX THORNE

ARE YOU SIGNED UP FOR DRAGONBLADE'S BLOG?

You'll get the latest news and information on exclusive giveaways, exclusive excerpts, coming releases, sales, free books, cover reveals and more.

Check out our complete list of authors, too!

No spam, no junk. That's a promise!

Sign Up Here

www.dragonbladepublishing.com

Dearest Reader;

Thank you for your support of a small press. At Dragonblade Publishing, we strive to bring you the highest quality Historical Romance from some of the best authors in the business. Without your support, there is no 'us', so we sincerely hope you adore these stories and find some new favorite authors along the way.

Happy Reading!

CEO, Dragonblade Publishing

Prologue

IT WAS LOVE at first sight.

Her breath was stolen the moment she walked out into the sunlight and the soles of her soft leather boots crunched the tops of the dewy morning grass. In all her ten years, Miss Myfanwy Wright had never encountered something so disparate from the welter of her ordinary life.

Myfanwy's tears had been left at home; the solitary misery that had filled her days and nights had been whisked away by the hushed breeze of the open field. Its vastness had lain before her like a magic carpet ready and willing to carry her anywhere. She'd been ripe for the picking, and she'd never stood a chance against the fresh allure of it all.

Myfanwy's father held her hand that day as they'd surveyed the pitch. His grip was warm and strong while he dragged her from end to end, eagerly reciting everything he knew about the game and the players. It was a revelation to her—every little bit of it. The men with their grass-stained white flannels, the numbers and statistics that tripped and rolled from her father's mouth like he was speaking in tongues. The experience was religious and unorthodox, otherworldly and yet very much on the mortal plane.

Myfanwy had been nervous for the match to begin. When

they took their seats in the pavilion, she had assumed her father would forget her as he had done over the past months. Her young heart hadn't the strength to blame him. Losing one's mother was one thing; losing a soulmate was another. And her parents had truly been that—soulmates of the highest order. So, she could bite away the disappointment whenever he seemed to look through her as she spoke, or when he would flee from the dining table abruptly without any sort of apology. If her mother's unexpected death had taught Myfanwy anything, it was that men weren't particularly equipped to deal with pain.

That was women's work.

Men like her father, the Viscount Newton, needed diversions. They needed games and play. They needed cricket.

Up until that day, Myfanwy hadn't thought she needed anything. Her mother was gone; *needing* would now become a thing of the past, a childlike luxury that she could no longer afford.

But then the teams took the pitch, and that naïve thought soared from Myfanwy's youthful head faster than the first bowl.

Because that was when she first saw him.

And in a year when Myfanwy's life had cracked and splintered and ultimately shattered, it changed one more time. Her father's excited voice picked up, buzzing in the background, but it was lost to her. A different kind of humming had taken hold of the young girl, a humming she had never experienced before. A verve, an energy, sparked repeatedly inside her, making it hard to sit. Myfanwy tucked her hands underneath her thighs and leaned forward on her bench, absorbed by the action.

To the outside observer, cricket can be a head-scratching thing, an incredibly British game where rules—both arbitrary and not—are dealt with in the most respectable of fashion. It was a game for Englishmen. More importantly, a game for *gentlemen*.

But Myfanwy was no gentleman, and neither was the man she watched on the field that day. And yet she was still drawn to the allure.

Looking back, she often wondered if the sport would have

had the same effect on her had her mother not died. Surely her father wouldn't have taken her to the match in an attempt to get her out of her room and repair what had been so recently fractured.

Without that stinging loss, would Myfanwy have been able to appreciate the spine-tingling crack of the ball off the bat, or the dizzying spin of the ball as it shot up from the ground? Would she have been able to understand the steely determination in her player's eyes as he tramped up to the wicket?

Would she have understood cricket—and him—so plainly without her heartache?

But despite being a game with so many rules, so many players, so many scenarios considered after each and every ball thrown, at that moment, it was remarkably simple to her and would be forever after.

As he lined up his stance, gripping the bat, he held his destiny in his hands. He had to withstand.

Withstand the bowler who was trying to bowl him out.

Withstand the fielders who were trying to catch him out.

With every bowl, he had to fight just to stay alive, to stay in the game. Every swing could be his last; every stroke of his bat could be his downfall.

So, you took it one bowl at a time, one hit at a time, one run at a time. Because when it felt like everything from God to men and even nature was trying to force you to your knees, you only had yourself.

And you stayed alive no matter what.

It was so obvious to Myfanwy.

Cricket wasn't a game. Cricket was life, and for the first time in a long time, she felt alive.

It was love at first sight.

Chapter One

London, England 1848

SAMUEL EVERETT WAS in a foul mood. But that wasn't anything new. His left leg smarted like a bastard. That wasn't new either. What was unique about his situation was that he was behind his bar instead of sitting at his corner table, as he preferred most nights. He was pulling pints instead of downing them. It was enough to make a thirsty man growl, and Samuel was very thirsty.

"Where's Tim?"

Samuel looked up from wiping a pint glass to find Joe Danvers leaning over the bar counter. One wouldn't be able to guess it now, but Joe used to be so fast, he could smack a ball right at the defense and still make it to the wicket before the fielder could throw down the stumps. He was a hell of a cricketer, and now he was so bloated and red-faced that he could barely hold himself up from the counter with those once-famous legs.

"Tim's out tonight," Samuel answered, filling the pint glass he'd just cleaned with fresh ale. "His wife's going through it again. Said he had to stay by her side."

He placed the pint glass in front of the old cricketer even though it almost killed him to do it. The last thing Joe needed was more to drink, but who was Samuel to deny him? No longer his captain, Samuel was a genteel proprietor. He owned the Flying Batsman Tavern and Inn, and proprietors needed customers.

Joe scooped the ale up quickly and was about to dump it down his gullet before he remembered his manners and held it up for a salute. "You're a good one, Sam. Much obliged. I'm sure Tim's wife appreciates the time you're giving him."

"I don't know about that." Samuel chuckled, stroking a hand over his smooth chin. "This is their seventh child. I should probably be keeping Tim away from his missus as much as possible."

Joe laughed in his drink, his grizzled face taking on such a wistful expression that Samuel could almost see the boy inside the beaten man. "Oh, to be so in love. Good for the couple. I remember what that's like, to be so obsessed with a lass that you couldn't be away from her for longer than a few hours."

All this maudlin talk only made Samuel's leg ache more. "Shut it, you bastard. You know as well as I that the only thing you ever loved was cricket."

Joe sniffed, and for a terrifying moment, Samuel worried that his old friend might break out into tears. "No," he said softly. "There was a girl once. A long, long time ago."

"I call bullshit to that!" a man next to Joe said, slamming into his side. Benny Hardcastle. The only cricketer that Sam knew who valued bowling balls into a man's crotch more than taking wickets. With his three chins waving as he chortled, Benny had also seen better days. The Flying Batsman was turning into a mausoleum for dreams long gone.

Joe shrugged off the interloper. "Stop fooling with me, Benny," he grumbled before taking another long swallow of the amber liquid. "I was in love, I was. Still am."

That was enough to sober Benny—metaphorically. "Oh, you know I didn't mean anything by it. Go on, Joe. Tell us all about her."

Samuel could have kissed the old bruiser. With Benny at the

helm, Samuel could slide away from the sentimental cricketer without Joe noticing. That was why he preferred to drink in his corner. No one bothered him with old, sappy stories of bygone days there. In the corner, Samuel could drown his own sorrows while he watched everyone else make him rich.

If he had told his eighteen-year-old self that he would one day own a successful inn and tavern on the outskirts of London, he wouldn't have believed it. Back then, Samuel only had eyes for one thing—sport. Earning a fortune was the farthest thing from his mind. Getting out of Nottinghamshire was the main reason Samuel woke up early in the morning. Proving to his father he could make it as a professional cricketer, and not a bricklayer like him, was a close second.

Luckily, Samuel's youthful stupidity and lack of forethought had been noticed by a wiser, older gentleman. For some reason Samuel would never understand, Viscount Newton had noticed him on the pitch one day while he'd been playing for the county and taken a liking to him. The older man had created a project out of Samuel, making sure he didn't piss away his earnings on women and alcohol like his fellow players. The viscount advised Samuel away from the drink and taught him the importance of saving and investing. Till his dying day, Samuel could never thank the man enough. As his teammates continued to play into old age due to debts and lack of options, Samuel had been able to walk— or hobble—away from cricket on his own terms with a tidy nest egg. And he refused to look back. Walking without grimacing was a chore, and one of his eyes was all but dead, but Samuel's hands were still sound, and he would hold on to his dignity with every ounce of energy in his body.

However, there were downsides to owning successful inns. And they were similar to his years as captain of all his various cricket teams. When everything went to shit, all eyes flew to him, and damned if Samuel ever let a team down.

Having said all that, he wasn't above claiming the spoils of his fame. He hadn't run onto a cricket pitch in three years, but his name still preceded him most places he went with hushed awe. *Samuel Everett...one of the best cricketers to ever play the game.* He never wasted money on women because he never had to. Women came to him. Even with his milky eye and spoiled temperament, Samuel remained a man that women were drawn to. Like flies to honey, the female gaze still sought him out, and as long as they didn't yearn for a sweet word after the fact, he was only so happy to oblige them.

Like the brown-haired woman sitting between two older ladies at the far table in the corner. She'd been giving him come-hither looks for the past hour. Samuel didn't pretend not to notice. What was the point? Subterfuge wasn't a language he spoke. Blunt honesty was what made those liaisons palatable. The woman seemed perfect for what he needed at the present. Not too young, not too old—hopefully a widow. Just passing through from *I don't care* to *who knows where.* She would slake a need, and he would dutifully do the same.

Samuel was a professional. More than anything, he understood the value of a transaction. Nothing in life was free—cricket and sex were no exception. If you were going to play, you had to make sure you gave as well as you got. And that was why Samuel could still hear people shouting his name—on the field *and* in the bedroom.

He offered the woman a lazy half-smile. It felt so rusty, he could almost hear the hinges squeaking around his jaw, but it did the trick. The woman's cheeks bunched merrily as she grinned, and her eyelashes batted with blatant invitation. Samuel wondered if she was sharing a room with the older ladies or if she had her own. No matter—a woman like that could always be counted on to find a way downstairs after her traveling partners retired. He had a hunch that this wasn't her first foray into the nighttime habits of inns. And Samuel kept an office in the back that could work in a pinch.

He just had a few more hours. A few more hours of pulling pints and pretending to listen to the old cricketers who desperately wanted to relive their better days. A few more hours of standing on this bastard of a leg before he could sink himself into her plummy flesh, losing the pain and sorrows and responsibilities, if only for a little lonely while—

"Oh, bartender," a familiar feminine voice sang from down the counter, breaking off his prurient ruminations. In the process of cleaning a new glass, Samuel gripped it so tight he thought it might shatter. "I'm awfully parched and have been waiting for what seems like hours. Are you always so slow to serve your customers?"

Samuel slammed the pint on the wood and limped over to that grating, oh-so-womanly voice. His body must hate him. The cockstand that had started to grow at the thought of his upcoming interlude doubled in size with the emergence of the new voice. The hindrance of a wench was trying to get under her skin, and she had no idea how well she achieved that goal.

He kept his eyes downcast when he reached her, his words coming out guttural and fierce. "Go home."

He could hear the smile in his ward's response. "Oh, that's no way to greet a paying customer."

His jaw clenched. "Go home, Myfanwy."

"I was home," the lady said easily. "But I needed to talk to you."

"How did you know I was here?"

Myfanwy shrugged. "Where else would you be? Besides, Benjamin told me I should look for you here."

"My butler would never do that," he returned icily. Samuel might not be refined, but his butler most certainly was. And Benjamin would never send Miss Myfanwy Wright, a viscount's daughter, to a pub this late at night—or ever.

Myfanwy shrugged again. He wished she would stop making that motion. The dainty way her shoulders bobbed made Samuel want to lift his head and stare at her, and he wouldn't be doing that. He'd done it once before—the day she'd shown up at his home with her father's will in one hand and a valise in the other—and he was still recovering from the magnificent sight.

Up until then, Samuel had only ever seen Myfanwy from across the field when her father would bring her to his matches. Buttoned up and proper, she'd appeared blandly similar to every other young lady with her bonnet and matching parasol. But that day—up close—as she'd stood dejected yet defiant in his foyer, Samuel was proven woefully wrong. He could still remember the way her small hands trembled as she'd handed him the papers, the way Myfanwy's lips tightened in a fierce line to keep her tears at bay. Her long auburn hair molded to her frame like an expensive mourning shawl, showing that she'd been too desolate to care how she came to him. She'd come as perfection. Broken, but still perfect.

Samuel had no idea why Viscount Wright had left him as his daughter's guardian in his will. Quite defenseless, Samuel had allowed her to pass over his threshold that afternoon because she simply wouldn't allow him to turn her away. He couldn't be positive—he'd just finished a bottle of gin and might have still been drunk from the night before—but he thought he'd tried to send her back to her aunt's home; however, the silly woman wouldn't budge. The Honorable Miss Myfanwy Wright had stormed into his life with all the power of a tornado, and she hadn't stopped swirling around him ever since. This was why Samuel did his best not to look, not to talk, not to approach as much as possible. With only one stable leg, his balance was bad enough as it was.

In cricket, if you put the ball in play but decided not to run to the opposite wicket, the other team couldn't get you out. You stayed alive for another chance. When Myfanwy was in his presence, Samuel never ran. He never even swung the bat. One couldn't be too careful.

Out of the corner of his eye, he saw her drum her lovely, long fingers on the counter. Her pearl-like nails were short and efficient. Samuel liked that. He liked just about everything to do with her—except her obstinate personality. "I've told you before that you cannot be here," he seethed. "Your father wouldn't approve."

"Well, how fortunate I am that he isn't here to stop me," Myfanwy countered.

Samuel heard her suck in a breath. After a pause, he replied, "You shouldn't say such things."

Myfanwy's hands flattened against the bar. "I shouldn't *do* a lot of things. And yet here I am."

Yes. Here she was. And as much as Samuel wanted her to leave—*knew* she should leave this place of tortured men and resolute delusions—he couldn't force her. He would have to touch her to do that, and that was even worse than looking at her. As weak as Samuel had become, both in mind and body, he'd refrained from ever putting his hands on Myfanwy. Only late at night, when his imagination was at its deadliest and the alcohol was at its worst, did he contemplate the softness of the lady's skin, the dewiness of her lips, the silkiness of her hair.

"Hey, Sam," Benny called down the counter, raising an empty pint glass in the air. "When you can?"

Samuel threw the bruiser a curt nod before ducking his head again. His neck always hurt after Myfanwy confronted him. He could never tell if he hated or loved the effect. "Just spit it out, then. Tell me what you want so you can go."

Myfanwy stiffened away from the counter. He'd offended her. It was for the best.

"Well…" she began slowly.

Samuel tersely waved his hand in between them. "I'm busy," he snapped. "Get to it."

Myfanwy exhaled an irritated breath. "Fine." She leaned against the counter, and it acted as a shelf for a small, lovely bosom. Samuel groaned inside. He finally lifted his gaze to her face, the lesser of two evils, not to stare, just to look…briefly.

Myfanwy's dark brown eyes widened at his sudden shift, and for a tantalizing moment, words stalled on her tongue. Her full eyelashes fluttered wildly, and Samuel's irritation grew—and he could feel another part of himself continue to grow at the sight. Her eyelashes had none of the guile and suggestion of the woman in the corner, and yet they appealed to every inch of his lonely body. Covertly, he dropped his arm under the counter and pulled at his trousers.

"Um...right...yes," Myfanwy said, eventually finding her voice. "As you know, I, along with my single friends, play cricket—"

"Another thing you shouldn't be doing."

"—and we had a meeting today."

Samuel scoffed, shaking his head. "Meetings in cricket..."

"And they—not I, mind you—decided that we need a coach."

"I could have told you that. Everyone needs a coach."

"They think it should be you."

"Not like a coach would help a bunch of gently bred—" Samuel stopped. And stared, completely forgetting what it would do to him. Luckily, he was too incensed to fall under his insane ward's spell. Well...to *completely* fall under her spell.

Now, it was Samuel's lashes doing all the fluttering. "What... How... Why... I don't...?"

A tiny smile formed on Myfanwy's plush pink lips. "Funny. I said the exact same thing."

There was nothing funny about this. Samuel planted his palms on the counter and bent over it as menacingly as he could, making sure his white eye was on full display. It wasn't totally useless; he could make out forms and shapes, but that was of little help nowadays. What did help was the way it made people cower away from him.

Only, it wasn't doing that now. If anything, Myfanwy only peered more intently at the offending orb. "I already know what you're going to say," she said.

"Then why did you ask?"

Her mouth pinched, showing an adorable dimple on the one side. "Because my team told me to. We took a vote, and I lost. We are a very democratic club."

"Well, I'm sorry for that," Samuel said, sliding away. He couldn't take being that close to her. Even in the musty, hoppy, sweaty fumes of the pub, Myfanwy's perfume captured him. It was soft and sweet and reminded him of the jasmine that grew wild back home around his mother's garden. "But it looks like you lost again."

She backed away as well. "It's not really a loss if I knew I was going to lose."

Samuel's laugh was bitter. "A loss is always a loss, whether you expect it or not. And you call yourself a cricketer."

Myfanwy rolled her eyes and dumped her reticule on the counter, furiously searching inside the tiny thing. Mesmerized and confused, Samuel watched her for long seconds. How could such a paltry bag hide anything inside?

"So, you won't even consider it?" she asked. The tip of her tongue stuck out the corner of her mouth while she continued to dig. "We're not bad, you know. We're actually quite good."

"From what I hear, you're on quite the losing streak."

She stopped rummaging and regarded him squarely. "What do *you* know about it?"

Samuel shrugged, glancing over her head as if this conversation meant absolutely nothing to him. Cricketers usually made good actors. "A lot of players come into the tavern. I hear things."

Her smile was sly. "You mean you listen for things."

"Hardly."

"And what do you hear when you aren't listening?"

Benny called out to him again, and Samuel held up his hand for his friend to wait. He settled his forearms on the counter. Myfanwy studied him warily. Samuel never had a sweet tooth, but he thought he could live a happy life swimming in the chocolate of her eyes. "I hear your little team—"

"Don't call us little."

"—has gotten positively wrecked by—"

"Hardly wrecked."

"—the matrons for the past three years."

Myfanwy *tsked*, and, again, the tip of her tongue peeked out of her mouth. Samuel shifted his stance once more. He needed her to leave. Now.

He adopted a steely tone. "And that's not all I hear."

There. That got the reaction he was hoping for. Myfanwy's tanned cheeks flushed. Like all the other female cricketers, no doubt she wore a hat when she played to ward off freckles and sun, and yet her complexion was as smooth and rich as a field of wheat.

"I also heard that after your last match, one of your teammates made a rather desultory comment...something along the lines of wishing that she was married so she could finally be on the winning side."

Myfanwy's almond-shaped eyes narrowed menacingly, and her throat rippled from a swallow. "You don't know what you're talking about."

"Oh, I think I do. I also read it in the papers. Sad quote, it was. Seems like you're having a difficult time keeping your players happy. Your losing is driving them to the marital yoke."

As he held her stare, the lights seemed to dim and the conversations that had been swirling around them lowered to a distant pitch. Immediately, Samuel was reminded why he didn't—*couldn't*—engage with this woman. Everything else fell away to nothing whenever she was near.

Myfanwy broke their moment, pillaging her ridiculous bag again. At long last, she found what she'd been looking for and pulled out a single coin. Unceremoniously she lobbed it on the counter and backed away.

"For your time," she said, escaping toward the exit.

Samuel sneered at the offending item. "I don't need your money," he yelled after her.

Myfanwy didn't turn back. "Maybe not, but you need something," she returned.

Chapter Two

DISAPPOINTMENT—THE MOST DANGEROUS kind—hovered around Myfanwy like nine pairs of knitting needles poised and waiting to stab her in the arm.

"I just don't understand why you won't ask him again," Lady Everly complained, folding her hands into her lap in a way that could only be described as exasperatingly polite.

"Well," Myfanwy began, keeping a tight hold on her patience, "it's not as easy as it seems."

Miss Anna Smythe took a brisk, perturbed sip of her tea. "But you live in the same house as Mr. Everett," she replied, clinking the cup as she returned it to its saucer. "It seems incredibly easy to me. You could ask him again over his morning coffee."

Myfanwy's shoulders hiked to her ears. "Mr. Everett is not at his best in the morning hours." *Or any hours after that.* "It would be challenging to maintain his attention."

Lady Everly *humphed*. "Perhaps you're not trying hard enough. Here." She placed her teacup on the table next to her and brushed her hands together. "Tell us what he said to you this morning, and we'll help you think of a way to divert the conversation to our ends."

Myfanwy sighed. This was not the way she'd seen this Single Ladies Cricket Club meeting going. Fifteen minutes into it, she'd assumed they'd be debating slow pitches and spinners by now. *Fun* things. *Important* things. Not incorrigible degenerates.

She tilted her head to study the intricate relief ceiling of her best friend's drawing room. "Let me think, let me think," she drawled. "What did Mr. Everett say to me this morning...? Ah, yes. He came into the dining room while I was finishing up, sat down in his chair, and put his head in his hands. For a good five minutes, I wondered if he was asleep or dead. He confirmed it was only the former when out of nowhere he told me to 'Stop thinking so hard, because that whorish devil is making my head pound like the blazes.'" She crinkled up her nose. "I think it actually had less to do with the devil and more to do with his propensity to drink all night."

Myfanwy returned to her audience. She was certain she could hear a pin drop on the Venetian carpet.

"Well, did you?" Anna squeaked. "Did you do as he asked?"

Myfanwy stared at her friend, who was absolutely—and not surprisingly—serious in her question.

"I...tried?" Actually, she'd answered Samuel by slurping her tea as loudly as she could, but she kept that information to herself.

The ten other members of the cricket club sat around her in a circle, consternation and agitation evident on their genteel faces as they attempted to make sense of her current living arrangement with her guardian. *Good luck to them,* Myfanwy thought balefully.

Unlike Lady Everly, the other women avoided meeting Myfanwy's eyes. It made sense that Lady Everly was the first one to speak up. Slightly older than the rest, as well as a widow, the lady had life experience—and the boldness that came along with it—which never made her short of an opinion.

But I'm the captain, Myfanwy reminded herself, smiling confidently for her teammates. *And there will be no mutinies under my watch.*

"Look. As I've told you, I asked, and he said no. There's no point in asking again," Myfanwy declared firmly. She met Lady Everly's intrepid countenance. "Mr. Samuel Everett is not interested in coaching us, and I think we should move on to other options."

"That's the point," Lady Everly insisted, leaning forward in her chair, crinkling her silk dress with the abrupt movement. "There are no other options. If we want to beat the matrons this year, we need to be serious—"

A chorus of affirmations rose from the other women. "Please, ladies, one at a time," Myfanwy said, ringing the tiny silver bell for attention. "That's better. Now, you know very well I *am* being serious—"

The door to the drawing room shot open and a maid promptly entered. "Did you need something, ladies?" the young woman asked, face flushed and shining with anticipation.

Myfanwy's best friend, Miss Jennifer Hallett, smiled apologetically at the expectant maid. "We're so sorry, Agnes. We didn't mean to ring you. We don't need anything at present. Thank you."

Agnes bobbed and swiftly exited.

Jennifer nodded to Myfanwy. "Sorry about that. Please, go on."

"I am being serious," Myfanwy repeated to the group. "Mr. Everett is not a viable option for us at the present time."

Lady Everly didn't miss a beat. "As unattached women, we can't just dance all over town asking old cricketers if they want to spend their afternoons with us, honing our craft. Mr. Everett makes the most sense. My late husband said he was the greatest cricketer to ever play the game...could take on whole teams by himself. Not to mention," she added with a disapproving arch of her brow, "you live with the man. He's your guardian, and, as you've pointed out in the past, he's not busy, since he's still recuperating."

Myfanwy frowned. Yes, she had said that, though it hadn't been the full truth. Samuel Everett's preferred method of recuperation seemed to chiefly involve finishing off a bottle of gin each night. So, in that respect, he was very busy indeed.

"Lady Everly, please," she started. *Damn.* She'd lost her train of thought. Taking her time, she scanned over her friends and teammates. Each of them was as hungry and dedicated to beating the matrons this year as she was. Each of them also loved cricket as much as she. Which was why it killed Myfanwy to deny them. They simply didn't understand what they were asking. They didn't know Samuel as she did—and even after living in his home for the past year, she barely knew him at all. One thing she was sure of was that he would throw their offer back in their faces once more, and Myfanwy had too much heart—and ego—to deal with another rejection.

Closing her eyes, she placed her fingers on her temple, where she could feel her veins beat out of her thin skin. Through her haze of thoughts, she heard Lady Everly ask under her breath— the cheek!—if Myfanwy even wanted to beat the matrons this year.

What an asinine question! Of course Myfanwy wanted to win; she wanted to win so badly she could practically taste it. This cricket club wouldn't exist if it weren't for her. It was Myfanwy who'd invited the others to join the group three years ago and bond over their love of the sport. And it was Myfanwy who'd found out that there was a similar group of married women who also practiced as a team and asked them if they wanted to play against each other. And what a triumph! Last year's match had roped in close to a thousand spectators. One thousand people who'd watched the single ladies get walloped by sixty-seven runs. The match might have been successful, but it was still an ignominious defeat. As had been the one the year before that.

The single women were sick of losing. And Myfanwy understood sport well enough to know that when a team was upset, there was only one person to blame—the captain.

A light hand touched her shoulder, and she opened her eyes to find Jennifer regarding her kindly. "Are you all right?" her friend asked.

Myfanwy nodded softly and took a calming breath.

Jennifer smiled before turning back to the others. She rang the bell until all the little conversations halted. Her voice was remarkably soft and worked to shift the tense atmosphere in the room. "I think we can all agree that no one wants to win more than Myfi," Jennifer said, using Myfanwy's childhood nickname.

The drawing room door whipped open, and again the maid tripped through. "Did you need me, miss?" she asked, rather breathlessly.

"Oh, so sorry, Agnes. No, again, we were just ringing for order," Jennifer replied. "How about this? For the time being, whenever you hear this bell, just ignore it."

The maid nodded and rushed off.

Jennifer frowned when she realized the room's collective attention was still pointed at her. "Where was I?" she whispered to Myfanwy.

Myfanwy leaned into her best friend's side. "You were telling them all how amazing I am."

They shared a smile. "Right. Yes." Jennifer squared her shoulders. "If Myfi says that it's pointless to keep asking Mr. Everett, then we should all believe her and put our minds together to think of other alternatives."

Myfanwy's heart swelled with relief as the others nodded. She should have known her lifelong friend would help her out of this mess. If anyone understood Myfanwy's distaste for confronting Samuel, it was her. They'd wasted enough teatimes discussing the man's horrid qualities.

Myfanwy opened her mouth to add to the little speech, but Jennifer beat her to it. "However," she said, raising one slender finger and instantly eliciting quiet, "I think it's only fair that the group takes a vote. This cricket club was founded on democratic principles, and we should employ them now." She winced, giving Myfanwy a remorseful look. "None of us are above cricket club law."

"Quite right," Lady Everly said adamantly, shaking her thick blonde hair so that her braids almost came loose from her bun. Out of the team, Myfanwy had the hardest time enjoying this particular member. Maybe because they were too alike. It was rare that Myfanwy found someone as competitive as she was. Though, Myfanwy had to admit, Lady Everly had incredibly strong motivations. She was the only member of the cricket club to have played for *both* the matrons and the singles. After her husband died two years ago, she'd been informed by the matrons that she had to switch to the singles team. Hardly surprising, Lady Everly had stomped into her first club meeting with a sizeable axe to grind.

Now, like a general on the cusp of battle, the widow stared down the members. "All in favor of asking Mr. Everett to be our coach, please say *aye*."

Myfanwy could have plugged her ears, and she still would have heard the chirps of enthusiastic *ayes* clear as day.

Lady Everly flashed her an indulgent grin. "I don't think we have to ask for the nays, do you?"

Myfanwy shook her head glumly.

The ladies went back to her tea. It was all so civilized. But, then again, cricket was a civilized game for civilized people.

If anyone knew that, it was Myfanwy. Unfortunately, she couldn't say the same about Samuel.

"I'M SORRY I couldn't be more helpful," Jennifer said. The meeting had closed, and she and Myfanwy were doing their part, putting the chairs away and getting the drawing room back in the order that Jennifer's mother approved.

Initially, Myfanwy had hosted the club at her father's townhouse; however, now that she lived with Mr. Everett, it made more sense to pass the baton to Jennifer. Her mother was only so happy to have the group (which boasted of wealthy members of the peerage) in her luxurious home, though there were stipulations. Along with setting the room to rights, Mrs. Hallett demanded that the club be an open space for discussing a variety of topics outside of cricket—including suitors and men who were of decent marriage potential.

Mrs. Hallett never hid the fact that she didn't approve of Myfanwy. However, she also didn't hide the fact that, since Myfanwy was a viscount's daughter, she was a catch of a friend for Jennifer, who was merely the child of an incredibly wealthy soap merchant. Like many good women before her, it was Mrs. Hallett's dream to marry her daughter off to a member of the peerage. Spending time in a cricket club with the Honorable Myfanwy Wright was a necessary evil in that endeavor. Besides, the older woman had wondered, how much cricket could a gaggle of girls really talk about in one hour over tea? Surely, available men were truly the *objet du jour*, and cricket was merely a ruse?

Ha! Myfanwy would have felt sorry for Mrs. Hallett's naivete if the woman had treated her with less disdain.

"It's fine," she grumbled while sliding a heavy chair across the floor, upsetting the carpet in its wake. She straightened the corner with the toe of her slipper. "They don't understand, since they won't be the ones he laughs at after he says no. *Again*." She sighed. "But I'll do it and then I'll come back and say, 'I told you so,' right in Lady Everly's long face."

"Don't blame Jo," Jennifer replied in that infuriatingly rational way of hers. "She's just frustrated." Myfanwy could never understand how a termagant like Mrs. Hallett could create such a forgiving and beautiful girl like Jennifer. Evil must skip a generation.

Gracefully, Jennifer brushed a strand of blonde hair off her forehead. Everyone always remarked on Jennifer's elegance and applauded her for it. Myfanwy did as well, but purely from a mercenary point of view. Jennifer's unfaltering balance was why she could hit for a fifty without breaking a sweat. In contrast, by the end of her innings, Myfanwy would be as drenched and messy as a young pig who'd just discovered her first mud puddle. However, she didn't begrudge her best friend's habit of staying cool under pressure. Jennifer could be as pretty and dry as she wanted, as long as she kept hitting the daylight out of the ball.

"We're *all* frustrated," Myfanwy said, flopping into a chair to mark her frustration. "But we don't have to look outward to get better. I spent most of my childhood watching cricket matches with my father. I know the game backward and forward. We just have to keep working and practicing. There's nothing Samuel Everett can teach us that I don't already know."

Jennifer hesitated, wrinkling her brow in indecision. "Well…" she said slowly. "Obviously, there are *some* things he must know more of. He played professionally for years."

Myfanwy folded her arms in a huff. "And has one eye and one leg left to show for it." Immediately, her chest pulled tight. The man could be a taciturn bastard, but that was indecorous even for her.

"Wait," Jennifer said, cocking her head. "I thought he still had both eyes and legs."

"Oh, he does," Myfanwy rushed out. Her voice wobbled with shame at her previous comment. "Both legs still work, although he limps something fierce. I never hear him say anything, but it must be excruciating."

"And the eye?"

Myfanwy's brow furrowed. "The eye…I'm not sure. It's not all cloudy, like you see in some who are blind. It's only white in the middle, and it's surrounded by this ring of startling blue. It's quite beautiful, actually."

If Jennifer heard the wistfulness in Myfanwy's voice, she didn't point it out. "How horrible to have such ailments when you're still so young. He couldn't be more than thirty?"

"He…*might* be thirty," Myfanwy replied absent-mindedly. She was laying it on thick because she knew perfectly well that

Samuel Everett was thirty-one. She even knew his birthday: December 22.

Jennifer took a seat next to her friend. "Well, no wonder you say he's always in a foul mood. He could still be playing, and instead, he's stuck in his home—"

"With me," Myfanwy ended with an evil grin.

Jennifer laughed. "That's another reason why I know he must be a decent man. Your father would have never elected him to be your guardian over your aunt if he was some rampant deviant."

Myfanwy squinted disbelievingly at her friend. "You knew my father. He loved rampant deviants!"

"He did not!" Jennifer replied, shaking her head. "He loved cricketers, and he loved Samuel Everett."

"For some reason," Myfanwy groused.

"For some *probably* very good reason." Jennifer paused. "And Samuel—Mr. Everett—loved your father too."

"Because my father was his patron and helped him when he was younger," Myfanwy replied.

"And now," Jennifer said, lifting her chin, "it will be Mr. Everett's turn to help his patron's daughter. That's why I am sure he won't say no to our cause."

Myfanwy slumped in her seat like a petulant child. "I wish I had your confidence—"

Just as Myfanwy finished speaking, the drawing room door opened, and Mrs. Hallett sailed in with an overwhelming bouquet of roses in her arms. "Darling, look at what just came for you—" Her smile vanished the second she noticed that Myfanwy was still in the room. "Oh...you still have...company. I thought I told you to be ready for the Lawfords' musicale. We're leaving soon. Surely Miss Myfanwy should be moving along."

Jennifer shot to her feet, smoothing down her dress in front. "We're almost done, Mother. Myfi didn't want to leave until the room was put to rights."

Furtively, Myfanwy rolled her eyes. *Sweet Jennifer.* She could try all she wanted, but Mrs. Hallett would only ever see that the most helpful thing about Myfanwy was her bloodline. And since the death of her father, even that wasn't as important as it once was.

"The flowers are beautiful," Myfanwy announced instead. "Are they for Jennifer?"

A tall, angular woman, Mrs. Hallett curved her lips into a smile that made her nose seem ever longer. "Naturally. Sir Bramble sent them. His second bouquet this week."

Mrs. Hallett shoved the flowers into the girls' faces, and Myfanwy recoiled in uninterest. On second thought, she decided, the bouquet wasn't so pretty anymore.

"Sir Bramble, eh?" Myfanwy said as the older woman whisked away from the girls, fussing and arranging the roses into a vase near the window that looked out into the street. No doubt, she wanted the whole neighborhood to take note of them. If ever there was a coup for Mrs. Hallett, Sir Bramble was it. Even though he was merely a baron, his title was old and distinguished.

Myfanwy whispered out of the corner of her mouth, "I thought you called Sir Bramble boring at Lord Sinclair's."

Jennifer peered down at her hands as a light blush formed over her cheeks. "*He* wasn't boring," she answered slowly. "I said the topic was boring."

"But he's the one who came up with the topic."

"No," Jennifer argued. "Lord Jameson did. He's mad for breeding quail, and it's all he would talk about. Sir Bramble was being polite."

"So…he's boring, but at least he's polite about it?"

From the window, Mrs. Hallett issued a dramatic sigh and started ringing the silver bell.

"Why do you dislike Sir Bramble so much?" Jennifer asked.

Because he's threatening to take you away from me. The words were on the tip of her tongue, but Myfanwy reeled them back just in time. She had to remind herself that Sir Bramble wasn't the first man to express an interest in Jennifer and wouldn't be the last. Unlike her mother, Jennifer was a hopeless romantic and wouldn't settle for anything less than her soulmate. Myfanwy was certain that Sir Bramble wasn't it, even with all his flowers and polite dullness.

"I don't dislike him," Myfanwy said with a dismissive shrug. "I just don't want you to lose focus. The match with the matrons is less than two months away. You can be as politely bored as you want after that, but until then, I need you to keep your head on straight. Men weaken the legs, remember that."

Jennifer swatted her playfully on the arm. "That is not true."

Mrs. Hallett rang the bell like she was announcing the birth of a prince.

"It *is* true!" Myfanwy replied to her friend over the incessant noise. "You're one of my best batsmen. I need you in fighting shape. Promise me, please." She took Jennifer's hands in hers, stifling her friend's laughter. "No engagements, no kisses, no secret letters until the match is over. We've worked too hard to lose now. And after we win, everyone will be knocking down our doors wanting to be members of the Single Ladies Cricket Club."

Mrs. Hallett slammed the bell on the table. "I swear, what is wrong with that maid? How long do I have to ring this bell? Has she gone deaf?"

Chapter Three

THE FUTILE TASK given by her teammates was still fresh in Myfanwy's mind the following day as she readied to meet her aunt.

She tried tying her bonnet ribbon into an aggravating knot three times before she could finally get it into a suitable bow underneath her chin. Myfanwy loved it when her father's sister came to visit her, but today she couldn't bolster her heart to feel anything but stiff, unyielding discontent. Usually, she loved being proven correct, but she didn't relish going back to the club and telling the members that they still didn't have a coach to help them beat the matrons.

"My dear," Mrs. Abigail Moreland said grandly as she waited at the base of the staircase for her niece, "pick up your feet. You trudge any harder and you'll fall right through."

Myfanwy attempted to lighten her steps, but it was a paltry effort. "I'm sorry, Aunt," she replied glumly. "I'm in a mood."

"On a day such as this?" Mrs. Moreland replied, snatching her niece tight for a quick peck on each cheek. "It's marvelous outside. The perfect weather for a garden party. I demand you cheer up immediately."

A smile fought its way onto Myfanwy's face. It was difficult to stay curmudgeonly around her aunt, who was the late Viscount

Newton's one sibling and the only relative that Myfanwy held any type of relationship with. Though she'd married Sir Richard Moreland, Aunt Abigail never had any children of her own and doted on Myfanwy something fierce. Oddly enough, they disagreed on virtually everything under the sun—from politics to art to women in sport. However, the ladies maintained a strong bond, most likely because they both knew what it was like to navigate through the world alone. Sir Richard died soon after they'd wed fifteen years ago, and Aunt Abigail had never cared to consider another husband, even when she'd been pressured by her family. Myfanwy would never consider herself a romantic, and yet she'd always appreciated that conviction in the older woman.

"Oh, Aunt," Myfanwy said, her expression as gloomy as the day was fine. "I just don't think I'm up for a garden party today."

"Pish!" her aunt answered. "You absolutely must go. It will look poor if we don't show and play nice. I won't have people saying you're bitter about the whole thing."

Bitter? Myfanwy hadn't even thought about that.

Her aunt went on, "It's the viscount's first garden party. Can you believe that? He took over your father's title a whole year ago, and this is the first time he's invited anyone in. Most likely nervous, the drab thing, his being a newspaperman and all that before this was all thrust on him. He probably doesn't have the faintest idea how to act and what to do."

"I suppose," Myfanwy answered slowly. In all honesty, the moment she moved into Mr. Everett's home, she'd barely given a second's thought to the new viscount or how he was settling into his role. All she knew was that he was a distant cousin who'd written for one of the daily newspapers before he was notified of his stroke of luck. At least, Myfanwy assumed that the new Viscount Newton considered the title good fortune. Most people would, anyway.

It occurred to Myfanwy that her aunt thought she was reluctant to go back home because it would be her first time returning since her father's funeral. She adored Holly Lodge and always would, but Myfanwy had always known that it wouldn't be her forever home, and she didn't begrudge the new viscount his due.

"Please don't think I'm upset about going home—I mean to Holly Lodge," Myfanwy began. She turned to accept her parasol and reticule from the maid waiting behind her. "I just don't feel like standing around talking to people. So, you have nothing to worry about on that account."

"Nothing to worry about?" her aunt retorted, quite aghast. The pale red curls framing her round face shook with her vehemence. "How can you say that? It's all I ever do, poor girl. How can I not when you're living in this house with that...with that man!"

Myfanwy sighed, sliding a few feet toward the door, hoping her aunt would follow instead of breaking out into a fresh tirade. It didn't work.

"I loved my brother," the older woman continued. "He was everything an older brother should be. Gallant and beautiful. But for the life of me, I will never understand what he was thinking when he wrote his will. I should never have listened to you; I should have contested it."

"You know as well as I that it wouldn't have done any good. Father was in perfect health and of sound mind when he created it."

Aunt Abigail droned on. "I take solace in the fact that you won't be here much longer. Only twelve more weeks until you reach your majority. Although, what you have planned next makes me even more tormented. Dearest, please tell me you aren't *actually* going to live alone."

"That's the plan," Myfanwy announced with a grin. "Which reminds me, I still haven't found a house that's perfect. The one we toured in Hampstead Heath didn't sing to me. Will you go out with me to look some more next week? Nothing feels quite right."

"Because there's no husband attached to it!" her aunt scoffed, shivering at the thought. "How can a house feel like a home when you're planning to live in it all by yourself? Come live with me. I won't take no for an answer."

"You'll have to," Myfanwy said. "I told you. I don't care about my reputation or my social standing or a husband. All I care about is starting a cricket club for single ladies. Once I reach majority and take control of my dowry, I'll be able to purchase a small house with a proper spot of land for a cricket pitch. There we'll be able to play and compete without always asking for permission to use the men's fields. It's the only way."

Aunt Abigail appeared positively crestfallen. "But you are the daughter of a viscount. You can't just do whatever you want."

"Why not?" Myfanwy asked pointedly. "You do."

"Yes," her aunt replied drolly, "but I got married first. You have to do one before you can do the other. Those are the rules."

"Not my rules. If I marry, then all my money belongs to my husband. What if he decides to change his mind one day? What if on a whim he feels like betting it all on a hand of cards? I can't risk that. Men can't be controlled."

"What about love?"

"Ha!" Myfanwy laughed, aghast. "From what I hear, love is the very opposite of control. There's no place for it in my life."

Aunt Abigail tugged at her gloves. "I don't know who's giving you these horrible ideas. It's the golfer, isn't it? I knew he'd be a bad influence. Wicked, wicked golfer—"

"He's a cricketer."

The older woman sucked in a heaving breath. "He's lascivious—"

"You mean he's a bachelor."

"—he comes from Lord knows where—"

"He's from Sutton."

"—and who knows what kind of parents he had?"

"His father is a bricklayer, and one of his brothers is a physician and the other is a barrister."

Aunt Abigail *humphed*, acknowledging Myfanwy with a

pointy arch of a brow. "Well, they can't be any good at their jobs if they choose to live all the way out there in the middle of nowhere."

Myfanwy tossed up her hands. "It's Nottinghamshire, not Siberia. Some people enjoy the country."

"Odd people. *Odd* people prefer the country."

"And yet here you are, dragging me to a garden party."

"Oh stop." Aunt Abigail chuckled grimly. "Garden parties aren't the country. They are, however, the only sensible way to experience the outdoors. With tents and shade and drinks and entertainment. If you're determined to ruin your reputation, I have to do my best dragging you into decent Society as much as you'll allow—" She stopped, surveying her niece's ensemble shrewdly. "You aren't really wearing that, are you? You're going to catch a cold. Go upstairs and change at once. Honestly, Myfanwy. We don't have time for this."

Myfanwy shook her head. She'd been trying to herd the loquacious woman out the door for the past few minutes. "Of course I'm wearing this. Why? What's wrong with it?"

She followed her aunt's gaze and looked down at her pale yellow muslin dress. It was simple and plain, but the sleeves added a bit of a punch with their short, flowing ruffles. Most importantly, it was cool and airy for a late June day.

"You'll catch your death," her aunt said.

"I will not!" Myfanwy replied. "You said it yourself: the sun is out. I don't want to spend the day sweating."

Aunt Abigail's eyes rounded as large as cricket balls. Her pert nose went straight up in the air. "What are you talking about? Ladies don't sweat."

Myfanwy laughed and then sobered quickly when she realized her aunt was not joking. "You're not serious?"

"Of course I am!"

"Everyone sweats."

"Ladies don't."

"Yes, they do!"

Aunt Abigail made a sound from the base of her throat that could only be categorized as a growl. "Although I consider myself extraordinary in all things, alas, I am an average woman, and I do *not* sweat. It's physically impossible."

Myfanwy continued to gawk at her aunt, incredulous. "Well...I do!"

"Fine, fine," the older woman said, putting her hands up between them as if worried that her niece might sweat on her. "Just don't tell anyone."

"I only told you!"

"Well, don't do it again."

"Believe me, I won't!"

Fortunately, steps could be heard coming down the stairs, and the two women were diverted from their unsavory disagreement. Aunt Abigail craned her neck around Myfanwy and lit in a generous smile. "Ah, Mr. Everett, how lovely to see you this afternoon."

Myfanwy rolled her eyes. Her aunt was never at a loss when describing her guardian's numerous faults, and yet she lit up like Vauxhall Gardens whenever the man graced them with his presence.

It was a very nice presence, though, Myfanwy had to admit. She twirled around as her guardian made his way to the foyer. Samuel looked nothing like the barman he was the night before. Instead, he was the picture of gentility with his freshly pressed white shirt and impeccably tailored jacket. His trousers were a dark brown, and though loose as the style dictated, they weren't loose enough for Myfanwy. Her gaze traveled along the long lines of his leg muscles that hinted just below the surface like an Egyptian treasure waiting to be discovered underneath the hot desert sand.

Plus, he'd combed his dark blond hair. Which was usually enough to turn a vagrant into a gentleman for a day.

Samuel's smile was tight and in no way made it up to his eyes. However, it was enough to bring out the dimple on his left cheek, though not the one on his right. Myfanwy hadn't seen that one since she was very young.

"Mrs. Moreland, always a pleasure," he replied adequately, following it with a curt bow.

"Awfully dressed up for the tavern," Myfanwy drawled. She was baiting him, naturally, but she received no satisfaction when Samuel continued to focus on her aunt.

"No tavern today. I suspect we are traveling in the same circles," he said stiffly, keeping his gaze averted from hers. This shy action remained a considerable curiosity for Myfanwy. She'd noticed his lack of eye contact with her when she first moved into his townhome. Assuming it was because of his embarrassment over his injured eye, she'd gone out of her way never to stare at the white spot. But it didn't matter how nonchalantly she behaved. Samuel made it a point to not look at her as much as possible.

He didn't mind looking at her aunt, though. Samuel wasn't charming the older woman in the slightest, but he wasn't avoiding her either.

"You're off to Viscount Newton's garden party?" Aunt Abigail asked, trying and failing to hide her amazement.

Samuel nodded, amused at her failure. "Indeed. I've known him for a long time, ever since he used to write cricket features for the *Standard*. He was ruthless but fair."

Myfanwy stepped forward. "And you're...friends?"

"I wouldn't say that," he answered, ducking his head, giving Myfanwy a good view of the bump in his nose. Surely he'd broken it—a few times. "We're acquaintances. I'm only going because Sir Bramble told me he would be there, and he wished to speak to me about investing in my new business."

"The sporting goods business?" Myfanwy asked.

Samuel's jaw clenched. "The very one."

Aunt Abigail chuckled, obliviously unaware of the tension between the two younger people. Perhaps only Myfanwy was aware of it. Samuel seemed as at ease as ever—or as at ease as he could ever seem.

"You are an interesting man, aren't you, Mr. Everett?" Aunt Abigail remarked. "So many eggs in so many baskets. An inn, a tavern, and now a sporting goods business. Whatever can't you do?"

"Oh, I have my limitations," he said. Wrinkles fanned out from the corners of his eyes as he winced at the flattery. He tapped his hand against his left thigh. "If you ever asked me to dance, we might have problems."

Aunt Abigail's cheeks went red, and she giggled like a schoolgirl. "Oh, I doubt that. You forget, my brother used to drag me to your matches from time to time. I bet those legs still have life in them. I might ask you to dance just to prove you wrong. Something on the slower side."

Was Myfanwy's aunt flirting? *With Samuel Everett?* And worse yet, was he blushing?

While her stomach curdled, Myfanwy watched as Samuel's Adam's apple bobbed over his starched collar. "I should be going," he said with another stiff bow. "I don't plan to stay long, so I want to get there early."

"You can ride in my carriage with us," Aunt Abigail said, perhaps a little too eagerly.

"Ah, no thank you," Samuel replied, perhaps a little too quickly. "The fresh air would do me good after spending the evening in the tavern."

And as if he vanished into thin air, he escaped seconds later, his bad leg not hindering his swift exit.

Both Myfanwy and Aunt Abigail were quiet for a long pause, finding themselves alone again. Then, in a frenzy of movement, Aunt Abigail dug into her pelisse and located her fan. She utilized it instantly and furiously.

"I can't believe it," she said, her brow reaching up to her hairline. "It seems you were right, niece. Ladies can sweat after all."

Chapter Four

DESPITE HER RESERVATIONS, Myfanwy was actually enjoying herself at the viscount's garden party. A few of her friends from the cricket club had also accepted invitations, and the women had hidden themselves away in a corner of shrubs to amuse themselves.

Myfanwy didn't have time to fixate on her old home or her father's heart issues that had led to his passing that fateful night when they'd been sharing a quiet evening together. Looking back, Myfanwy could only be grateful for how quickly everything happened. One moment her father was sitting in his chair, chuckling over Charles Dickens, and the next he was slumped over, lifeless though still smiling.

After the initial grieving process, Myfanwy determined that if she was ever fortunate enough to meet the author, she would tell him thank you. The viscount had died happy, and, even at twenty, Myfanwy was old enough to understand that one couldn't wish for more than that.

At the present, unfortunately, she was also wise enough to know that when a group of women were standing together chuckling, entertaining each other with in-jokes, a man must come to spoil all the fun.

"What could possibly have you in such thrall, ladies? You

must tell us at once."

With a put-upon sigh, Myfanwy turned to see Sir Bramble creeping on the outskirts of the group with Lord Cremly close at his heel. She wasn't sure what upset her more—the interruption or Jennifer's barely contained grin when she spotted her suitor. Honestly, what did she see in Sir Bramble?

If someone forced her, Myfanwy could acknowledge that the baron was a decent-looking man with dark brown hair cut short to his head and delicate—dare she say it—almost pretty, feline features. He was tall and fit and always up for a laugh. Myfanwy found that the most disturbing. Nothing seemed to perturb the man. Sir Bramble was positively tickled by all and sundry—even her dour expression whenever he ventured too close!

"Oh, we weren't discussing much," Jennifer said blandly. "Nothing important."

Myfanwy shot her friend a confused look. "Yes, we were. We were talking about batting setup... When to be aggressive or when to play it safe. You know, back foot, front foot, that sort of thing."

Sir Bramble appeared lost. He was a terrible cricket player, and Myfanwy was well aware he had absolutely no idea what she was talking about—which was precisely why she'd said it. How could Jennifer—an amazing athlete—consider this man as a life partner? Her children might be as terrible at sport as he, and *then* where would she be?

True to form, Sir Bramble never lost his smile, and his white teeth glistened against the sun. "You ladies," he said, wagging his finger, "are always discussing cricket. What lively creatures you are."

The other women tittered with polite laughter, which was well and good, since it drowned out Myfanwy's groan.

Lord Cremly sauntered to the side of his friend and hung an arm around Sir Bramble's neck. It was the only time Myfanwy saw the baron appear remotely uncomfortable. She couldn't blame Bramble for that. Even at a far distance, Lord Cremly—

with his arrogance and unctuous attitude—made her skin crawl.

Damn fine cricketer, though. Myfanwy had to admit that. She'd first seen him play when he represented Eton in the famous Eton vs. Harrow match at Lord's. That was years ago, but he was still one of the best amateurs in London.

"Cricket. Now that's a wonderful idea, girls," Lord Cremly said. He issued a disgruntled frown across the garden toward the viscount's home. "Our host has left us out here without any worthwhile diversions. Who's in the mood for a match?"

Myfanwy clapped her hands together before she could temper her delight. She shuddered when Lord Cremly slid an appreciative gaze up her body.

"It looks like Miss Myfanwy is game. Anyone else?" He cocked his head in her direction. "By the by, you should smile more, Miss Myfanwy. You're a changed woman when you do."

Myfanwy bit her tongue so hard she thought it might bleed, simultaneously stopping any smile *or* sharp retort.

Her friends saved her from an ignominious action as they expressed their agreement for the lord's proposal. It proved infectious, and in no time, Lord Cremly had rounded up a handful of men to join them in the sporting endeavor.

"All right, now," he said, surveying the crowd with a critical eye, hands on his narrow hips. Years spent playing cricket had weathered his skin, giving him a distinguished quality. His luscious black hair kept most of the women in the *ton* in a constant state of flighty agitation. He ran a confident hand through his locks now, causing some ladies to hide their dreamy sighs behind their fans. "We've got enough for two teams of five. How do you suppose we divide it up?"

Myfanwy opened her mouth to respond, but Sir Bramble beat her to it. "I'd like to be on Miss Jennifer's team." Without an ounce of shame, he added, "She's a wonderful player, and I need her to help me look good out there."

Jennifer lowered her head, blushing mightily under her straw bonnet. Myfanwy might have thought the entire scene adorable if it didn't infuriate her so much. Jennifer was her teammate—not Sir Bramble's!

Casually, not conspicuously in the least, Myfanwy meandered over to the couple and inserted herself between them, slightly— very slightly—nudging the baron further away from her friend. "I always think girls against boys is more interesting, don't you?" she asked, raising her chin toward Lord Cremly.

He responded with a slow smile.

It was a political maneuver. Like would always identify like, and Myfanwy understood Lord Cremly's reputation well enough to know that he hated to lose just as much as she did—even in friendly matches like these. Due to his unfounded prejudices, there was no way he would welcome a woman on his team.

"But there aren't enough women," Miss Anna Smythe stated from across the circle. Myfanwy leveled her with a weighted look, but Anna wasn't getting the message. "It would be four of us against six of them… Hardly fair."

Myfanwy swooped in. "We'll be fine—"

"Oh, come now, Miss Anna," Lord Cremly purred, cutting Myfanwy off. "Do you really take us men for such blackguards?"

It soothed Myfanwy's soul that not one woman responded to that question, leaving the answer up in the air where it belonged.

Lord Cremly meandered to the middle of the circle. "You didn't truly think that the men would play to full strength?"

Myfanwy stepped forward. "Well, yes, of course. Why wouldn't you—"

He cut her off again, this time adding a rude swipe of his hand. "We wouldn't dare embarrass you like that. Besides, we want to have fun as well, and beating you easily wouldn't be fun at all. What do you say, men? Should we play left-handed?"

Masculine laughter answered Lord Cremly all around.

"Not good enough. How about with one hand tied behind our backs?" a gentleman called out.

"Not good enough," another responded. "How about with our legs tied together?"

"What about no hands at all? Would that make it fair?"

"Let's wear blindfolds!"

Lord Cremly's grin dripped with condescension. "Now, now, gentlemen. Let's not go that far. I've seen some of these women play. The matrons versus singles game is quite…adorable."

Adorable?

Myfanwy gripped the handle of her parasol and thought she heard the wood crack. The men were being ridiculous and childish. She had grown up with most of them, and, other than Lord Cremly, they could use four arms and it wouldn't make any difference.

"I hardly think that will be necessary," Anna said, her voice higher than usual. Myfanwy nodded at the woman. By the heightened color in her cheeks, it was clear Anna was just as offended as she was.

This was why the ladies needed a safe place to play cricket, away from the whims and prejudices of these kinds of men. Unfortunately, it was these sorts of gentlemen who owned all the cricket fields and directed all the county leagues—the women played at *their* convenience. And Myfanwy had a feeling that it would never be convenient for these sorts of gentlemen to ever see the women as real cricket players. They were just amusements, diversions, entertainments for them to laugh at like exotic animals in a zoo. To the women, cricket was the game. To these men, the women would always be the game. And in their minds, men never lost.

Lord Cremly zeroed in on Anna, patronizing her with a hefty exhale. "I applaud your confidence, miss"—he placed his hand over his heart—"but as a gentleman, I have to insist. We'll all play left-handed. What say you, men?"

The others closed the discussion with a slew of *ayes*.

But Anna, dear, stubborn Anna, wasn't having it. "No, no, I still say it isn't right. The women need one more player to make it fair."

Lord Cremly dropped his hand from his heart, vexation deep

and evident. He spun wildly, eliciting more laughter from his friends. "I'm afraid I'm at a loss. No one else is here—no one else you'd want on your team, anyway. I suggest you just take the terms I've set for you. I'm looking out for your best interests, after all."

"Oh, I doubt that," came a hard voice from outside the group.

Heads swiveled side to side, searching for the man who'd spoken. Bodies split until a path opened up with Samuel Everett standing alone and looking rather bored on the other end. Myfanwy thought she was seeing things as Samuel inspected his nails and continued in that lazy drawl. "From what I remember," he said, "the only interests you ever look out for are your own."

Crunching grass and silk rustling were the only things to be heard as everyone nearby shifted on anxious feet. After an uncomfortable pause, Lord Cremly chuckled, but nothing about the man was amused. "That's hilarious coming from you, Everett," he returned easily, "considering you won't even walk onto a pitch or pick up a cricket bat without a promise of payment first."

Samuel shrugged as if he'd heard the insult many times before, but his lips curled back from his teeth in a menacing way when he responded, "A man has to make a living. Professionals get paid so others can enjoy watching the game."

"Ha!" Lord Cremly sneered. "It's professionals like you that ruin the game, jumping from team to team. No loyalty, no beauty—only playing for the highest bidder. Amateurs like me are who people come to see. Amateurs are the only ones maintaining the integrity of the great sport."

Myfanwy's ears were pounding, but she still heard a few gasps break from the crowd. She scooted next to Lord Cremly, fearing that Samuel might throw himself on the man and tear his throat out. She had no love for the lord...but she didn't want anything to get in the way of playing the game that afternoon.

"Gentlemen, we're losing the light," she began. "I suggest the ladies go to bat first."

But no one budged. She didn't even think anyone heard her. All were too engrossed in Samuel's next move.

However, those expecting more drama were sadly thwarted. Because all Samuel did was laugh, clasping his hands behind his back. Myfanwy had a sinking suspicion he did it to keep himself from throwing the first punch. "Is that why you ruined Benny Hardcastle's benefit match last year? To maintain the game's integrity?"

Myfanwy turned to Lord Cremly. He wasn't squirming...though it was close. "I ruined nothing. The conditions were terrible that day. My side determined—as a whole—that it was the safe decision not to play."

For the first time, real anger sparked from Samuel. His eyes flashed and he took a quick step forward before containing himself. "It was barely spitting rain. You just wanted to deprive the man of income. All because whenever he faced you at the bat, he made mincemeat out of you."

Was that true? Could the lord be so spiteful? Myfanwy wondered. Benefit matches were incredibly important for cricketers who were retiring. Since there was no pension or way for them to earn money after they quit, clubs and friends hosted benefit matches, donating most of the proceeds from the event to the player and his family. Good benefit matches gifted a man with thousands of pounds that could see him living comfortably while he figured out what to do with the rest of his life. Bad benefits left a man with little more than well-wishes and money for dinner that night.

Myfanwy had never heard of a player ruining another's benefit match *on purpose*. That wasn't just unsportsmanlike—that was plain cruel.

The sardonic grin stalled on Lord Cremly's face as the crowd waited for him to speak. When he did, his lips barely moved. "Was there a reason why you interrupted us, Mr. Everett? Surely it can't be just about old grievances. It's bad form to speak like this in front of the ladies. Even a bricklayer's son knows that."

Samuel's eyes flickered to Myfanwy, landing with the force of a brick. They narrowed as he held her gaze for a long while, saying so much, but in a language she didn't understand. "Oh, I don't know," he said wistfully. "These women are stronger than you think."

Lord Cremly shook his head and turned away from Samuel. Addressing his friends, he said, "Let's forget about that, shall we? Now, what did we decide about the teams? If I remember correctly, the ladies were searching for another player—"

"I'll play," Samuel called out, stopping the crowd of people from cutting him off from the circle. Once more, it widened at his announcement.

Lord Cremly gritted his teeth. "Thank you, but the men don't need another player. Maybe next time."

"Not with you," Samuel spat. He nodded toward Anna. "Them. I'll play with the women… If they'll have me, that is."

Lord Cremly snorted before granting Anna a disbelieving grin. "I think you can do better than that. The man can barely walk…or see, for that matter. Here. Let me go into the house. I think there's a six-year-old boy who wants to learn to play. Even he would be a better option for you."

"We'll take him," Myfanwy called out instantly.

Samuel clapped his hands and began to jog out to the far field. "Fine. I thought the talking would never end. Let's play, shall we?"

Chapter Five

SAMUEL WOULD PAY for this later, but as of now—this lovely moment—he didn't feel a goddamned thing. No, that was wrong. He felt pure, unadulterated hatred wafting from fucking Lord Cremly whenever Samuel had the ball in his hands—which was just about the entire time he was out in the field.

It was almost too easy.

With the men's team batting left-handed, Samuel bowled all but one out, hitting the wickets off the stumps in five straight deliveries. Sir Bramble managed to make contact with the ball; however, that was pure, dumb luck, since his eyes were closed when he swung. In any event, he popped the ball up and Samuel was able to race over and get under it for the catch, single-handedly dismissing the entire men's side without breaking a sweat.

When it was the women's turn to bat, he insisted that he go first. Was he being a bit aggressive? Perhaps. Myfanwy didn't hide her exasperation as he yanked the bat out of her hands and marched up to the wicket, but she didn't make a meal out of it. He knew she wanted to win, so she eventually stopped harassing him and let him face the bowler.

Naturally, it was Lord Cremly, and naturally, Samuel slammed the ball so far that Sir Bramble called it for an automatic six runs, meaning Samuel didn't actually have to go back and forth between the two wickets to count the runs.

Samuel could have kissed the unathletic man. He'd die before acknowledging it, but his leg was throbbing like someone had taken a hammer to his kneecap. It was taking all his resolve to walk as evenly as he could, but he refused to give Lord Cremly the satisfaction of limping. The bastard had taken his eye from him that day three years ago, and Samuel wouldn't allow the man to take his pride at a garden party too.

In the end, the match only lasted thirty minutes before the elusive viscount emerged out of his hiding to announce a light supper was being served inside the house. And Samuel had stayed at bat for the majority of that time.

Because they couldn't finish two innings, the men were forced to forfeit and the women walked off the field to polite applause as the victors with forty-seven runs to the men's zero.

Samuel growled when the servant took the bat from him, upset that he hadn't been able to hit for fifty. It didn't matter how long he'd been away from the game—the competitive spirit died hard.

He had no intention of following the others to the house. Samuel had already done what he'd set out to do that afternoon and had discussed his business plans with Sir Bramble— embarrassing Lord Cremly had just been a lovely bonus. With everyone heading inside, he thought to slide away without notice.

Samuel should have known escaping wouldn't be that easy. As the field cleared, Myfanwy stayed behind, obviously waiting for him, the jacket he'd taken off to play hanging from her arm.

"Looking for this?" she said, holding it out to him as he ap-proached. Samuel accepted it with a nod of thanks before reluctantly putting it back on. The last thing he wanted to do was add another layer of clothing. Her glare could have melted an iceberg. "Did you enjoy yourself?" she asked.

Samuel took his time, fastening his last button, and then his arms fell helplessly by his sides. "You won, didn't you? There's no reason to be angry at me."

"Oh, I'm not angry," she shot back. "I'm bloody furious."

"You're furious at the wrong person, then. Save it for Lord Cremly and his ilk. I made him look like a fool for you—doesn't that count for anything?"

Myfanwy shook her head, and Samuel had to stop himself from staring at her marvelous hair. Even pulled back at the back of her head, the copper locks caught the light in such a brilliant fashion, startling him with their glorious shine. That was another reason why he'd been so domineering during the match. If his head was in the game, it wasn't on her—the way she moved so fluidly on the pitch, the way her gown flowed around and in between her legs when she ran. Myfanwy was as graceful as any dancer; her motions were always purposeful and true. He couldn't help but wonder what a woman like that would be like in the bedroom, so sure of herself and in tune with her strong body.

She snapped her fingers in front of his face, causing Samuel to blink and release the erotic visions from his head. "Are you even listening to me? I said I don't believe for one second that you made Cremly the fool because of me. You did it only for yourself."

Samuel swiped a sweaty hand over his face and began to trudge away. The limp was back, as was the mounting pain. "Does it matter?" he challenged.

"Yes!" she yelped, latching behind him like a shadow. "I wanted *us* to beat him—the women. And we could have if you hadn't gotten in our way. By monopolizing the game, you made it seem like we were incapable. Yes, you helped us win, but you also helped prove their point."

"And what point is that?"

"That they're better. That...that...we need help and we don't deserve to be taken seriously!"

Samuel spun around, but he was stopped from saying anything by a grating chuckle he knew all too well.

"Of course I take you seriously, Miss Myfanwy," Lord Cremly replied in his pandering, confident way. "Why do you have it in that pretty little head of yours that we men have such a negative image of women?"

Goddamn Cremly! Why couldn't the bastard just leave them alone and lick his wounds somewhere else? Samuel could answer his own question—because Lord Cremly's title and fortune prohibited him from ever having true wounds—nothing like Samuel's, anyway.

"I'm sorry, my lord," Myfanwy said tightly, rubbing her eyes. "Would you mind giving us a moment? We're in the middle of an important conversation."

"I can see that," the marquis said, meandering even closer. Samuel instantly locked his hands behind his back. He would not punch him. He wouldn't lay his bricklaying hands on the son of a bitch, giving him the opportunity to crow to the entire party about Samuel's lack of discipline. His parents couldn't give him much in life, but at least they'd given him that.

"I *love* women, by the way," Lord Cremly added, licking Myfanwy with another of those lascivious glances. Samuel clutched his hands together tighter. "I especially love watching you run around on the pitch like chickens with your heads cut off. It's positively delightful. Not to mention all the money I make betting on the matrons when they beat the single ladies every year. What about you, Everett? You've been known to throw your money on a bet. Have you made some of your paltry fortune on the matrons? Did it pay for that sweet little inn of yours?"

"I'm afraid that won't be happening again, my lord," Myfanwy said testily. "I assure you that the single women will be taking home the victory this year."

Lord Cremly tilted his head toward the clouds, musing as if he hadn't heard Myfanwy at all. "You know...I always thinks it's odd that the single ladies continue to lose year after year. All those girls, no doubt angry and frustrated that they have no husbands, could use that aggression and despair in their play. Can you imagine? All that pent-up energy…" He lobbed his gaze back to Myfanwy, full of pity. "Did you know the matrons have asked me to be their coach this year?"

"No… I…" Myfanwy stammered.

Lord Cremly reached out and plucked a blade of grass off her shoulder. "Perhaps it's time you just got married. Like Miss Jennifer. I have it on good authority that Sir Bramble is going to propose soon, despite her father's profession. Don't you want to be like your friend and know what it feels like to win…in all areas of life?"

Samuel followed this interaction, knowing he was balancing on a thin wire. He lived with Myfanwy; he knew she could handle herself. More importantly, he knew she *wanted* to handle herself against villains such as Cremly, and yet it was becoming harder and harder to stand back and not interfere. If he had his way, he would have busted Cremly's nose the second his arm extended in Myfanwy's direction. Samuel had assumed she would edge away…or maybe snap the lord's finger. But she didn't do any of that. In fact, she didn't do anything. It was as if Myfanwy was paralyzed, frozen by the lord's callous words.

Cremly, pushing his advantage, reached across Myfanwy's torso to her other shoulder. As he was poised to pick off another piece of grass, Samuel had finally had enough.

"Touch her again and I will break your fucking hand," he stated evenly.

Cremly frowned, dropping his arm to his side. "Excuse me? Who do you think you are, speaking to me that way?"

Samuel stepped in front of him, blocking Cremly's view from Myfanwy. "I'm her guardian, that's who I am. And her coach." Myfanwy gasped, and he felt the heat of her breath on the back of his neck. Odd, that the heady sensation made Samuel want to batter the bastard's hand even more.

Cremly backed away. "Her coach? What coach?"

"For the single ladies," Samuel remarked matter-of-factly. "They asked me, and I accepted. So, it seems we have a date soon on the pitch." He found his first true smile of the afternoon. "Just like old times."

Cremly let out a mirthless snort as the men gave one another deathly expressions. Then, slowly and maliciously, his attention fastened on Samuel's bad eye. "I feel sorry for those poor girls," Cremly said softly. "They deserve someone better than a used-up old cricketer who can barely see two feet in front of him." He paused, his teeth curling over his lips. "It really is ugly, isn't it? I've often wondered why you don't wear a patch over the frightful sight."

"Why should I? So you don't have to see what you did?"

"I played the game, Samuel. That's what gentlemen do. It's not my fault you couldn't move fast enough to get out of the way. Blame your pathetic leg for that. Everyone has moved on. I suggest you do the same."

Move on? Move on? When the son of a bitch took everything from him? His livelihood, his youth, the only thing Samuel had ever truly loved? "If you're a gentleman, then I'm glad I'll never be one."

The marquis barked a flippant laugh. "Well, luckily for all of us, there's no danger in that happening." Then, without waiting for a reply, Lord Cremly bowed low to Myfanwy and walked away, whistling as he went.

SAMUEL'S HAND CLUNG to the lip of the tub. He hissed as he lowered himself inside the freezing water, and the ice clinked and bobbed as it made room for his shivering body. Taking a deep breath, he finally submerged himself in one quick movement, knowing the longer he pussyfooted, the worse the experience would be.

"I've grown soft," Samuel muttered as he let the glacial water swallow him up to mid-chest. That was precisely why he'd asked the maids to fill the entire tub. He only needed to ice his bad leg, but decided at the last moment that it wouldn't hurt to give his entire body the frigid treatment. When he'd played cricket full-time, it had been nothing to submerge himself in an ice bath... Now, he dreaded it more than the pain he was working to alleviate.

"Fuck," he rasped, leaning his head back against the tub and closing his eyes. What a disaster of a day. Not his meeting with Sir Bramble—that had gone well, with the baron agreeing to invest in the sporting goods venture. However, just like every-thing else in Samuel's life, the second the sky appeared clear...the rain came pounding down.

Samuel didn't know the first thing about coaching. He was a cricket *player*. One of the best England had ever seen. And he knew even less about coaching girls. He'd grown up with two brothers; when disagreements happened (and there had been many), they were solved with fists and cutting remarks. The coaches that he'd had the benefit of playing under in his youth had resolved matters in the same, belligerent way. Pats on the back were few. Screaming and foul words were the only motivations.

The gentler, weaker sex was...well, gentle and weak.

Perhaps Samuel was overthinking this. Since the single ladies would never make good cricket players, maybe he didn't need to be a good coach. Only a decent one. Good enough for them to slaughter Cremly's team.

But that thought put him in an even worse mood. Samuel didn't have it in him to do anything perfunctorily—especially when it came to cricket. If these women wanted him, then he would give his experience in its entirety. Shame on them. They should have known better. *Caveat emptor.*

One woman, in particular, should have known better.

What the hell was he going to do about Myfanwy? The moment she'd needled her way into his house, Samuel had made a point to keep their interactions to a minimum. And he'd been doing a damn fine job, too. Now, in only a matter of days, he'd agreed to spend more time with her—intimate time. Because, to Samuel, there was nothing deeper and more personal, private and profound, than the cricket pitch. It was the only place he'd ever truly felt his soul quicken and transcend his body, the one place he ever felt like the man he wanted to be. Even bloody and bruised, it was the one place he was whole.

Sharing the pitch with her would be dangerous.

A knock sounded on the door. "I told you I needed more time," Samuel called out, desperately trying not to move. He'd gotten a handle on the cold, but when he jostled in the water, it was like a million ice picks stabbing into him all over again. "Come back in ten minutes."

"No, I don't have ten minutes," a resolute voice answered as the door swung forward.

Samuel's eyes flew open, and behind him, he heard determined footsteps stall on his bedroom carpet.

"What are you doing?" Myfanwy yelped.

Samuel shot straight up to sitting, frigid water be damned. "What does it look like I'm doing? Get out of here!"

But his ward didn't budge. Instead, the damn girl seemed to tiptoe even more into his room. "Is that ice?" she asked with naked curiosity.

Samuel cupped some water and splashed it on his face. He had to be dreaming, but nothing was waking him up. "Of course it's ice."

"Oh...you're *naked* in there!"

Samuel swiveled around in the bath to see Myfanwy—wide-eyed and impertinent—craning her neck toward the tub. "Of course I'm naked! Why wouldn't I be?"

She twisted her fingers fretfully. "I have no idea! I just didn't expect it!"

"This my room," Samuel returned dryly. "A reasonable person would expect it."

Myfanwy shook her head. Her copper hair was down, and it swayed across her shoulders like glorious church bells. "I told Benjamin I needed to speak with you; he said now would be a good time."

Samuel gripped the lip of the tub. "My butler wouldn't do that."

"He did."

"He wouldn't." *Or would he?*

A pregnant pause fell over them. Samuel could almost hear the wheels spinning in her head. "Why are you sitting in ice water?" she asked.

"Because," he lamented wearily, realizing she wouldn't leave until she got her answer, "it's the only thing that stops my leg from feeling like it's been set on fire."

"Because you played with us today?"

"Yes. No. It hurts every day, but playing on it didn't help."

"You could have fooled me. For a moment there, when I was watching you…" Her voice took on a dreamy quality that pricked Samuel worse than the ice. "I thought… Well, I thought it was like I'd gone back in time. You seemed like the old you."

"And now I'm paying the price for it."

"Is there anything else you can do…for the pain?"

"No."

"Truly? Forgive me, but this seems like torture."

No more than speaking to you alone in my room with only one set of clothing between us. "I'm used to it," Samuel said, annoyed that the more he told himself not to engage with her, the more he engaged. "Just… Will you please go back to your room? I'll be there momentarily, and then I can answer more of your ridiculous questions."

Myfanwy was about to step away but stopped herself. "Wait, no. Can I just say what I have to say? It won't take long. Please?" A small smile curled onto her face. "I won't look, I promise."

Samuel continued to glare at her. That little smile told him that trusting her was the last thing he should do. But he wasn't in the best position to debate. It wasn't like he could pick her up and throw her out. Or could he?

"Fine," he gritted out. Samuel resumed his position, leaning against the back of the tub, his eyes closed. "It's not like there's much to see anyway."

"I don't understand."

Samuel chuckled. "Good." He'd let her husband inform her about the delightful consequences of cold water on a man's balls. His chuckle died a hasty death. Thoughts of her future husband usually had that morose effect. "If you're going to stay here, go over to the far side of the bed," he instructed her, claiming a modicum of respectability in this improbable situation.

Myfanwy released an exasperated exhale, but at least she listened. However, once Samuel heard the telltale squeak of the mattress, his eyes shot open once more.

"Don't sit on it!" he yelped, splashing ice cubes out of the tub.

Myfanwy hopped off the mattress like it was covered in poisonous snakes. "What's wrong now? You told me to come here!"

"Not to sit! Just to stand."

She tossed up her hands. "What does it matter?"

Oh, it matters. Samuel couldn't let one ounce of Myfanwy perch on that bed. If he saw her in that position, all the ice in all the world wouldn't matter to his inflamed flesh.

"You're being ridiculous and mean," she announced, leaning against his bedpost. *Fine. Leaning is fine.* As long as she didn't lean *too* much. "All I wanted to do was come in here and say thank you. That is…" Myfanwy bit at her plump lower lip, and Samuel came to the stark conclusion that leaning *was* too much. He needed more ice.

"What?" he growled, a little too harshly even for his own ears. *Dammit!* It couldn't be helped. He was naked and she wasn't—which was the way it was supposed to be, but not the way he wanted it.

A streak of red traveled from Myfanwy's neck, flushing the

skin up to her cheekbones. "I'm worried that you only told Lord Cremly that you'd be our coach to get back at him and that you didn't truly mean it."

"I mean what I say."

"Yes, but..." Myfanwy lazed against the bedpost, hugging it with her torso, and Samuel had never wanted to be a piece of wood so much in his life. "Do you really want to do it, or do you just want to beat Lord Cremly?"

Samuel splashed more water in his face. This was what separated professionals from amateurs. Professionals wanted to win at any cost; amateurs seemed to only care about the optics of winning. It never made any sense to him.

"You're worried about the wrong thing," he said evenly. "Who cares why I'm helping you? All you need to know is that with me as your coach, you will beat the matrons. Isn't that what you want?"

Myfanwy squinted while she paused to mull that over. "Yes. I suppose..."

"There's no supposing; there's winning and losing. That's it. Now, I'll ask you again. Do you want to win?"

"Yes."

"Good, then—"

"But I also want to know what changed your mind," she said, cutting him off. "You seemed adamantly against the idea the day before. I never took you to be someone whose mind could be changed so quickly."

Samuel stared into the water where the ice cubes were melting at a faster rate than he would have expected. The notion of honesty banged around in his muddled head. Honesty between a guardian and his ward wasn't necessarily needed; however, honesty between a coach and his player...that was something else.

Myfanwy continued, her voice soft. "I wasn't aware that it was Lord Cremly who did that to"—she nodded toward his face—"to you. It's understandable that you would want revenge.

I suppose I only hoped that it was more than that."

"It is." Samuel cleared his throat. "It is more than that." He trailed his fingers through the water, watching the perfect and fluid way the liquid cut across his skin. "I didn't like the way he looked at you. It was wrong."

"How did he look at me?"

Samuel's gaze remained down. "Like he owned you," he said gruffly, "or thought he could have you."

Myfanwy's laughter surprised him. She untangled herself from the bedpost and perched on the edge of his bed. With his latest admission, Samuel no longer had the strength to stop her. "Clearly, you have no experience being a woman," she replied.

"What does that mean?"

Her laughter subsided. "Men always look at me like that, at women like that. Well...most men do, anyway. You don't. I've lived with you for a year, and it's rare to get you to look in my direction."

Samuel's entire body screamed at him to stay quiet, but he dragged the next words from his lips. "Do you want me to?"

"Look at me?"

He nodded.

"Yes...I believe I do."

Samuel's gaze soared to her in an instant, and he watched that shy little smile come back to her face, making his chest tighten. He also noticed her focus latch on to his bad eye.

He motioned to it with his hand. "I find it's easier for every-one if I don't look at them. It can be distressing. I actually tried wearing a patch, but I hated feeling like a pirate."

Myfanwy didn't laugh. "I'm not distressed."

Samuel cleared his throat again. "No?"

She shook her head, and then slowly peeled herself from the bed and walked toward the door. Samuel was numb, and it had nothing to do with the water.

"I like it when you look at me, Samuel," Myfanwy said softly before leaving.

After she closed the door, Samuel inflated his lungs and plunged himself under the water. When he came up, he could still smell her perfume.

Chapter Six

"I THINK I'M going to ask Samuel Everett to be my lover."
Jennifer dropped her cricket bat to the ground.

Myfanwy, attempting to be nonchalant after her frank admission, kept her gaze forward and away from Jennifer's astounded expression.

Eventually, she heard her friend issue a resigned sigh. "Can you at least wait to ask him until after practice is over?" Jennifer replied, mimicking Myfanwy's casual manner. "I'm nervous enough as it is."

As usual, Jennifer's response was exactly what Myfanwy needed, and the two of them burst into laughter while biding their time for their first practice with Samuel to begin. With still a few minutes until they were scheduled to start, the entire team was already present and accounted for at the agreed-upon location—the vacant plot of land adjacent to the Flying Batsman. Samuel may have agreed to be their coach, but he wasn't willing to travel far to do it.

Jennifer wasn't the only one that had a touch of nerves. Most of the women fidgeted while they anticipated Samuel's arrival, toeing their boots into the dirt and grass, issuing anxious smiles while fiddling with their bonnets. Myfanwy wasn't immune to the jittery mood, recognizing it was most likely the cause of her outrageous—*though truthful*—admission.

Jennifer picked up her bat and rested it over her shoulder before turning to Myfanwy with a confused look. "But weren't you the one who told me that now wasn't the best time for men because they 'weakened legs'?" Her gaze narrowed. "Or is that only when it applies to me?"

"Not at all," Myfanwy replied breezily, keeping her nose high in the air. Captains needed to betray confidence on the field—even when discussing such delicate matters. "Men *do* weaken legs when you get all moony over them. That is not the case with me. My situation with Samuel is purely physical. My birthday is soon, and I'm set to be my own woman with my own money and home. Taking a lover wouldn't be unreasonable."

It was obvious that Myfanwy was desperately trying to appear worldly and matter-of-fact, and Jennifer wanted to keep pace. But her voice cracked, coming out noticeably high-pitched, when she replied, "Oh, and the fact that you've been in love with him since you were a girl has nothing to do with the decision."

"Certainly not," Myfanwy retorted, warmth creeping onto her cheeks. So much for being mature. She had a decided lack of knowledge of worldly women, but assumed they probably didn't blush when discussing potential lovers. "And I haven't been in love with him for all these years. I've been merely interested."

"Ah," Jennifer said, nodding, not even pretending to believe what Myfanwy was telling her. "And I suppose seeing Mr. Everett naked in his tub didn't influence your decision either. Which reminds me, you haven't told me nearly enough about that encounter." She glued herself to Myfanwy's side, dropping her voice into a breathy whisper. "How was he?"

Myfanwy elbowed Jennifer in the ribs with a giggle, sending her back a few steps. "He was…acceptable."

Jennifer rolled her eyes, her mouth falling into a pout. "I'm so glad you've not taken up the pen. You'd make a terrible writer. *Acceptable?* That's it?"

A small smile curled its way onto Myfanwy's face as she

threw her friend a look out of the corner of her eye. "He was...very acceptable."

Jennifer's lips twisted. "Ah."

"Yes. Incredibly *ah*."

Apparently content with that answer, Jennifer turned back to the field, where a sour-faced *and late* Samuel was finally making his way across to join them. His footsteps long and measured, the man looked as surly as a goat. He'd left his hat and his jacket behind and came to them only in his plaid waistcoat and white linen shirt, his hair blowing wild off his high forehead.

Myfanwy couldn't stop her mind from traveling back to the night when she'd surprised him during his ice bath. In the week that proceeded, Myfanwy wasn't sure if Samuel was actively avoiding her or if she was being sensitive. It wasn't as if they'd existed in the same orbits before, but that hadn't stopped her from hoping.

She'd never know what it was that spurred her to say those things to him that night. Maybe it was because he was incapacitated. Save for a fire (and even that was debatable), there was no way Samuel was going to jump out of that tub and run her out of his room, and that had helped loosen her tongue...and her desires.

Seeing him there, his tight, honed muscles on display, awakened a need in Myfanwy she'd managed to hide so well for so long. Even her father never had a clue as to the reason she'd insisted on going to all those cricket matches when she was younger. Yes, it had been for a love of the game, but it had also been for *him*. Samuel, in all his youth and vitality, had been such a marvel to watch. The fluid nature of his body as he ran the field— all childish vigor and unrelenting enthusiasm—had left Myfanwy transfixed from the beginning.

Now, standing on the field next to her mates, regarding Samuel as he frowned ferociously at all of them, she couldn't help but wonder if asking him to come had been a bad idea. Everything felt so entirely personal. Myfanwy lived in two worlds: cricket and everything else. All of a sudden, mixing the two seemed perilous, almost heartbreaking.

"Well, for your sake, I hope he's a better lover than a coach," Jennifer whispered in her ear as Samuel continued to glower.

"He's just getting his feet wet," Myfanwy whispered back, hoping he'd prove her right and speak before night fell. "He'll get there."

"He better," Jennifer replied doubtfully.

Anna, bless her heart, broke up the awkward monotony. "Is this really where we're going to practice?"

Samuel's hawkish focus immediately zeroed in on the woman, and Myfanwy was proud that her pint-sized friend didn't melt under his harsh—and rude—perusal.

"I own it," Samuel said, glancing over his shoulder at the field. This was news to Myfanwy. She had no idea he'd made the purchase or when. It was a decent-sized spot of land but needed work. Though it was large and open, there was more dirt than grass, and no fences or natural hedges that could work as a boundary for the pitch. "It's free to use and available anytime we need," he continued, catching Myfanwy's attention with a knowing look. "We won't have to wait or ask anyone's permission to use it. It is yours and only yours for the foreseeable future."

Joyous expressions lit up around the group. The team had never had its own field before. The ownership of this one—however limited—was a gift that would not go unappreciated.

A few of the players began to clap, but Samuel quickly quashed it with a flick of his hand. "We don't have time for all of that. Just get out there."

The women's smiles were eclipsed by frowns. "What do you want us to do?" Lady Everly asked.

Samuel answered with a smirk, "What the hell do you think? Play." He cocked his head. "*And* impress me."

꘎꘎꘎꘎꘎

AND THEY TRIED. They *really* did. For her part, Myfanwy ran faster, threw quicker, and swung harder than she ever had in her life. But nothing seemed to matter.

When Samuel wasn't barking out barely coherent orders, he was always standing there on the edge of the field, studying—always just studying—with a horribly displeased look on his face.

It took no time at all for Myfanwy to completely give up trying to ascertain what was going on in that mind of his or why he was making certain decisions. Most of the practice was taken up by drills. Drills, drills, and more drills! Running drills, throwing drills, balancing drills, catching drills. There was no practice game, no strategy.

By the time the miserable, unrelenting sun was starting to decline, Myfanwy's thighs were shaking from the overuse, and she was certain she wouldn't be able to lift anything heavier than a teacup for days.

Perhaps that was why she stopped right in the middle of yet another interminable drill where Samuel had the ladies first catch a ball in the air and then throw it at the two bails lying across the top of the wicket as quickly as they could. Myfanwy simply stepped out of the line. She was tired, drenched in sweat, and ready for an uplifting comment from her coach. She couldn't go on. She didn't *want* to go on, and that made her furious at herself. She'd never had that thought before. And *that* made her furious at Samuel.

Her curmudgeonly coach didn't notice the mutiny at first. Anna and Jennifer finished the drill before he spotted Myfanwy on the outskirts of the group.

The tendons in Samuel's neck began to flare, and Myfanwy readied herself for another tirade.

"Get back in line," he yelled.

Myfanwy shook her head. "I'm tired," she called back. "We

need a break."

Samuel tilted his head to the blue sky as if asking the Lord for patience with dissident players. "I didn't ask if you were tired. I know you're tired. You *should* be tired. This is practice. So, get back in line and practice."

The other players stopped the drill, not knowing what to do, but also not wanting to miss the spectacular argument that was surely coming.

To be honest, Myfanwy didn't know if she had it in her to fight. She'd never been so exhausted in her life. "I don't understand why we are doing all these drills. We came here to play cricket. This isn't cricket."

Myfanwy could see the muscles under Samuel's bad eye twitch as if she'd just confessed to kicking his favorite dog. His arms locked to his sides, and his hands remained clenched as he started to come toward her. His gait wasn't hurried or erratic, which made it even more terrifying.

The tips of his shoes were almost skimming hers by the time he spoke again. "You came here to play cricket?" he asked softly, causing the other ladies to bunch in closer to the couple. "Huh. Well, I came here to coach. And you will play cricket when I tell you to play cricket. Get back in line." He glanced at their audience. "I didn't tell you to stop!"

The others ran to restart the exercise, but Myfanwy held her ground. They continued their stalemate for long seconds. Samuel's nostrils flared, and she wondered if he could smell her with the same ferocity with which she could smell him. He was sweaty and flushed, with a damp sheen over his upper lip. Myfanwy was thirsty (and clearly delusional), because a vision of licking it off him came to her, causing a cold chill to shiver up her spine. Actually, it had nothing to do with her physical thirst. It was an emotional need, pure and simple.

"If you don't want to play by my rules, then you can leave," Samuel said. "You asked me to make you better players, and that's what I'm doing. I can't have you questioning me every time you feel a little tired. Tired is good. *Hard* is good."

Myfanwy was transfixed by Samuel's mouth as he enunciated each and every word as if he were spouting Shakespeare. "I like hard," she replied.

Samuel blinked. She thought his lips inched up on the side before he clamped them back in their tight grimace. "Then do as I say and get back in line—"

"And I like questioning you."

Samuel palmed his face and groaned.

"This isn't a dictatorship, Samuel," Myfanwy went on. "I'm the captain of this team. If I don't speak up for us, then no one will. I just want to understand—"

"You don't need to understand," he roared, sliding his hand down his haggard face. "You just have to listen!"

In an instant, he swiveled his neck to the side like a hunting dog who'd just gotten a whiff of a fresh scent. "Wait, you there! Brown-haired girl!"

Samuel snapped his fingers and hurried over to a tall, reedy young lady who held the ball at the side of her body, paralyzed as she was ready to throw it.

"Her name is Ruthie," Myfanwy called out in indignation. Samuel answered her with a rude flick of his hand over his shoulder.

"You...you..." He scratched the back of his neck as he came up to the girl, who now looked like she was ready to pass out from the attention. "What's your name, again?"

"Ruthie!" Myfanwy growled, sidling up to the pair. She nodded to Ruthie encouragingly. *Don't let him bully you!*

Ruthie clutched the ball nervously in front of her chest, digging her nails into its seam. "I'm Ruthie," she mumbled, casting her attention down at the pathetic grass.

"That's fine," Samuel said dismissively. "You were just about to throw the ball. Show me again."

Ruthie gnawed at her lips for long seconds before she gained the courage to do as he asked. Then, slowly, painstakingly, she lifted her arm to the side of her body and tossed the ball—in the same fashion that well-wishers would toss rice after a wedding— causing it to land a dismal few feet in front of her.

Samuel's jaw clenched, and Myfanwy readied herself to defend the young woman if Samuel decided to lose his composure. She knew that Ruthie needed work, but for all her trouble, Myfanwy still had not found a way to help her. Myfanwy wasn't even sure why Ruthie had asked to join the team this year. The poor girl was always too stiff and self-conscious to enjoy herself, and never laughed and joked with her teammates during breaks.

But Myfanwy refused to let Samuel harass her. Not only might Ruthie leave—and the team desperately needed the numbers—but the shamed lady might also never pick up a cricket bat again, and that was unconscionable.

Myfanwy decided to strike first, patting Ruthie's upper arm consolingly, but Samuel's sudden movement killed all action and thought.

In a flash, the insane man reached out with both arms and grabbed at both of Ruthie's shoulders. He fisted his hands on the fussy muslin fabric and...*yanked*. He yanked like the devil trying to keep a man out of heaven.

A collective gasp rang out from all the ladies as Samuel tore off Ruthie's sleeves in one fell swoop, leaving her arms completely bare.

And completely unrestricted.

Ruthie's mouth dropped open, but she didn't even let out a squeak.

Myfanwy realized her mouth was in the same gawking position. "What in the world do you think you're doing—"

"There," Samuel said, stepping back to admire his handiwork. He wiped the sweat off his forehead with the ruined pink fabric and then tossed it on the ground. "That's better. Now you can throw the ball. Show me again."

Myfanwy couldn't believe her eyes. No one said a word. No one balked at their coach's unorthodox and Neanderthal-like behavior. If anything, the other ladies appeared curious and studied Ruthie with genuine anticipation.

Ruthie squared her body to the wicket and gripped the ball with renewed determination. She lowered her forehead to the target and brought her elbow back and high toward her ear.

Samuel nodded, his concentration fixed on his player, like she was the only person on the planet. "Good. Now, step and throw and sail the arm through. The elbow leads and the arm follows. Go on."

Myfanwy almost couldn't believe it. Samuel sounded almost...encouraging.

And it was exactly what Ruthie needed, because she did as he asked and the ball soared in the air, just shaving the wicket on its right side. The bails didn't fall, though they did teeter.

Ruthie clapped her hands together, hopping up and down. "I did it," she squealed. "I did it. I've never done that before. I didn't think I could."

"Of course you could," Samuel sneered. Was he trying not to sound cheerful? "Only your ridiculous clothes were in the way, and you didn't have the right form. Now you do. Let's move on."

He turned to Myfanwy and graced her with a pompous smile. "Now, you, back in line. Unless you have anything else you need to get off your chest."

Myfanwy thought her teeth might crack, she was gritting them so hard. But she had to give credit where credit was due. The incorrigible man had seen what Ruthie needed and given it to her. That was more than Myfanwy had been able to do.

"Well?" he taunted her when she continued to stare, slack-jawed.

Myfanwy was just about to get back in line when Lady Everly stepped forward. "I have something to say," she said sternly.

Samuel groaned, rolling his eyes while he muttered something that sounded an awful lot like *damn women*. "What?" he barked.

The lady lifted her covered arms out in front of her as if she were waiting for someone to put her in handcuffs. "Do it to me next?"

Chapter Seven

SAMUEL HEARD A *crash!* outside the drawing room. Leaving the comfort of his gin and solitude, he ventured to the garden attached to the back of the townhouse. As he stepped outdoors, his lungs immediately filled with the odd mix of nighttime scents of succulent, meaty family dinners and fruity roses. The private, high-walled garden was lined on all sides with the blasted fragrant flowers thanks to the previous owner. Samuel didn't mind the cloying, powdery smell, but he didn't love it either. It reminded him too much of funerals.

It appeared that his ward didn't approve of the robust flower either. He spied Myfanwy on the pebbled walking lane that framed both sides of the garden, a ball in her hand, ostensibly lining herself up to bowl down the path.

Silently, he regarded her unusual behavior, admiring her lithe form as she ran down the lane, winding up her arm to bowl. With astonishing speed, she whipped it at one of the plants at the far end, taking off half of a juicy red rose in one striking slice.

Samuel clapped slowly as he emerged from the shadows, causing Myfanwy to yelp and clutch her hands to her heart as if to keep it inside her chest.

"You scared me!" she shrieked, fetching her ball from the battered plant. Samuel noticed her stride past a broken flowerpot, which he surmised had been the source of the earlier noise.

"You know," he drawled easily, enjoying the round, plush view of Myfanwy's backside as she bent over to search for her ball under the bushes. "Plants are expensive. I'm not as rich as the gentlemen of your acquaintance, you know."

With a triumphant "ah-ha!" Myfanwy shot up straight. She tossed the ball in the air and caught it. "Oh, please. You're richer than Croesus. My father told me all about your investments. You do know that, don't you? He told me everything."

Samuel didn't know what he knew anymore. Not when her sunburst red hair sat all disheveled and enticing around her face. Half of him wanted to run his fingers through it—try to tame it—and the other half never wanted her to wear her hair any different for the rest of her life.

Myfanwy cocked her head, waiting for him to answer. Samuel cleared his throat. "Um...yes... You know what I mean. Someone put a great deal of money and time into this garden."

"Not you?"

Samuel almost laughed. "No, not me. I bought it this way, and I'd hate to have to spend money to repair it after you're gone."

Myfanwy took deliberate steps back to the top of her makeshift pitch, her brow furrowed. She had a very kissable brow as well, Samuel surmised. In fact, every spot on her body deserved to be kissed by him. Especially her arms, which were bare since she'd changed after practice into a cap-sleeved gown. She'd been the only woman who hadn't asked him to tear off her dress sleeves at practice—almost as if she was being spiteful. Or maybe she just didn't want Samuel to touch her.

He didn't like that thought, not one bit.

"Where am I going?" she asked.

"Excuse me?"

Myfanwy tossed the ball up in the air again and caught it. "You said 'after I'm gone.' Where am I going?"

Oh. Samuel locked his hands behind his back and waded

further into the garden, being sure not to get too close to her. It was safer that way for reasons he didn't want to contemplate. Myfanwy had divulged that she liked it when Samuel looked at her; however, she'd never said anything about his touching her. No, that was his wishful thinking.

Realizing that he'd pushed his leg too far that afternoon, he sat on the little bench against the brick wall facing her. "When you get married, obviously." Did his voice always sound this rough? Why was he so thirsty all of a sudden?

Samuel pulled at his collar while Myfanwy chuckled mirthlessly. "I thought I already told you that wasn't going to happen."

Samuel pulled harder. "You never told me that."

"I'm positive I did."

"When?"

She shrugged. "Before."

"Before what?"

How could she continue to look at him so incredulously? *She* was the one who wasn't making any damn sense! "Before everything, just before," she answered sharply. "It's not a secret. I'm sure I told you when I first moved in."

Samuel winced. He wasn't at his best in that period, so soon after the fateful circumstances that led to his retirement, not to mention his friend's passing. If Myfanwy had divulged anything at that time, she would have had to shout over all the booze he'd been drinking. And alcohol could be awfully loud.

"Never mind," he stated, shifting on the bench. He desperately needed another ice bath tonight. His hip muscles were screaming. "Just tell me why I won't have the pleasure of seeing you leave anytime soon."

Myfanwy's shoulders slumped. "Do you always have to be such an ass?"

Samuel didn't respond. It wasn't necessary, since they both knew the answer.

The woman sighed. "You don't have that long to wait, actually. As I'm sure you know, I will reach my majority soon, then I'll be able to take my money and live on my own. You can plan a party for me at that time if you'd like. I adore lemon cake."

"I already knew that."

"You did?"

Samuel caught the hopeful note in her tone—and the way it made his heart thump at odd intervals. He cleared his throat again. "Where will you go, if you don't mind my asking?"

With another huff, Myfanwy turned away from him toward her target. She started her windup down the pitch and managed to take off an entire rose head this time. *Not bad.*

Her chest heaved from the exertion, and that damn hair was flying all over the place once more, bracketing her face like she was a picture of the Madonna and Child. "I don't have to tell you," she said, panting. "But since I'm certain you won't try to stop me, I might as well. I'm going to buy a little bit of land and a small house—nothing too hard to manage—and start a cricket club. A real one. A place we can all be ourselves and call home without men or mothers skulking about, begging to give their opinions or make us doubt ourselves. A proper clubhouse. Just for us women."

More parts of Samuel's body were screaming now, but he couldn't pinpoint where they were. They were too deep inside. Questions, so many questions, ran through his mind. Rational questions. Logistical questions. But they all fell to the wayside as the only one that mattered charged out of his mouth. "Why do you think I won't try to stop you?"

In the process of going after her ball, Myfanwy froze. She stared at the ground for a couple of heartbeats before lifting her gaze to his. "You've made it clear that you'd like me to leave," she said softly.

Samuel hauled himself to standing. If his entire body hurt when he was sitting, what was the point of not being on his feet? "I've never said anything of the kind," he muttered gruffly, striding past her toward the bushes. He heard him follow on his heels.

"In the past, you've made it quite clear that you'd like to see me married—"

"I said I wanted to do right by your father."

"So...you want me to be happy!"

"Yes," Samuel replied. "Happy *and* married."

"Those aren't always the same thing."

Samuel got on his knees and scooted under the bush, throwing out curse after curse as the thorns waged a silent war on him. Myfanwy seemed only too happy to let him do this chivalrous deed on his own. His hand finally cupped the ball, and he escaped with his clothes mostly intact.

He offered it to Myfanwy with a cocky half-smile. She started to take it from him, but then her hand diverted sharply. Her fingers dove into his hair. "You have petals on your head." She laughed while rustling it about.

Samuel had to stop himself from closing his eyes. He hadn't been touched in so long. He'd forgotten how beautiful it was, how goddamn transcendent. A shudder escaped him, and Myfanwy's hand whipped away.

Thank the Lord it was dark outside. Samuel swore that he was blushing. "Um...thank you," he said. He shoved the ball in her hand and made a fuss of dusting the dirt off his palms while backing away a few steps. Space was needed. They could be in different rooms, and they would still need more.

Myfanwy seemed embarrassed by her action—or maybe his—because she shuffled her boots in the pebbles. The grating, grinding sound seemed like it was coming straight from his rusty, sluggish heart.

What would happen if he held her right now? Samuel wondered. He almost believed that she would let him, maybe even *want* him to. Then he would know what the pearly skin of her arms felt like. He could trace his hands over the goosebumps that he would surely cause, and experience the vibrant muscles just under her surface. Because this woman was strong. So very strong. But she was not his. She was a viscount's daughter. He was a bricklayer's son. And although he had money, and maybe even a little bit of celebrity, they would never be on the same level.

Once more, Samuel locked his hands behind his back and gripped tight. "What of your friends?" he asked quietly. "They will all get married and won't be able to play with you anymore. Joining the matrons is a way for you to counter that."

Myfanwy *humphed*, crossing her arms. "I will never play for the matrons."

"Because they're married?"

"No," she spat, her composure breaking. Hugging her middle, she continued. "Because they're pompous and rude and completely forget about their friends once they put rings on their fingers. Not just forget…they pretend like they never existed in the first place."

Samuel was beginning to understand. The viscount wasn't the only person that Myfanwy had lost. It appeared that she considered her married friends ghosts to her as well.

"Is that why you want to beat them so badly?" he asked.

Myfanwy bobbed a shoulder petulantly. "Perhaps."

"Oh, no, that's not good enough. I told you about my history with Cremly. Now it's your turn to do the same."

Myfanwy wanted to argue with him. He could see it in the glint of her eyes, but he also could see she was tired. Like a house of cards, Myfanwy collapsed from his pressure. "Fine," she said, brushing his shoulder as she moved past him. "But let's sit down, at least. Your leg is hurting you again."

"It's not," Samuel countered, but Myfanwy didn't turn around.

"We both know it is. You don't have to pretend with me, Samuel. I know you better than you think."

Samuel frowned…but hobbled in her wake to the bench, setting a mental reminder to ask her everything she thought she knew about him—which couldn't be much.

He took a seat next to her and leveled her with a *there, are you happy now?* glare. "Explain."

Myfanwy rolled her eyes, keeping her attention in front of her, giving Samuel an ample view of the swanlike column of her neck. The tendons pulsed and tightened as she deliberated over her words. Samuel wanted to shake her—and kiss her—and then tell her not to measure her conversation with him. He wanted off-the-cuff comments, ideas that just sprang in her head, no filters between them. Samuel was never comfortable in this world—his injuries and his family had seen to that—and yet he wanted Myfanwy to feel unfettered with him.

"Jennifer—Miss Hallett—is my very best friend in the world. You know that, correct?"

"I do."

Myfanwy nodded. "Well, she wasn't my only best friend. We had another. Lilly Gladwell. It was always the three of us. All the time. I thought nothing—not even a slip of paper—could ever come between us. And then…"

"And then?"

She inflated her lungs. Samuel prepared himself for the worst. By his own admission, he wasn't superb at consoling others, but he'd be damned if he fell short with Myfanwy.

"She got married."

Her nails cut into the leather of the ball. Samuel hesitated, hoping there was more to the story.

There wasn't.

"That's it?" he asked after a couple of beats. "She got married?"

Myfanwy's eyebrows crowded angrily toward her nose. "What do you mean, 'that's it'? She got married. That's plenty."

Christ. Samuel was so far out of the game, he couldn't even see the pitch. How was he supposed to console the woman when he didn't understand why she was so upset? And she *was* upset. It was obvious. Even with her head facing front, he could see her eyes shining with tears. He hoped to God they didn't fall. That would test his empathy skills.

"Explain more…please," he urged.

Myfanwy's eyelashes flickered, and Samuel held his breath, but no tears fell. She rolled the ball around and around; the tendons on the tops of her hands lifted up and down like piano keys. "I suppose men don't understand this sort of thing," she began. "Maybe it all could have been different, but the second Lilly got married, it was as if she turned into a different person. All her time and energy were spent on her husband."

Samuel's spine straightened. Now he was getting it. "And she had no time for ladies. That's to be expected in a new marriage, no?"

"No!" Myfanwy exclaimed, finally canting her body to his. It was then Samuel realized that her eyes weren't bright because she was close to tears, but because she was close to anger. Samuel felt enormously better. Tears he didn't understand, but anger and he were old friends.

Myfanwy went on, "Lilly had time for friends—new friends. Jennifer and I called on her, but she never called back. We saw her at balls and parties, but she pretended like we didn't exist. She wrote us out of her life and created an entirely new one. I didn't know what to do. I felt so…so…"

"Helpless?"

Myfanwy grabbed his hand. "Yes! Helpless! Thank you."

Samuel resisted the urge to move his hand underneath hers so their palms were facing each other. He mustn't tempt himself, because then he would tangle his fingers in between hers and all hell would break loose in his soul.

She glanced down at their hands, and her eyes widened at what she'd done…but she didn't take hers away.

Nor did Samuel remove his. Instead, he coughed because he was afraid of what his voice would sound like if he didn't. "Um… So, revenge. That's where your lust for winning comes from. I suppose that's as good a reason as any."

Myfanwy squeezed him, and Samuel almost jumped out of his seat at the utter bliss of her inflamed touch. There was so much intensity to this woman, and he wanted all of it to be directed at him.

"No, not revenge," she stated firmly. "I'm better than that."

Well, shit. Samuel was quite certain he was not.

"I have a plan," Myfanwy continued. "If the single women win—and if we continue to win—then the ladies will want to stay with me, with my new club. And...maybe..." She looked away hastily. "Maybe some of them won't see the need to marry at all. Maybe they'll recognize other options. Maybe, like me, they'll be curious about...alternative lifestyles."

Samuel's gaze narrowed. "Some of them...like Jennifer?"

Myfanwy flinched. "What about Jennifer?"

"You actually believe that she won't get married—that she won't leave you—if you win."

Suddenly, Myfanwy's entire body shrank, as if she was being stuffed into a cage. "It could happen."

The poor, naïve girl. Samuel understood there were many who wondered if he truly had a heart inside his beaten body, but now he knew for sure, because it positively shattered at Myfanwy's pathetic words. He'd never considered her a lonely person; however, it appeared that his ward's loneliness rivaled his own.

But there was a major difference between them.

Samuel's cricket career had been so successful because he'd craved autonomy. Being alone, affording his luxurious townhouse, not having to plan his days around a bricklayer's schedule, was all he'd ever wanted. Myfanwy, on the other hand, valued winning as a way to keep the ones she loved around her. They'd both experienced loss in life, and they each had reacted to it in completely different ways.

But Samuel could help her. Beyond a doubt, he knew he could. Even if that meant she would eventually leave him, he would do it. Because that would make her happy, and Samuel realized there were no limits to what he would do to keep her so.

He heard a sniffle. And it just came to him. As natural as

breathing, as faithful as a dog at her feet, Samuel raised his hand to her face. Slowly, with utter devotion, he used his thumb to wipe the tears from her cheeks. He didn't flinch once. Didn't even hesitate.

Myfanwy returned a sad, shy smile. "I'm sorry. I don't know what has come over me."

"It's fine," Samuel said, amazed at how level his voice was, how smooth and confident it escaped from his mouth.

Tiny tears collected on Myfanwy's eyelashes, and he was reminded of the fairytales his mother used to tell him and his brothers before they fell asleep at night about desperate princess-es and lovestruck knights. He'd loved those stories—loved any stories that got him out of Sutton, if not in body, then in mind.

Chagrined by her emotion, Myfanwy rustled about, using her fingers to stanch the flow of her tears at the corners of her eyes. Even so, Samuel didn't take his hand away. As if it had a mind of its own, it remained holding her cheek. No, that wasn't true. It wasn't doing it on its own. It was Samuel.

Her brown pupils swallowed her face, and she stared at him. Samuel couldn't read her expression. It wasn't fear that kept her locked with him, though it wasn't desire either. It almost looked like recognition, like Myfanwy was encountering something she hadn't seen in a long time.

Her next words gave credence to that thought. "I'm glad that I have you here, Samuel," she said tentatively. "I...I...uh...wanted to ask you something, ask you if you'd be amenable to something...with me. But now I can't ask it." She blushed prettily, ducking her head.

She spoke so low, so timid, that Samuel bent his torso to her. "Why?" he asked, echoing her soft tone, hoping to feel her next words brush against his lips.

"There's something about you," she said gently. "Something different, but also the same." Myfanwy shook her head. "I don't know." She licked her bottom lip with the tip of her tongue. "You remind me of someone long ago. Someone who..." She angled her head, and her hair skimmed over the top of Samuel's hand, scorching him.

"Someone who...?"

Again, her smile held a hint of sorrow. Somehow, Samuel knew she was speaking of him—the man he once was—and he wanted to kiss the anguish from her. More importantly, he wanted to kiss that memory away, because that man was gone and never coming back. There was only the man that he was now.

He pressed his hand against her cheek and nudged her closer, so close that the features of her face ceased to be. Freckles, dimples, cheekbones, syrupy eyes, all were lost. The only thing that remained was Myfanwy.

In a life filled with long shots, impossibilities, and pure luck, Samuel took the biggest gamble of his life and simply laid his forehead on hers.

And just as he'd wanted, Myfanwy's next words did caress his mouth—but they were the wrong ones. "Someone who...someone who once truly loved something."

Samuel's face flinched back. Myfanwy's eyes were closed. She'd been waiting for his kiss. And he'd moved away, struck by her comment.

"What?" he asked.

Myfanwy blinked like someone just waking from a confusing dream. "What?" she repeated.

"What did you say?"

She shook her head. "I just said—"

Samuel dropped his hand. "No, I heard you, but I don't understand—"

The door to the garden opened. "Mr. Everett, sir?"

Myfanwy shot up from her seat, dropping the ball to the pebbles as she smoothed her dress down on her lap.

Benjamin was too good of a butler to announce his surprise at finding them together, though Samuel did detect a slight rise in his voice. "Ah, hello, Miss Myfanwy. I didn't know you were here. Uh, Mr. Everett?"

Samuel got to his feet as well, although not as quickly as Myfanwy. "What is it?"

"There's a caller for you."

"At this time of night? Send them away."

Benjamin's mouth tightened. "I really think you should come and speak with them," he urged. "You'll want to see this."

Samuel could feel Myfanwy's gaze on him, and he almost tasted her disapproval. Clearly, she thought it was a woman. Who else would come this late? He almost wanted to tell her that she didn't know him as well as she thought, since he never had women come to the house. He always went to them.

Samuel nodded and began to move. Of course, Myfanwy was right behind him.

She followed him all the way to the foyer, her feet pounding louder and louder into the floor as they went. He couldn't wait to see the look on her face when he proved her wrong. He couldn't wait to ask her what she thought she'd find.

When they reached the door, he turned to give her one smug grin before reaching for the handle.

But Samuel should have known. The night had been much too sunny for him. Again with the damn rain.

His expression fell the moment he opened the door and saw the child on the other side. Two children, really.

A rough-looking urchin—couldn't have been more than ten—shoved a note into his hand. "She needs you," was all the boy said before taking off in a flash, leaving the younger child woefully behind.

Since the little one barely reached Samuel's busted kneecap, she couldn't be blamed. Besides, the child was beyond terrified and on the verge of hysterics as she sucked her thumb and gazed up at him helplessly.

Samuel didn't bother reading the note. He already knew what it said anyway. He knew by the color of the child's head. Red.

"Goddammit," he whispered. "Not again."

Chapter Eight

MYFANWY RAN LIKE she'd never run before. But it was too dark. The boy was too fast. And he wasn't chained down with three petticoats. But she couldn't just stand there, like Samuel, staring at the poor little girl.

Nevertheless, she called her search off after three blocks, avoiding the odd stares of the well-to-do couples enjoying their nightly strolls. Retreating to the house, she only had one thing on her mind, and the anger and indignation of the words she planned to say to Samuel built and built until she thought they would explode out of her.

Myfanwy slammed the door closed as she entered Samuel's house and found him in the drawing room, where he was pacing back and forth in front of the fire, his hand still clutching the note the boy had given him. The little girl was nowhere to be found.

Samuel didn't look up when she planted herself in a hard stance in front of him. *Coward.* "I had Gertie take her upstairs," he explained quietly. "Sit with her until she fell asleep."

"What are you going to do?" Myfanwy asked, crossing her arms. She needed the extra barrier between them. Myfanwy felt so incredibly raw, like she'd slid across the grass with nothing but her shift on. She couldn't believe that just minutes ago she'd opened up to this man, showed him places inside her that she hadn't shown anyone. And this was how the universe rewarded her.

Eventually, Samuel's somber gaze lifted. She was struck by how haggard and weary he seemed, as if he'd aged ten years in the time she'd spent searching in the streets. Deep bluish-green bags settled under his eyes, and his mouth was impossibly grim. Myfanwy had to stop the pity that was threatening to dampen her fury. The only person that deserved pity was the little girl who clearly needed her father.

Samuel's jaw moved, almost like he was chewing his words into smaller, more palatable bits before he let them go free. "I don't know what I'm going to do."

"You don't know? How could you not know?" she said. Then her eyes alighted on the glass of amber liquor Samuel was holding in his other hand. Quickly, she snatched it away and dumped the contents unceremoniously into her mouth.

Fire! Incandescent flames scalded her throat.

"Holy hell!" she yelped as coughing spasms overwhelmed her. She clamped her hand over her mouth so she didn't spit up. "Is that what you drink every night? That's revolting!"

Samuel remained in place, the expression on his face signaling she'd gone mad. "Only on rare occasions do I drink that."

"Because it's rancid?"

Samuel huffed, took the tumbler out of her hand, and placed it on the table. "Because it's expensive. Go to bed, Myfanwy."

"No," she said, bracing her legs. "Not until you tell me what you're going to do with her."

Emotion finally sprang from his countenance. "I told you, I don't know!"

"But you said, 'Not again.' So, obviously, you have experience dealing with bastard children."

Samuel winced at the word. Myfanwy did too. She hated the term and was ashamed that she'd used it. It wasn't a child's fault that it was born out of wedlock, and yet it seemed that Society was hellbent on making it pay for it for the rest of its life.

Samuel glanced at the note once more before balling it up in his fist and tossing it into the fireplace. Myfanwy lunged to reach for it, but he wrapped his hand around her upper arm, staying her action.

Myfanwy shrugged him off, though she had to acknowledge that Samuel had simply let her go. "I've dealt with it only once before, and it wasn't pleasant," he said. "This time is clearly different, but I will handle it."

The calmness in his voice struck her like a blow to the stomach. How could he sound so cavalier? It was like they were discussing a lost puppy. It made her hate him, and Myfanwy never thought that would happen.

"Do you know who the mother is? Perhaps we can contact her."

Again, with one of his curious looks, almost as if there was something she was missing. Myfanwy dashed that thought aside. She might not be as hardened and jaded as Samuel, but she wasn't so naïve that she didn't know that men had natural children all the time. The aristocracy was full of stories and gossip about them. Silly her—she'd always assumed that Samuel was different. Not a gentleman...but better.

Myfanwy's father had once told her that she should never be in a rush to meet people she admired. They were always bound to disappoint, since they were made from flesh and blood like her. She'd laughed him off at the time; however, she wasn't laughing now.

Samuel rubbed his eyes and limped to a chair. His gait always got worse by the end of the night. "Why would I have any idea who the mother is?" he said, tilting his head back to ponder the ceiling.

Myfanwy planted her hands on her hips. Was he being obtuse on purpose? There was no time for games! "Are you trying to impress me with all your ladies? You have so many that you can't remember whom you fathered a child with?"

Samuel's brows came together, and slowly he leveled his gaze back on hers. "What did you say?"

He seemed mystified—and also frightening. Myfanwy struggled to maintain her composure. "You heard me."

He came to his feet, even though she could see how much it cost him. "Are you trying to imply that the child is *mine?*"

Myfanwy's confidence and ire shattered. "I...I," she stammered. "You know I am."

Samuel laughed then, a great, booming laugh that was completely devoid of joy. His legs unsteady, he knocked into her shoulder as he wobbled to the table, where he poured another drink into the empty crystal glass. Just as Myfanwy had, he knocked the drink back into his mouth, finishing it in one swallow. He handled its noxious taste much better.

Samuel blew out a long breath, tapping his fingers on the crystal as he contemplated her. "So, this is what you really think of me? I knew you didn't have a high opinion, but I thought we were getting somewhere."

"I'm sorry," Myfanwy replied, growing cagey and uncomfortable under his scowl. "But a man must be judged by his actions—all of them."

"Indeed," Samuel said, placing the glass back on the table. "Did you happen to notice the child's hair?"

It was an odd question, made even odder by the offhand way he asked it. "What of it?"

"Did it strike you as similar to anyone you know?"

"What?" Myfanwy jerked back. She tried to picture the child in her mind. It had all happened so fast; nothing stood out to her. She was a girl. Small. Tiny, really. What was there to notice?

Samuel's gaze flickered to the top of her head. On impulse, Myfanwy clutched a hank of hair running down her side. "What are you implying?"

Samuel let out a mirthless sound and dropped into his seat once more, crossing one leg over the other. "You're a smart one. And since you're so ready to branch out by yourself, own a home and club, I suppose you don't need to be shielded anymore by life's indelicate matters. What do you think I'm saying?"

Myfanwy clamped her eyes shut and took a steadying breath, but it was no use. Her heart felt like it was in between her ears. It couldn't be. Could it? She would have known. *He* would have told her. They spent all their time together. Surely she would have suspected...?

Samuel studied her silently, no doubt reading all the erratic thoughts fighting for purchase in her mind.

Tears came, and Myfanwy rubbed her arm over her face to catch them before they fell, but it was too late, and there were too many. Samuel didn't play the empathetic hero this time, as he had in the garden. In fact, he became increasingly uncomfortable as recognition slapped her across the face.

Myfanwy began to shiver like Samuel had dunked her in one of his tortuous ice baths. "He couldn't have done this. He wouldn't. He was better than that."

Now, Samuel's smile was sad, wilting with pity. "He was a man. Just a man."

"No," Myfanwy whispered plaintively. "He wasn't a man. He was my father."

⇒⇒⇒≪≪≪

HOURS LATER, MYFANWY was still tossing and turning in her bed. Her mind was too restless; the betrayal cut too close to the bone. How could her father do this to her? More importantly, how could he do it to her mother's memory? The viscount and his viscountess had been soulmates, the darlings of the *ton*. To this day, Myfanwy was still stopped by old friends of theirs who recounted stories of her parents' great love affair.

Looking back, she understood that her relationship with her father had only truly blossomed after the death of her mother. They were all each other had in the world, and clung to one another like shipwrecked men left behind on a remote island.

Only now, Myfanwy knew it was all a lie. Her father had been a man—a needy, lonely man who had sought the company of other women to take the place of his dead wife. And he had done it in the most irresponsible fashion. Like the other fine men of the *ton* who boasted loudly of honor but acted with very little of it.

Myfanwy had forced Samuel to tell her everything. He'd hated every minute of it. Samuel had loved her father too. The viscount had believed in the young cricketer, been a patron and father figure when he'd had no one. And Samuel still loved him despite his failings. Myfanwy was unsure if or when she would be able to do the same.

Because it hadn't just been one baby—one accident. There had been another. Samuel explained that after the funeral, he'd been confronted by an opera singer who found herself with child. She insisted the viscount was the father. She said she would go to the papers if he didn't give her the funds to raise it. Naturally, Samuel had complied. He saw no other choice. The idea of anyone ruining the old man's good name made him sick to his stomach. Everyone had ghosts in their pasts, he'd told himself, some more flesh and bone than others.

Samuel had paid for that child for an entire year before he learned that it had died hours after its birth. The opera singer fled to the Continent after Samuel exposed her perfidy, never truly knowing if she'd been telling the truth about the father or not.

He'd thought it was over. He'd assumed if there were any more children, they would have come into the light. But he'd been wrong.

Slamming her head down into her pillow, Myfanwy stifled a cry. *Never meet those you admire...* Yes, and never grow up with them either. Did everyone disappoint in the end? Was that what growing up was all about? Learning to cope with everyone's failures?

How cynical she could become if she let herself.

Well, Myfanwy wouldn't become cynical. She couldn't.

She crawled out of her bed and left her room, creeping down the chilly corridor to the guest room at the far end. She'd never been in it before, for the simple fact that Samuel never had visitors. It was only ever them in the house, along with the servants who knew better than to be noticed.

Myfanwy opened the door as quietly as she could, tensing at the squeak in the hinge as if it were a firecracker. Peeking her head inside, she relaxed as she spied the little girl asleep in the giant bed, swallowed in the covers that the maid had piled on.

She *was* going to let it end there. However, she couldn't hear the child breathing. Surely she was, but Myfanwy just needed to be extra sure. Tiptoeing closer, she leaned over the bed and found the girl's head at the top end of her toasty cocoon. Myfanwy placed her hand near the girl's mouth and waited for the telltale signs of life. When a warm puff of air caressed her skin, she released a breath of her own. It was so loud that the girl shifted in the covers, but thankfully didn't wake up.

Myfanwy didn't know how long she stayed there, staring at the little one. She yearned to touch the girl's hair and see if it felt the same as hers. A profound, overwhelming feeling gripped her, and suddenly, without a doubt, she knew they were half-sisters. As Samuel had pointed out, the red color was too similar to discount. And her father was there in the little girl's features. It was faint, but evident in the elegant thickness of her lips, the line of her eyebrows, which slashed above her eyes instead of curving like rainbows.

If Myfanwy was going to be honest with herself, she might acknowledge that she'd known the instant the front door opened. Maybe that was why she'd run after the boy like her life depended on it. Because it had.

Myfanwy exited the room, this time closing the door without making any noise. She'd begun the journey back to her bed, hoping sleep might finally take hold, when she heard a click. A doorknob twisted, and then Samuel appeared in front of her, wearing a navy-blue robe and a surprised expression.

Then he nodded, and Myfanwy understood that he was checking on the girl, just as she was. Like two ships in the night, they passed each other. Silently. Slowly. As if this was just a secret.

Later, when Myfanwy was dozing off to sleep, she would wonder if Samuel had truly taken her hand and squeezed it as he'd passed, or if it had all been a dream.

Chapter Nine

THEY WERE AT loggerheads. The little girl was more stubborn than Myfanwy thought. The following morning over breakfast, she tried everything. She was sweet. She was kind. She was fussy. She was funny (at least, she thought she was funny). But it was to no avail. The child would not speak to her. She wouldn't do more than nibble on her toast and smile at the maid whenever Gertie ventured into the dining room to deliver more milk.

"Such a sweet thing," Gertie cooed, filling up yet another glass. She caressed the little wisps of hair off the girl's face. Myfanwy frowned, trying not to feel too left out. Gertie had been the one to help the child to sleep the night before. Clearly, that was where the camaraderie had bloomed. But Myfanwy couldn't help the uncomfortableness pricking at her skin. She'd heard children could sense the good in others. Did that mean they could also sense the bad? Had the girl already found her wanting?

Gertie had pegged the girl to be around three years of age, which meant that she should be talking. She kept silent at the table; however, Myfanwy got the distinct impression she'd spoken to Gertie before. What was wrong with *her*? Didn't the girl recognize Myfanwy's hair color? Couldn't she sense a familial bond?

Although, in the light of day, the hair seemed to be the only feature the two had in common. Whereas Myfanwy's nose and chin took after her mother's and were pointy and pronounced, the little girl had a round face covered in freckles that swallowed her eyes so much that Myfanwy couldn't tell what color they were. Despite the current predicament, the girl had obviously been well taken care of. Her dress was of a good quality, and the fullness in her cheeks showed that she wasn't missing any meals. Plump and pretty, she didn't seem at all unaccustomed to her fine surroundings.

"Oh, good. You're here," Samuel said, striding into the room. "I'd hoped to speak with you before I left."

Myfanwy had never seen her guardian this early in the morning and was shocked to find him turned out so well. Wearing a fitted, dark jacket with gray trousers, he was dressed in what her father would have called his "Sunday best," though Myfanwy had her doubts that Samuel was on his way to any sacred ground on this day of rest.

He stood at the head of the table and nodded to the girl, though he directed his question to Myfanwy. "How have you been getting on this morning?"

She played with her spoon, tracing it over the white tablecloth. "Oh, fine," she answered breezily. For some reason, it killed her to let him know of her shortcomings regarding the child. All women were maternal, weren't they? Somewhere in their bones was the information on how to deal with children. Perhaps Myfanwy just hadn't located the secret yet. She straightened her spine. "We're just getting to know one another."

Samuel nodded once more before addressing the girl. "And you, Annabelle? Did you have a nice sleep?"

"Annabelle?" Myfanwy squeaked. "How did you know that was her name?"

Samuel frowned. "She told me last night."

Incredulous, Myfanwy threw up her hands, flopping them on the table with a thud. "Has she talked to everyone but me?"

Annabelle smiled into her toast, but naturally, said nothing.

Samuel's sigh regained Myfanwy's attention. "I'll be gone for most of the day. I spoke to Tim Nevil at the tavern, and he's agreed to send his eldest daughter over this morning to take care of Annabelle. You won't need to watch her for long."

Myfanwy flinched. "Watch her? Me? What about Gertie?"

Samuel leveled her with a weighted look. "Gertie has to do the shopping this morning, along with everything else she does in the house. It will only be for an hour at most. You can handle it."

That rankled her. "Of course I can handle it, but…but I had plans."

He lifted an imperious eyebrow. "Plans?"

"Yes, I am to go to Jennifer's for tea. She's expecting me." Her words fell off at the end. Even Myfanwy knew how pathetic her excuse was. Was she actually scared to be alone with her own sister? In her defense, she'd never spent any time around children before; she hadn't the faintest idea how to occupy them. Myfanwy desperately wanted to get to know Annabelle, but that was a double-edged sword. She wasn't sure if she was ready for the girl to make any early, premature assumptions about *her*.

"Invite Jennifer here. Introduce her to Annabelle. I trust her to be prudent," Samuel replied easily. "I'm sure the child will love meeting her. Jennifer seems like she'd be wonderful with children."

Maybe Myfanwy was just being sensitive, but she thought Samuel put a little too much emphasis on his last sentence. What was he trying to imply? That Jennifer would be better with children than her? Well…obviously! She had three younger sisters!

"Please, Myfanwy. I'm begging you," Samuel said. "We all need to do our part until we fix this…situation. There are a lot of questions to be asked, information to be gained, and we need to do it as discreetly as possible. Then we'll be able to make the best decision for Annabelle."

"Where are you going to be?"

Samuel backed away from the table. "I have a meeting," he stated firmly.

On a Sunday? But then it dawned on her. Samuel was never home on Sundays, and he didn't spend them at the tavern either, because she'd gone there looking for him once before and was told as such. It seemed that her father wasn't the only man in her life good at keeping secrets. However, that mystery would have to wait for another day. A woman could only take so much.

Samuel attempted to leave again, and Myfanwy clawed at the edge of the table. "But what do you want me to *do* with her?"

Samuel stopped, tearing a hand through his hair. "How in the world should I know? She's a girl. You were once a girl. Surely you know about girl things."

Suddenly this conversation was immensely entertaining. Myfanwy rested her head in her palm, drumming her fingers on the side of her chin. "Please tell me. What are girl things?"

Samuel's shoulders hiked to his ears. "How am I supposed to know? Dolls! Talk about dolls!"

Myfanwy rolled her eyes. "You don't talk about dolls; you play with dolls."

"Then play with damn dolls!"

"I don't have any *damn* dolls. I'm twenty years old. Besides, I never had dolls to play with."

"What the hell did you play, then?"

"What the *hell* did you think? Cricket!"

Samuel turned to leave. "I don't have time for this," he muttered irritably. Thinking better of it, he twirled back around. "Play cricket with her, then. She's *your* sister. Do whatever makes you both happy."

Myfanwy frowned. She hadn't considered that. And it wasn't every day that someone told her to do what *actually* made her happy. What an idea! Someone to play cricket with all the time. Was this what it felt like to have a sibling? Such adventure!

She awarded Annabelle with a mighty grin, but the child ignored her for the toast. Myfanwy decided not to blame her.

Toast was mighty important in the morning. One couldn't play cricket on an empty stomach, after all.

"She looks exactly like you," Jennifer remarked thoughtfully, sitting next to Myfanwy on the garden bench. After receiving Myfanwy's note, she'd wasted no time hurrying over to the house, even with her mother's various objections.

Myfanwy regarded Annabelle with the stolid objectivity of a physician. "Do you really think so? Besides the hair, we have absolutely nothing in common."

The earlier positivity of the morning had quickly evaporated after Samuel left. To say Myfanwy's plans had not gone as well as she'd hoped would be an understatement.

Jennifer smiled at the little one as Annabelle sat near a rose-bush, picking off the blooms that had managed to stay alive despite Myfanwy's best bowling efforts. "What does having anything in common have to do with it?" she asked with a laugh. "My mother says that she and I are practically twins, and you know that we have very different constitutions."

Myfanwy snorted. Jennifer's mother loved to say the two looked alike, and no one ever had the heart—or courage—to counter that notion, recognizing that it was mostly wishful thinking on the older woman's part. Jennifer was beautiful. Her mother was handsome, at best.

Myfanwy cringed as Annabelle threw a handful of petals in the air and clapped as they rained down on her. She needed those roses for practice. "I just thought...she would enjoy me more...since we are sisters."

Jennifer sniffed. "Clearly, you've never had sisters. Most of the time, there is very little to enjoy. In fact, I've come to believe their entire goal is to burrow under your skin and scratch until you can't take it anymore."

"Yes," Myfanwy said softly. "Yes, I can see that now."

"Myfanwy!" Jennifer exclaimed. "I wasn't speaking about Annabelle. She's only three, correct? She hasn't had time to provoke you yet—Oh, wait." A shadow dropped over her face with the force of an anvil falling from the sky. "Three? You said she was three?" Jennifer's lips tightened as if she didn't want to say what they both were thinking. "Does that mean…?"

"Yes," Myfanwy replied, picking at the dirt underneath her fingernails. "It means that unlike the other child that Samuel told me about—the one that died—Annabelle was born *before* my father passed away."

"Do you think he knew about her?"

Myfanwy shrugged, dropping her hands in her lap. "I don't know, and I won't know until I find the mother. She's the only one who can explain his actions, because I surely can't. And she'll also be the one to explain why she thought Annabelle *needed us*."

Jennifer reached out and took her hand in a comforting hold. "Maybe the mother is dead?"

"Maybe," Myfanwy allowed. "Or destitute. Is it horrid of me to hope the mother has passed? That would answer why the child needs us. But if the mother is alive and in need of funds… I just don't think I can accept that my father had a child and left the mother in such a horrible predicament without providing any financial relief."

"People are strange beings that do strange things. You mustn't let this affect your feelings for him, especially since he cannot defend himself."

"How can I not?" Myfanwy argued. "Either my father knew about the child and never told me or didn't know about the child and neglected his duty. It's…it's…" She slumped. "I don't know what it is."

Jennifer lengthened her spine as if shouldering the burden for the both of them. "Well," she stated firmly, "we know for certain that none of this is Annabelle's fault. She's innocent in all of this."

Myfanwy couldn't debate that point. The child was the picture of purity with her rosy complexion and toothy smile, but she seemed determined not to want anything to do with her older sister. And that felt too close to losing for Myfanwy to take kindly. She flashed her friend a thankful smile, though it died quickly.

Jennifer continued, seeming to understand Myfanwy's disappointment. "Did you try to play with her? I've found that children enjoy it when you get down on their level to join in games and such."

Myfanwy responded with an irritated *tsk*. "Of course I tried to play with her! I showed her how to hold the cricket bat properly and threw balls at for a quarter of an hour, but she wouldn't swing. Not once. She just looked at me like I was insane!"

It wasn't lost on Myfanwy that her best friend was looking at her in the same way now. Jennifer's countenance was sweet—it was always sweet—however, her eyes sharpened, telling a different story. "Dearest, Annabelle probably didn't like you throwing balls at her. I don't think most children would."

"I would have loved it!"

Jennifer patted her hand. "Yes, but you weren't exactly a normal child, were you?"

"*I* thought I was," Myfanwy grumbled.

"What else did you try?"

"Well…naturally, I thought that maybe she would like to bowl the ball instead, so I taught her the proper way to so while I was at bat—"

"Myfanwy!" Jennifer interrupted with a start. "Did you do *anything* else besides teach the child how to play cricket?" Myfanwy's mouth screwed up in a pout and her friend released an exasperated sigh. "No, I didn't think so," Jennifer replied. "What about dolls?"

"Again with the dolls," Myfanwy muttered. "I don't have any blasted dolls!"

"Right." Jennifer nodded, focusing on the girl again. "You'll have to remedy that. Ask Samuel to go out and purchase new toys for Annabelle. She'll need new clothes as well, everything that will make her feel at home. That's the only thing that's important right now. Not *cricket*."

Home. In the excitement of the day, Myfanwy had completely glossed over the possibility that Annabelle might be staying in Samuel's home for an indeterminate amount of time. How would he take that? He already had one ward; he could hardly want the trouble of another, especially when neither was related to him in the slightest. Most men would send the child away to an orphanage if family couldn't be found, providing money for its care.

But Samuel wasn't most men. And Annabelle wasn't just another potential orphan on London's streets. She was Myfanwy's sister. And as exciting as it was to know she had a sibling, it was equally confusing. Even when her father was alive, Myfanwy's life was incredibly solitary. For the most part, all she ever had to worry about was her wants and needs. Adding another to worry about—care about—would require an energy that Myfanwy didn't know she had. She had one goal in her life— the cricket club was everything, and it was almost in her grasp. That dream looked extremely different with a child at her side.

But Annabelle *would* stay at her side. Myfanwy understood that now. It didn't matter what family Samuel found. If Annabelle's mother had truly passed, then Myfanwy would keep her. Her mothering skills might be lacking; however, her sense of family and decency wasn't. Learning to handle and love a child would be like any other skill she'd had to master. Myfanwy hadn't come out of the womb understanding the mechanics of throwing a leg-spinner. She'd had to work at it! For hours and hours! Practice was the only thing that led to success, and those who thought differently were only fooling themselves.

Myfanwy would practice. And she would make perfect.

Suddenly, everything seemed a little bit brighter in the garden, even as Annabelle ripped off the heads of more target roses. "Yes," Myfanwy said jovially, raising her face to the sun. She allowed the rays to soak into her skin, reviving her fledgling courage. "I will make her feel at home. And *then* I will teach her to love cricket."

Myfanwy thought she heard Jennifer sigh, but she was too busy enjoying the light and her newfound confidence.

Chapter Ten

S AMUEL'S STEPS WERE sloppy. He was dead tired, not an unusual occurrence after his Sunday trips. Though, to be fair to this body, the meetings depleted his mind more than anything. If only he had the courage to stay away, to announce he would no longer take part... But it was a ridiculous idea. He knew he wouldn't. He knew he couldn't.

The house was quiet and cold. The candles had all been snuffed out and everyone was most likely in bed. He'd hated being away so long on Annabelle's first day in the house. But at least it afforded the sisters a chance to get to know one another. That could only be a positive outcome, and his presence would have prohibited that. Besides, his time on the road had helped him come to terms with what he must do. If his searching came to nothing, and no immediate family could be found, the child had to stay. That was obvious. He would never turn his back on Viscount Wright, and if that meant housing every one of his children, then he would. Having a ward really wasn't that difficult anyway. He'd managed to do so with Myfanwy for the past year, and they'd hardly had any interaction at all. However, that was for different reasons altogether.

His mind went back to Myfanwy at the dining table this morning, and he couldn't help but chuckle. The woman was out of her depth. Handling a child would take her down a peg or two. Myfanwy was so used to being absurdly capable at everything, commanding everyone around her. A captain was always a captain. But, he had no doubt, she'd get the situation straightened out in no time. Who could resist her? Yes, the intrepid wench was stubborn and vexing, troublesome and a pain in his arse, but she was also exuberant and fun, a lightning rod of possibilities of what could be. She saw the future—and herself right in the middle of it—so clearly. That kind of energy was impossible to ignore. He knew that better than anybody, because he'd tried and was desperately failing.

Samuel stopped at the base of the stairs, his hand hanging listlessly on the newel cap. He should check on the little girl, but his leg was biting into his sanity. Sleep would elude him if the pain continued. One drink would dull it enough for him to close his eyes. One drink and then bed.

He limped to the library, debating whether to start a fire. He hated wasting the firewood, but the summer night had a briskness to it. And he wanted to feel cozy. There was nothing cozy about whom he'd shared his day with, and something inside Samuel screamed for a little special attention, if only from himself.

However, it seemed that he wasn't the only one with that intention. As he ventured closer to the room, he noticed light spilling through the door crack. He opened it warily and saw a blur of a body scattering spastically.

As Samuel's eyes adjusted to the light, he found Myfanwy sitting primly on the couch, a book in her lap, with an intimate fire at the end. It was a lovely tableau, worth painting—or it would have been if the book she was pretending to read wasn't upside down in her hands and she didn't look like fifty shades of hell.

Samuel entered the space wordlessly, taking the book from her, making a point to turn it right-side up so he could read the title. He cocked his head. *"Accounts of the Sandwich Islands* by Lady

Louise, Countess of Somerset?" He squelched the urge to laugh. "Going somewhere, are we?"

Relaxing her spine, Myfanwy deflated against the couch cushions, folding her arms tight to her chest. The poor thing looked as drained as Samuel felt. She was still wearing her day dress, but there were dark smudge marks across her skirts, as if she'd been crawling in the dirt. Her hair was just as ragged, not that he minded. Samuel adored it when it was wild and disheveled, pouring over her shoulders. It made him want to do things. Particular things.

He tossed the book on the table and clenched his hands into fists at his sides. "Bad day?" he asked, falling onto the couch next to her. His weight shifted Myfanwy, causing her to knock into him. Neither of them had the energy to right themselves. Or maybe, he thought, they just didn't want to.

Samuel wasn't sure where he found the courage, but he casually lifted his arm and rested it along her shoulders while he hooked one leg over the other. Once more, Myfanwy didn't move. She laid her head against Samuel. Just like that. Like this was just something they did and nothing out of the ordinary. Was this the miraculous effect of children? Make their parents so fatigued and careless that they collapsed into each other's arms at night? If so, Samuel liked it immensely, and had a whole new appreciation for parenthood.

"You caught me," Myfanwy said sleepily. "I was dozing on the couch when I heard you come in."

Samuel began to trace little circles on the top of her shoulder. A few inches lower and he could do it to her bare skin, but he considered that might be too much temptation. Her skin was like the Holy Grail to him—once he had it, he would never be able to let it go.

He closed his eyes, trying to stay on top of the conversation. However, all that did was make him want to imagine being on top of something else. *Dammit, man! Concentrate!* "Why didn't you go up to bed?"

Myfanwy huffed and gestured to her legs. "I tried, but they just don't want to move."

He wished she hadn't directed his attention to those legs, which were colt-like and lean. He could see the indentation of her muscle from under her thin skirts. She was being so agreeable tonight. Would she stop him if he placed his hand there? Just on her thigh. That was all he wanted.

"Didn't Tim's daughter come to help?" he asked instead.

Myfanwy nodded and yawned, and her warm breath made him cozier than a thousand fires. "Sarah. And yes, she did come, just as you said she would. She was wonderful, but I wanted to help, so…"

"So?"

She shrugged, and the action moved her head even more toward his pounding heart. "I helped." She yawned again, and Samuel's conscience finally beat out his cock to grab his full attention. He should carry her upstairs and place her in her bed. But would he join her there? That was the problem. Samuel was too fatigued to know the answer, so he stayed where he was.

"How did you help?"

"Well," she began dramatically, "we bathed her and washed her hair, fed her more. The child is always hungry, though so am I, so I can't fault her for that. And then we played. All day."

"Cricket?"

"No," she said sulkily. "Annabelle made it quite clear she hasn't the affinity for cricket—yet. But I'll work on her."

Samuel smiled over the top of her head, enjoying the scene she was painting for him. He'd witnessed Myfanwy running back and forth between wickets countless times and never once seen her falter. One day with a child and she was like a wet rag, wrung out by an old laundress's heavy hands.

"So, if there was no cricket, what did you do?"

Her laugh was woefully depleted. "What didn't we do? We ran around the house, threw stones, drew pictures—"

Samuel leaned over to look at her face. "She talked to you,

95

then?"

Myfanwy's smile fled. "No, not yet, but we're getting there. It'll happen. She needs time to trust me."

Samuel tightened his arm around her. "She'll come around. I wonder why she remains quiet with you?"

"Who knows for sure?" she replied. "But she will one day."

"Of course she will. You're her sister."

"We need to find her mother, Samuel. Find out why she left Annabelle with us. Maybe we can look for that boy—the one that dropped her off. He'll have to tell us."

Samuel understood that Myfanwy was speaking but didn't have the slightest idea what she was talking about. She'd ruined that for him when her hand began to flutter. It was a small motion at first, just her palm resting on his chest; however, it didn't stay there. Her fingers began to caress him in tiny waves that made a sweat break out over his forehead.

Samuel placed his hand over hers, forcing her to stop. "Um... Yes, her mother. I, ah, sent a messenger to the opera house asking for any information regarding your father, but nothing came back. I'll try the gaming halls next. Maybe I'll go to the Lucky Fish. That's the preferred haunt of most of London nowadays."

She picked her head up off his shoulder, leaving a boulder-sized space of regret. "Can I come with you?"

"No."

She frowned. Her head was so close to him. Samuel's neck strained as he attempted to keep their distance. But he had no control over his good eye. It soaked up her loveliness, and he lost all restraint over the fullness of her lips, the richness of her sun-loved skin. He didn't even mind that she was staring at his bad eye. There was no sympathy in her countenance. Even if there was, Samuel wouldn't have cared. If she wanted to pity him, she could do it, as long as she was naked in his bed. Pathetic bastard that he was, he might even use it to his advantage.

Myfanwy was his. That realization hit him like a brick in the head. Not only was she his, but she was his for the taking. There was nothing to stop them from carrying their flirting to the next level. So why wasn't he acting on it?

Christ, what was he thinking? She was his ward! A viscount's daughter! He mustn't think of her in that way. The more he did—the more Samuel pretended that anything could develop between them—the more real it became to his feeble brain. But it wasn't real. Myfanwy deserved better. She was a gentleman's daughter, and if there was one thing that Samuel had been told time and time again in his miserable life, it was that he was no gentleman.

Myfanwy's hand dropped to his injured leg, where she continued to wreak all kinds of havoc on his senses. It took everything in Samuel to keep his head from falling back with a groan. It was such a light, innocent touch, but for a man accustomed to very little, it was like a choir of angels singing just for him.

Her eyelashes fluttered guilelessly as she met his tortured gaze. "Let me come with you to the hall. I can help," she whispered against his lips. How could drinking her breath be more erotic than actually kissing her? Maybe because Samuel hadn't actually kissed her yet.

"Go to bed, Myfi."

Her lips curled, and this time, Samuel could have sworn they touched his. "You've never called me that before."

"Should I not?"

"No, you can. I like it." She grew bolder, massaging the top of his thigh now, and even though it hurt, it also felt fucking amazing.

Samuel licked his dry lips, and Myfanwy flinched, her eyes wide—and then determined. Suddenly, she moved with greater intention. She pushed down on his leg to shift her body onto his—and, weak, stupid bastard that he was, he released a guttural yelp that stopped her from doing every beautiful thing she'd intended to.

Myfanwy froze and then fell back into her seat, no longer touching one blessed inch of him. "I'm sorry. I'm so sorry. I didn't mean to hurt you," she said, staring down at his useless appendage.

Samuel clenched his jaw in pain. It had nothing to do with his leg. He was used to that worthless son of a bitch. His cock was the source of more pressing matters.

He blew a ragged breath out from between his teeth and let his head loll back on the couch. "It's fine," he told the ceiling. "You didn't do anything."

"I did!"

"You didn't. It really doesn't hurt that much. I'll ice it later."

"I wish you would try something else."

Samuel swung his neck toward her and found a lazy grin. "Let's not talk about it. Truly, it doesn't hurt. I was just surprised, that's all."

Myfanwy chuckled self-consciously and answered with a shy smile. "Good surprised or bad surprised?"

"What do you think?"

She studied him for a long moment, and Samuel couldn't begin to guess what was going on in her head. When her focus shifted to his white eye—and then his leg—he knew. Without a doubt, he knew what she'd surmised. He was damaged goods.

And Samuel concluded that he didn't want to be pitied. Not even with Myfanwy naked in his arms.

His voice came out brutishly gruff, but it couldn't be helped.

"Go to bed, Myfanwy," he said once more.

She shifted in her seat, pressing her hands into the cushion as if to lift herself up, but paused. "You could come with me," she replied in a whisper that managed to scorch every patch of skin on his already inflamed body.

There it was. She was giving herself to him. But for all the wrong reasons.

Samuel shook his head. "Your room is no place for me."

"It could be," she said gently, "if you want it to be."

When Samuel didn't reply, Myfanwy eventually stood up and left the room. He couldn't ascertain who'd rejected whom in their situation, who was the winner and who was the loser. In the end, he had to admit that it was a draw. And a draw was worse than losing; it was worse than death. Any cricketer could tell you that.

Chapter Eleven

L ATER THAT NIGHT, Myfanwy was plagued with restlessness
yet again. With her weariness, she'd expected to close her
eyes the moment her head hit the pillow, but an unsettled feeling
ate at her, making it impossible to clear her mind.

It must be the child, Myfanwy thought, flinging off her covers. On only the second night in Samuel's home, Annabelle was
most likely still out of sorts. Even though Myfanwy had elicited a
smile from the little girl by the end of the day, she understood
that there would be a long period of readjustment for everyone in
the house.

But when she sneaked into Annabelle's room—and checked
to make sure she was still breathing—everything was exactly as it
should be. The only difference from the previous night was that
Annabelle wasn't completely hidden underneath her plush
covers. Her lovely, thick hair was spread out like a field of orange
tulips around her. Myfanwy reached out to stroke her sister's
forehead, mimicking how she'd seen Gertie do it earlier in the
day, and was delighted when Annabelle cuddled into the warmth
of her palm.

She was a sweet child. Odd and mysterious—almost like a
changeling baby—but Annabelle still managed to dig out a place
in Myfanwy's heart already. Funny, how fast things like that

could happen.

Love. When you were least expecting it. Even when it completely questioned her beliefs in her own father, Myfanwy still found love.

Keeping an eye on Annabelle, Myfanwy opened the door to leave and—

"What the hell are you—"

Myfanwy slapped her palm over Samuel's mouth. "Shh!" she hissed, pushing him out the doorway, swiftly closing the door behind them. He let her back-pedal him halfway down the corridor before he finally wrangled himself free.

"I'm quiet. I'm quiet," Samuel whispered. Again, he was wrapped in his navy-blue robe, but his feet were bare, and Myfanwy couldn't stop from wondering if anything else was bare underneath the expensive fabric. It seemed bizarre to imagine Samuel wearing a dressing gown and cap as her father had done. Bizarre and hilarious.

"What are you laughing at?" he asked, self-consciously pulling his robe tighter around his frame.

"Nothing," Myfanwy replied, pursing her lips. "I was just…"

"What?"

She shook her head. "Nothing."

Samuel gave her a hard look, telling her he didn't believe her for one second, but let it drop. "You should be asleep. What are you doing up?"

"The same thing you're doing," Myfanwy answered, flicking her chin toward Annabelle's door. "Checking on her."

Samuel hesitated, his gaze going to the door and back to her. Was he embarrassed that she'd discovered him, yet again? Did he not want her to know that he was a nervous hen, just as she was? Pity. She found she liked that about Samuel. It felt like a secret just between them, something only they knew because no one else would have believed it.

His lips screwed up, but eventually he let out words. "How is she?"

Myfanwy smiled. "She's fine. Fast asleep."

He frowned at the door. "So, I don't need to go in there…risk disturbing her?"

"I don't think so."

Samuel bobbed on the top of his feet and softly clapped his hands together. "So, I should go back to bed?"

Where else would you go? Myfanwy gave him a firm nod. "I think that would be the correct decision. It's late."

"So it is."

They continued to stand there. Myfanwy couldn't tell if he wanted to say something else. The man just waited there expectantly. Was she supposed to say something? They hadn't last night; they'd merely skimmed hands, and that had been worth a thousand words. Words that she would, most likely, ruminate over tonight as she tried to find sleep once more.

"Well," Myfanwy said, lifting her shoulders awkwardly. "Good night…Samuel."

Another pregnant pause. "Good night, Myfi."

Myfanwy had begun to walk past him, relieved the inelegant encounter was finally finished, when she felt the back of Samuel's hand lightly brush against hers once more.

However, this time, he caught her hand. And he didn't let go.

"Goddammit!" she heard him say, and then felt his hold strengthen around her wrist.

It all happened so quickly. One moment, Myfanwy was on her feet, and the next she was in Samuel Everett's arms with his mouth turning her entire body into warm butter.

She didn't have time to act—only *react* to what was happening to her. Bless his soul, Samuel was finally breaking.

For her.

Myfanwy wrapped her arms around his neck and held tight, even lifting her leg and hooking it around his good knee so that he didn't get any ideas. He was not leaving her. No second thoughts. Not until she was good and kissed.

Samuel growled and placed his hand just below her bottom,

hoisting her up even higher so that her one foot on the floor was now barely on its tiptoes. She was draped on him and learned—without a doubt—that this man did not sleep in a gown and cap at night.

Samuel's kisses were hard, punishing, as he angled his head to hers, sweeping his tongue into her mouth, groaning when Myfanwy got the hang of it. He walked her back to the wall and pinned her against it, holding her in place with the force of need and the insistence of his pelvis. Myfanwy was completely covered by him, enveloped by him, but she wouldn't be intimidated. Men like Samuel could make it so easy with their size and their appetite, but Myfanwy had an appetite too. She held his head in her hands and slowed his pace, drawing out the kisses, licking his full lips, sucking on the tip of his tongue when he thought to take over.

If life was a game, and there were always winners and losers, then this moment—this chance encounter—was even more important. Now was the time to write the unwritten rules of this sport, to let the other know what was fair and foul, no blurred lines.

"Goddammit," Samuel repeated huskily, nudging Myfanwy's head up so he could string a trail of kisses down her neck. She wore the nightgown that Aunt Abigail had purchased for her, which meant it was high-necked and puritanical. Samuel didn't seem to mind. Even with the cotton between them, she could feel his excitement, feel the lust in each and every flick of his tongue. She squirmed underneath him, and he locked her to him, his manhood stiff and hot in the cradle of her thighs.

"We shouldn't be doing this," he said, though he made no attempt to stop. He'd reached the top of her chest and stared at her breasts for heady seconds, pulling her nightgown on both sides, forcing the fabric tight against her skin. Glancing down, Myfanwy could see her nipples through the fabric, dusty pink and swollen from the feelings he incited inside her. She watched him lower his head and gloss one with the tip of his tongue. A frisson of excitement sparked up her inner thighs, and she rested her head back against the wall.

"We shouldn't be doing this," he said, traveling over to the other nipple, where he made her feel the same electric jolt.

"Stop saying that," Myfanwy said, closing her eyes to the sensations. "And don't stop."

She heard a guttural laugh. "I didn't say I was going to stop."

Myfanwy's eyes snapped open. She studied his, hoping to understand what he meant. Was he not going to stop...at all? Was that what she wanted? Myfanwy thought she knew the answer but was astonished by her hesitation.

Samuel's blue eye turned soft, melting her even further. His large hand replaced his mouth, and he fondled her breast, squeezing it in an intoxicating way that made her arch her back off the wall. "Fuck, Myfi," he purred. "I want this. I want you. I tried to stay way. I tried not to look, but I can't."

"Good," she said. "I don't want you to. Remember what I said that night in your room? I like it when you look at me."

Samuel leaned away. His white eye was so incredibly limpid, she wondered if he could see her in it. Only her.

"Why?" he asked. "Why do you want me? You could have anyone."

She smiled, running her hands up and down his arms. She loved the feel of them, so strong, so firm, so made for her. "I've only wanted you. Ever since I was a child. Ever since I first saw you on that field."

She didn't know what she'd said that was so wrong, but Samuel's face turned to thunder and he backed up even more, lowering her feet to the floor. "You want a different man. I am not the same as I was."

"You are."

"No." Samuel shook his head. "I can't lie to you, Myfanwy. And I can't allow you to give yourself to me, thinking I am who I once was, because I'm not. And deep down, you know that. I would ruin you with what I've become. You deserve better."

He cupped her face and traced her bottom lip with his thumb. He'd brushed her tears away before, but now she had none to give.

"What are you saying, Samuel?"

His smile was apologetic, and so very, very sad. "The last thing I want to do is take away your good opinion of the man I was. The man I can never be again. I'm sorry."

❧

"I THINK I'M going to have to seduce Samuel Everett."

Jennifer's feet stalled in place, and she snatched Myfanwy's arm so hard that Myfanwy had to hold back a yelp.

Walking ahead of them in the park with Mrs. Adams, Jennifer's mother twisted her long neck minutely, her straight nose in the air as if she could sniff the inappropriate conversation.

"Not so loud!" Jennifer hissed, frantically calming her expression before her mother turned her gimlet eye on the young pair.

"What's the matter?" Mrs. Hallett asked irritably.

"Nothing," Jennifer replied. "I think I have a pebble in my shoe, is all."

"Well, don't dawdle," her mother answered, issuing a put-upon smile to Mrs. Adams.

For once, Myfanwy was thankful the woman paid her next to no attention; she probably would have wondered why Myfanwy was rubbing her arm while her daughter was the one experiencing the alleged pain.

"That hurt!" Myfanwy whispered as Mrs. Hallett turned her back once more.

Jennifer's forehead furrowed. "I'm sorry. I didn't mean to pinch too hard, but you know my mother."

"I know." Myfanwy sighed. "That's why I had to come and see you today. I couldn't chance writing it in a letter because—"

"My mother reads them all."

"Yes," Myfanwy replied bitterly. *Insufferable woman.* She paused, allowing Jennifer to regroup. "So..." she began tentatively. "What do you think?"

Jennifer blanched. "Of seduction? I don't know the first thing."

Myfanwy chuckled, winding her arm around Jennifer's, tugging her back into the walk. "No, I mean, what do you think about my seducing Samuel? I can't keep waiting for him; I can't allow him to think. He won't take the lead, so I will."

Jennifer stared straight ahead, her features hidden behind her wide bonnet. But Myfanwy could feel the indecision in her frame, the way her legs seemed locked as they made their way down the dusty path. "Don't you have enough to worry about right now with your sister? And I feel inclined to remind you that he's your guardian and you're his ward... *And* your...*seducement*...might affect our cricket match."

"Yes," Myfanwy replied. "I'm well aware."

"And you don't think there's a problem with any of that?"

"Why would there be?" Myfanwy couldn't understand the wrong turn the conversation had taken. She'd expected Jennifer to be happy, excited for the adventurous lovers' tryst. But she was regarding Myfanwy the same way Myfanwy regarded her whenever Sir Bramble came up in conversation, and that almost made her high from the previous night disappear—almost.

"I don't know why you're behaving this way," Myfanwy grumbled. "I thought you'd be glad for me. You have Sir Bramble—why can't I have someone?"

Jennifer's head lowered, and her eyes darted nervously toward her mother again. "First off, I do not *have* Sir Bramble. He is a friend. A good, very good"—she blushed—"friend. Besides, if I had intentions for the baron, they are the marrying kind, as you well know. I do not want to... I do not want to..."

Myfanwy patted her friend's hand, hoping to help her out of her misery. "Seduce him?" she added.

"Yes!"

Myfanwy nodded. "Well, that is where we differ, then, dearest. Because, as *you know*, my end is *not* the altar. I want nothing to do with a husband, but that doesn't mean I have to miss out on the extras."

Jennifer placed a hand to her temple, closing her eyes like she was warding off a headache. "I have no idea what you are speaking about."

Myfanwy lobbed her a weighted look. "Of course you do. Don't pretend to be prudish with me now. You know exactly what I'm talking about." She lowered her voice furtively. "Do you mean to tell me that you and Sir Bramble haven't...you know?"

"I certainly do *not* know!"

Myfanwy snorted in disbelief. "Oh, please! I'm your best friend in all the world. Sir Bramble's been nipping at your heels for months. Are you trying to tell me he hasn't kissed you once? Not even a little peck in a dark corner?"

Jennifer's cheeks were on fire, and her lashes were fluttering so much that Myfanwy worried she might be having a fit. "No! Sir Bramble is not like the others. He's decent and kind and gallant. A true gentleman." Her lips twisted up nervously and then her shoulders deflated. "Why?" she asked. "Do you think that's bad? Do you think he should have tried? Maybe he doesn't desire me like Mr. Everett desires you?"

"Of course he does. The man is positively mad for you! Do you want him to kiss you?"

"Yes," Jennifer said instantly. "I think." She shook her head. "Yes, I do. But we're always being watched. My mother is always hovering, answering his questions before I get a chance to, making sure I—the family—is putting our best leg forward."

"Jennifer, sweet girl," Myfanwy said plaintively. "The only leg Sir Bramble cares about is yours. And he'd prefer to see it without your mother anywhere in the vicinity."

Jennifer liked that. She laughed to herself, relaxing and ambling into a stroll. "But I thought you didn't like Sir Bramble?" she asked. "Why are you so concerned about our...lack of affection?"

Myfanwy was ready for the question. She'd been rehearsing the answer all morning, reminding herself that she wasn't using her friend or playing with her affections—she was using Sir Bramble. "I have a favor to ask of you."

Jennifer's eyebrows went up again, and Myfanwy dashed away the ill feeling climbing up her back. "I should have known. No wonder you mentioned Sir Bramble without harassing him."

"I don't harass him," Myfanwy said. "I merely poke fun from time to time." *All the time.* "I just need help with something, and I thought he might be the perfect person to ask. And," Myfanwy added swiftly when she saw Jennifer open her mouth, "I thought you would be interested because it involves you too. It would be a way you could be around your baron without your ever-present mother."

Jennifer's mouth clamped shut, and she contemplated her friend for long seconds. Myfanwy tried to look as innocent as possible. "I'm listening," she finally said. "I don't know why I am, but I'm listening. What do you have in mind?"

Chapter Twelve

L ATER THAT WEEK, Myfanwy's plan came to fruition, and as she waded through the unconventional and diverse throng, she felt quite fortunate.

The Lucky Fish was living up to its namesake. If hardly being able to take a step without elbowing someone in their side meant business was good, then this gaming hall must be the most popular in town.

She could even see enjoying herself among the tables and people another time…with other companions.

Myfanwy glanced back at her unfortunate accomplices. How she'd managed to even get them through the door of the infamous establishment, she would never know. "Can you two please try to pretend that you want to be here?" she implored Jennifer and Sir Bramble, who were glued together. "People will begin to stare, and that's the last thing we need."

Unfortunately, it was the wrong time for Jennifer to swivel her neck. Just as she looked to her right, a very underdressed and very obvious woman of the night sauntered past her, batting her sultry lashes at the trio. Jennifer's eyes almost bulged out from under the black veil she wore over her face.

"Just breathe," Myfanwy said softly, as if she were dealing with a startled kitten. "Relax." She faced Sir Bramble, who also looked like he was one strong wind away from falling on his pasty face. "I thought you said you'd been here before? That's why I asked you to bring us in the first place. Why are you so shocked by the environment?"

Sir Bramble's Adam's apple bobbed under his collar. He attempted to gain his bearings and lifted his chin in the air. "Indeed, I have." He flicked a nervous glance toward Jennifer. "But never with...ladies."

Myfanwy rolled her eyes and turned to the crowd. Now, she *really* hoped those two never got married. What was expected of them in the bedroom might be too much for their delicate constitutions.

Speaking of bedroom activities...

Myfanwy stood on her tiptoes and scanned the room. If someone had told her that half of London was here, she would have believed them. *But where is Samuel...?*

It was difficult enough to recognize anyone behind her own dark veil, but the space was filled with a zephyr cloud of smoke from all the cigars. That didn't stop a smile from forming on her face. Myfanwy was utterly fascinated witnessing the opposite sex in its element. The Lucky Fish was a different country—nay, a different world. And she could be a different person in it.

Despite the establishment's hedonistic reputation, the atmosphere was much more genteel than she'd expected. Tables were scattered throughout the various rooms of the hall, each with a different game. The interior design was an interesting juxtaposition of the feminine and masculine, with the walls covered in dark wood panels and the windows lined with plush and delicate lace drapes. It gave the rooms a cloistered, intimate feel, almost as if she was visiting a person's home or, rather, what someone assumed a proper home should look like. The mastermind behind the ambiance must have had great knowledge of gamblers. If the den was cozy enough, there was no reason to ever leave.

"Do you see him?" Jennifer said over her shoulder, her voice still tighter than a grande dame's corset strings.

"Not yet," Myfanwy replied through her teeth. "Why don't you two wait for me in the corner, just over there?" she said, pointing to the farthest area she could spot. "I'll find you shortly, and then we can go."

Jennifer grabbed hold of her wrist. "I am not leaving you here to...meander alone with these people."

Myfanwy chuckled. She was hardly alone, and if Jennifer would take a good look around her, she would realize that "these people" were their people, just without all their saintly wives and disapproving mothers clucking in the corners. The trio had only been in the hall for ten minutes, and Myfanwy had already recognized one bishop and two Parliament members, only because she'd seen them enough times speaking to her father at cricket matches. It seemed that gamblers didn't have many scruples. They went where the games were—and the Lucky Fish had them in spades.

Jennifer tugged her again. "Just promise me we'll leave after he sees you. That's the plan still, right? You just want to surprise Mr. Everett, yes? Make him notice you, and then we'll run off before he makes a scene?"

Myfanwy frowned as she continued to examine the crowd. "He won't make a scene."

"He will!" Jennifer squeaked. "He told you that you couldn't come here. This isn't like showing up at his tavern, Myfi. This is different!"

Myfanwy smiled wickedly. "I know."

"He might throw you in your room and lock the door on you forever."

"As long as he's in there with me."

Jennifer grabbed her shoulder and whipped Myfanwy to face her. The stress was evident on the poor girl's face, and Myfanwy almost had a change of heart. She was asking too much of Jennifer tonight. Perfidy wasn't her strong suit. "Just be careful. You think you know Samuel Everett, but you don't."

Myfanwy huffed. "I live with the man."

Jennifer scoffed. "My parents have lived together for twenty-five years, and they're barely more than acquaintances. Listen to me when I tell you, people act differently in the light of day. I don't want you to be disappointed by what you find tonight."

Myfanwy nodded and backed out of Jennifer's aggressive hold. She didn't argue. How could she when Jennifer wouldn't understand? Myfanwy *did* know Samuel. She'd seen him at his worst, both when the sun was out and when it was not. And it wasn't the daytime Samuel that she wanted. Now that she'd had a taste of the man in the darkness, that was the only one she craved. She was certain she would find him here tonight. Maybe that would finally convince him that she wasn't still that little girl with a silly crush on a famous cricketer. Myfanwy was a woman now, and she wanted the man that he was—not some old dream, whether he liked it or not. And she had a feeling that Samuel *did* like it, even if he didn't want to.

Encountering him here—in this den of iniquity, of all places—might force his hand, incite Samuel to tear off his kid gloves when dealing with Myfanwy...and hopefully, strip off a lot more.

Myfanwy watched the nervous couple wind its way through the bustle, Sir Bramble shielding Jennifer with his skinny body from the drunken rabble like a knight protecting his lady fair from the marauding Vikings. She would almost think it was harmlessly sweet, if Jennifer wasn't cuddling him of her own volition. Myfanwy still didn't understand Jennifer's true feelings for the baron. It seemed innocent, friendly, and nothing like the low-simmering blaze that always burned when she and Samuel were in the same room.

She forced herself to dismiss them, reminding herself not to worry about Sir Bramble. He wasn't the one for her friend. It was obvious.

Myfanwy glided through the rooms, maintaining a low profile, keeping an aloof gaze on the participants. Jennifer had talked her into wearing the veil, and Myfanwy could now say she was happy for the intervention. A few times she was positively shocked by the Bacchanalian events surrounding her. It seemed that men's hands had a different set of rules at the Lucky Fish. They could grab just about any free part of a woman's body with or without her approval: arms, necks, waists...even backsides. The revelation insisted Myfanwy keep a wider berth in her musings.

A loud cacophony of laughter boomed from down the corridor. Myfanwy was just about to inspect the source of merriment when a large body stepped in front of her, blocking her path.

"Miss Myfanwy, isn't it?" the voice said, its tone a lovely melding of smooth molasses and crunchy biscuits. "I wasn't expecting you tonight. No, not at all."

Myfanwy raised her eyes away from the massive, wide chest to find Harry Holmes regarding her curiously, biting on a thick cigar. She'd only ever seen the gaming hall owner once before. He'd cornered the viscount at a cricket match while she was across the field with a group of friends. He'd vanished, like a thief in the night, by the time she ventured back to watch the match with her father.

"Mr. Holmes," she returned, thickening her tone with worldly poise. "I'm surprised you know me, as we've never met."

His gray eyes brightened, and he twisted the cigar slowly in the corner of his mouth. She couldn't be sure of his age, though she'd heard his name bandied about since she was a child. Harry Holmes could well be in his forties, but he had a generous amount of black hair, which he slicked back away from his face, highlighting his large, patrician nose. A smattering of white hair settled near his temple, oddly making his face appear even more youthful and golden. "I knew your father well. He pointed you out to me whenever we met on the cricket pitch."

She lifted an eyebrow. "And you didn't ask to be introduced?"

He laughed, a rich and bubbling sound coming from his cauldron-like chest. "The viscount wasn't a fan of Society's rules, but there were some that even he thought for the best."

"Like introducing his daughter to depraved men who take

advantage of the weakness of others."

Holmes's smile froze, though his cigar kept spinning. The muscles around his eyes twitched. "Take a look around you, Miss Myfanwy," he said. "Does it look like I'm taking advantage of anyone? Better yet, do you see anyone complaining about their weaknesses?"

Myfanwy didn't dare break from this battle of wits. And she didn't need to look around the room to know that everyone was still in the honeymoon stage of the night. It was too early for fortunes to be completely obliterated, for lives and reputations to be ruined. Hopefully, she'd be long gone before then.

"As you say, Mr. Holmes," she replied. The brackets around his mouth relaxed against the cigar. "Perhaps you can help me. I'm looking for—"

Holmes took her arm, guiding Myfanwy away from the corridor, back into the crowded room she'd come from. No bumping elbows this time. Holmes was like Moses—all he had to do was appear and a path opened before him. "You don't have to worry. He's not here."

Myfanwy frowned. "He?"

The gaming hall owner gave her a look that seemed to signify they were partners in crime. It was immediately off-putting and thrilling. "You don't have to pretend with me, Miss Myfanwy. I understand perfectly. A young, vivacious woman like yourself only wants to have a little fun without the shackles of her guardian clinking behind her. Samuel Everett is a friend. Well"— he cocked his head—"if I had friends, he would be one. Regardless, I will make sure no harm comes to you here. Being a gentle lady can be rather frightening, can't it?"

How very kind of him, Myfanwy thought drolly. "Thank you so much," she said with a pinched smile. "But I'm not worried or on the lookout for Mr. Everett. I'm...um..."

Myfanwy wasn't sure why she lied. Indeed, encountering Samuel was the only reason she'd come tonight; however, allowing this man to know that seemed plain wrong. Even with all the gambling and money being lost and won around them, Holmes was the kind of man who valued secrets as his main currency. Confiding in him—showing vulnerability—felt like a betrayal to her safety.

Holmes's lips curled up from his cigar. "You're...what? Meeting someone?"

"What? No!" Myfanwy had been doing so well maintaining a calm façade with the man, but she couldn't stop herself from flinching at his guess. Fortunately, across the room on a small dais, a woman wearing a blood-red dress broke out into song, and an idea instantly popped into her head. "I'm looking for information regarding a lady who might have come here with my father. Sometime in the past year or so. I know you have"—even with her affect of worldly poise, Myfanwy couldn't stop her cheeks from burning red—"women who stay here. Live here, I mean." She cleared her throat. "I was wondering if you knew of any that my father...took a forthright interest in."

The bastard was enjoying every minute of her discomfort. "*Forthright* interest?"

"Indeed."

His cigar again went round and round. To Myfanwy, it was the personification of his mind, always turning, always calculating.

"I know everything that happens in these rooms and hallways. I see everything," he said slowly. He raised his arms to his sides, like their savior on the cross, surrounded by the world and its sins. "And I can say with certainty that your father didn't come here that often, maybe a few times a month, and was always too busy talking cricket to show much...what did you call it? *Forthright interest?*"

Her father had managed to break her heart so much since he'd been gone, but that little bit of information worked to glue some of the smaller pieces back together. The man still had a way to go, though. However, Myfanwy couldn't hide the disappointment at the lack of new leads regarding Annabelle's mother, and

Holmes noticed.

He glanced over her head and snapped his fingers. "Holly, please come here for a moment."

A pretty girl with hair the color of sunflowers in full bloom sidled up to Holmes's side. Wearing a thin silk dress that conveyed to anyone with eyes that she was not wearing proper undergarments underneath, she was definitely one of the women who would have made Jennifer's eyes bulge out of her veil. "Whatcha need, Harry?" she asked, pleasantly enough.

He nodded at Myfanwy. "Miss Myfanwy wants to know if you saw the late Viscount Wright with any of the girls recently—"

"Not so recently," Myfanwy cut in. "It would have been a few years back." She shut her eyes, listening to her hopeless comment. Why would anyone remember a woman the viscount spent time with that long ago? He was an old peer, probably just like the others meandering around the tables, grabbing at all the succulent skin they could find.

"Sorry, no," Holly said. "The viscount didn't come around a lot, did he?" she said, confirming what Holmes had already said.

Myfanwy could feel a headache coming on. It was the various aromas in the room. She had a strong sense of smell, and there were too many perfumes, too many cigars fighting for pride of place. Although...one scent wasn't altogether that unpleasant. She opened her eyes to Holly.

"What is that you're wearing?" she asked.

Taken aback, Holly blushed through the mound of rouge caked on her cavernous cheeks. "You like it? A client—um, eh"— she threw an apologetic look to Holmes—"I mean, a gentleman friend made it for me, or his doctor did anyway, for my muscles. They can get mighty sore...from time to time."

Myfanwy almost wished she hadn't brought it up. The poor girl looked like she was going to faint during the windy explanation to save Myfanwy from guessing what she did for a living. Either Myfanwy appeared particularly innocent, or the woman was just being polite. Myfanwy concluded it was the latter.

She touched the woman's bare arm. "You smell delicious. Like happiness and Christmas all rolled up into one."

"You think so?" Holly asked, shifting awkwardly, not used to the praise. "I worry that it's a bit much. Most men like a more feminine smell, don't you know."

"I prefer your scent," Myfanwy replied. "What's in it?"

Holly's face brightened. "Oh! A whole host of things: wintergreen, belladonna, wolfsbane... And what's that last one? It's an odd word. I can never remember it..." She snapped her fingers. "Oh! Chloroform! That's it."

Myfanwy's nose crinkled. She'd never heard of that before. She had a vague knowledge of the other ingredients, though, and knew they had dubious reputations. Still...they must be safe to use if a doctor made the liniment and Holly was slathering it on her body for aching muscles.

She tightened her grasp around Holly's arm. "And you say it works? This liniment? For soreness."

"Are *you* sore, miss?" Holly asked.

"Not me," Myfanwy answered. "But a friend of mine suffers horribly. Can hardly walk after a long day."

Holly nodded confidently. "I completely understand. I don't know if it will cure her, but I give plenty of the girls this concoction after a hard night—um, ah, I mean a hard day—and it relieves a lot of the pain. Some even call it a miracle oil."

"I wouldn't suppose you have any extra that I could buy?" Myfanwy asked. "Or maybe I can speak to your business associate who gave it to you—"

"For Christ's sake," Holmes muttered. "You won't be going anywhere near that degenerate."

Holly snickered. "You're in luck. I have some extra bottles. Let me run and get you one before you leave."

Myfanwy thanked her and watched the girl fly off up the stairs. When she glanced back at Holmes, his head was shaking in his hands. "Don't you dare tell Samuel where you got that liniment from," he said through his long fingers.

Myfanwy blanched. "How did you—? I'm not buying it for Sam—Mr. Everett."

Again, Holmes gave her that co-conspirator's look. "Like I said, let's just keep it our little secret. I doubt Samuel would appreciate it."

"Oh," a deep voice said behind Myfanwy. "There are a lot of things I'm not appreciating right now."

Chapter Thirteen

SAMUEL SHOULDN'T HAVE enjoyed the way Myfanwy's eyelashes danced as she twirled to find him standing behind her. It wasn't like the action was appealing. It looked like the woman had a clump of dirt in her eyes and was desperately trying to get it out. However, it *did* show that he'd truly caught her unawares, and she was definitely off guard. *Good.* That was exactly where he wanted her.

"Ah, speak of the devil. It seems Samuel was here all along, miss. I must have forgotten," Harry Holmes remarked dryly, not looking half as guilty as he should have. The smarmy son of a bitch had the audacity to appear amused. He was lucky Samuel didn't break his fist over that damn cigar. The problem was that it wouldn't have done any good. Harry would have only been more entertained by the theatrics. It was always best to keep one's cool around the gaming hall owner. The man exploited vulnerability, pure and simple.

"Were your ears ringing?" Holmes asked coolly.

Every ounce of Samuel's blood was ringing, and it was killing him to remain stoic. "Oh, I'm used to being talked about," he drawled, keeping his gaze lazy and level. "I've learned to let go of what I couldn't control long ago."

Holmes's lips trembled in mirth. "Interesting choice of

words," he said, casting a look at Myfanwy.

Oh, Samuel knew exactly what the man was alluding to—the fact that he was having a damned difficult time controlling his sweet aristocratic ward. Ha! If Holmes only knew! However, Samuel had no intention of letting Myfanwy go anytime soon—especially not tonight.

"Time to say goodbye," he said, taking Myfanwy's arm. She blanched at his touch, making his temperature rise. Ever he played the gentleman in her presence; however, testing him at this moment was not in her best interest. Samuel would drag her out by her hair if he had to.

Myfanwy's eyes turned downcast. Usually, Samuel hated when women covered their faces in those ridiculously maudlin veils; they seemed to signify perfidy and subterfuge. And yet the net created sultry patterns across her face, illuminating her large, dark eyes in a positively sinful fashion that made his throat dry.

"I..." She coughed. "I...didn't come alone. I need to find my friends before we can go."

Jesus Christ in heaven! She'd brought *friends*? To the *fucking* Lucky Fish? The morning ahead was dire indeed. How many fathers were going to knock on his door and beat him to a bloody pulp? Samuel would have to let them. This was all his fault.

"Who?" he seethed under his breath.

Myfanwy's head dropped even further between her shoulders. "Jennifer."

Ah. Jennifer. That wasn't so terrible. Only one. If Samuel moved swiftly, he might be able to deposit her back in her room before her parents even noticed, forcing her to swear to secrecy—

"And Sir Bramble."

"What!" Samuel roared. Instantly, his knees locked, and he lifted his head above the crowd. "I'm going to kill him. How dare that mangy bastard escort two ladies—"

"Jennifer isn't a lady."

Samuel's jaw flexed as he continued to scan the room. "Two innocent women—"

Myfanwy chuckled. "And we are hardly innocent."

Samuel rounded on her, pinning her with a death stare. "Do you think this is funny?"

"I'll admit," Holmes interjected with laughter. "I'm rather enjoying myself."

"Fuck off, Holmes," Samuel growled before turning back to Myfanwy. "You. Go get Jennifer. Now. I'll deal with Sir Bramble later."

"Oh wait, you can't leave yet," Holmes said, taking hold of Myfanwy's other arm. Samuel saw red—fiery, lava-like, hell-in-the-middle-of-August crimson. If Holmes didn't get his dirty fingers off his ward, Samuel was certain everyone would be seeing red next—the bloody kind.

Holmes followed Samuel's eyes and withdrew his hold from Myfanwy like he'd just learned she was a leper. "Apologies, old friend."

"We are not old friends," Samuel replied caustically.

Holmes let out a mirthless snort. "I'm sorry to hear that. And I was just going to wish you luck in the cricket match."

Myfanwy's ears perked up, all contrition and embarrassment evaporating from her skin. "You know about that?"

Holmes gave her a quizzical look. "Of course I know about it, dear girl. It's all anybody is talking about...Cremly versus Everett. Should be one hell of a show. A lot of money is riding on it."

"It's also the matrons versus the singles." Myfanwy sniffed with indignation. "Just in case you forgot that vital piece of information."

A patronizing smile played on his lips. "I've insulted you. I didn't mean to, truly. Naturally, we are just as excited to watch you paragons of athleticism take the pitch. A lot of money is being placed on you in particular, or so I'm told."

Samuel should have pushed Myfanwy into moving along. Her ego was getting stroked by the gambler's attention, and no doubt she would cease regretting her decision to come to the Lucky Fish in the first place. And Samuel needed her to understand his point of view and displeasure. She couldn't just prance all over London like it was her playground—especially goddamn gaming halls! What would her father think? And what would he think of Samuel? That he was failing in his promise, that was what. That he wasn't taking adequate care and attention of the viscount's most valuable possession—his daughter.

"We need to go," Samuel said, but Myfanwy resisted the pull in her arm. She only had eyes—and ears—for Holmes.

"What kind of money?" she asked quietly, desperately interested.

Holmes could have turned green, for how much he reminded Samuel of the snake in the Garden of Eden. "Quite a fortune," he replied, milking her interest to the fullest. "It seems you and Samuel here are the odds-on favorites at the present. An upset could put a lot of coin in the hands of someone siding with Cremly." He laughed. "Not that anyone is doing that. You're a sure thing, my dear. And if gamblers value anything, it's a sure thing."

A sweet, ethereal smile lit up Myfanwy's face, and Samuel could imagine butterflies and rainbows and unicorns and whatever hell else gently bred ladies fantasized about dancing in her head. He had to shake her from that stupor—but it pained him to do it.

That was the weakness in man—wanting to make his woman happy, wanting to give her everything.

But Samuel was also Myfanwy's coach. And a coach couldn't allow his star cricketer's head to get big with praise from degenerates and things as vaporous as odds. The only number he wanted her to think about was her batting average.

Samuel guided Myfanwy away once more, and again Holmes beat him to it. His voice was heavy and promising, as if it were a basket laden with sweets. "I would love to talk about your match a little more some other time—if you're interested."

Samuel dropped Myfanwy's arm and charged forward, nose to nose with the gambler. Glaring into the depths of Holmes's black eyes, Samuel felt even more off-kilter. The inky depths were fathomless, no regret to be found. No soul either, for that matter.

"She's not fucking interested," Samuel said. A few heads turned his way, but for the most part, the evening was in full effect. Colors were high; inhibitions were low.

"Interested in what?" Myfanwy asked softly behind his back.

Holmes snorted and cocked his head. "Winning."

Samuel's hand clenched to a fist. He already had a bad leg, and now his hand would follow suit, because when Samuel Everett swung, he swung for the goddamn boundary every time. "Holmes, I swear to you, if you don't shut your fucking face…"

But a caress of fabric distracted him. A glove, as fine and translucent as gossamer wings, covered the ball of his fist, working it open. *Myfanwy*. She took his hand and, judging by her intensity, was not letting go anytime soon. It was a promise, and when he squeezed, Samuel accepted.

"Let's go, Samuel. Please," she pleaded gently, her lips close to the crook of his neck. "I shouldn't have encouraged him. Let's go home."

Home. Samuel recovered just in time. He gasped for a breath like he'd just erupted from the surface of the ocean. It was an odd sensation. The word on her tongue made him want to simultaneously shout from a rooftop and also hit his head against the door.

Samuel let her lead. He followed her skirts toward the entrance when Holmes determined that he would not be disregarded that easily. His indulgent chuckles filled the room along with the smoke. "Don't you want to know how to win?" he called out.

Myfanwy hooked her arm around Samuel's, locking him at her side. "Don't even think about it," she whispered. "If you break your hand, what kind of a coach will you be? How will you help me with my leg-spinners?"

She had a point, but she didn't listen to her own advice. Myfanwy twisted her head around and affected Holmes's confident tone. "I thought I was already going to win. You said it yourself."

Holmes's laughter took on gargantuan proportions. Like a tsunami, it threatened to chase them down and pull them under unless they got to higher ground. Not wanting to be left out of the joke, their audience chimed in as well, and Myfanwy's palms sweated through her gloves. "My dear girl, there's winning and there's *winning*. If you don't believe me, ask your guardian. Only a real professional can tell you the difference."

JENNIFER COULDN'T BE found. It seemed that Sir Bramble had grown some balls when Samuel entered the picture and had flown from the gambling hall with the girl as quickly as his skinny legs could carry them. It was for the best, Samuel decided, as he marched into the street, Myfanwy's hand still clasped in his. He trusted the baron to get the girl home safely. Besides, he had plenty to speak to his ward about on the way home, and none of it was fit for Jennifer. It was a family matter.

Family. Was that what they were?

Yes.

The night air was thick and foggy with the kind of humidity that made one's bones sweat, and it was made even worse by the insufferable tension radiating from his ward. Now that Holmes was behind them, it seemed their brief foray of solidarity was also dumped by the roadside.

Myfanwy allowed Samuel to direct her to the carriage, but her motions were stiff and brittle, as if one quick action might make her snap in two. She was just about to step inside the conveyance when a shout came from the place Samuel was trying so desperately to save her from.

"Miss Myfanwy! Miss!" a high-pitched voice rang out as heels pattered swiftly along the lane. Samuel turned and instantly closed his eyes on a groan. *For fuck's sake.* Why the hell was a strumpet chasing after them? And how in the bloody hell did she know Myfanwy's name?

The fallen woman caught up with them in no time, and it was easy to see why. Samuel wasn't trying to gawk; however, the strumpet's legs were clearly visible under her diaphanous gown. Nice and long. So were her arms... She'd make one hell of a batsman.

"Miss! You forgot this," the woman said, her lungs pumping like a bellows. She shoved a small brown sack into Myfanwy's hands.

Myfanwy's face erupted with a grateful smile. "Oh, thank you so much, Holly!" she exclaimed. "I'm so glad you didn't let me leave without it."

The strumpet—*Holly*—lowered her head shyly. It wasn't every day Samuel encountered a shy prostitute. On closer notice, this one didn't appear as old and withered as the others inside the Lucky Fish. Her face was heavily painted, and her cheeks sank so deep her cheekbones pierced like ice picks, but all of that could be remedied with a good bath and a steady stream of meals.

Samuel reached into his pocket for some loose coins and handed the younger woman everything he had. "For your trouble," he said, spinning toward the carriage.

Her eyelashes fanned wildly. "Oh no, I couldn't, my lord."

"He's not a lord," Myfanwy cut in. For some reason, that irked Samuel. Did she have to sound so jovial about it?

Holly tried again. "Sorry, sir, but I can't take it." She handed the coins back to him.

"Nonsense," Samuel replied, his irritation startling him. "Get something to eat."

"It's not that I'm not grateful," she said quickly. "Only..." She glanced down at her ensemble and raised her arms helplessly to her sides. "I don't have a place to put it, and my customers—ah, business associates—don't like to hear a jingle when they're in the middle of... For some reason, it makes them think badly of themselves."

Samuel pursed his lips. Bad indeed. Apparently, it was difficult to use a woman while you could hear the payment of her previous men clinking in the background. He dug inside his jacket again. Damn. He didn't like to travel with a lot of money on him. It was something he'd learned during his playing years. The less you had on you, the less people could steal. There were always sharks in the water.

He winced. "I'm sorry—"

"Let me," Myfanwy said readily, shuffling in her dainty reticule. She pulled out a five-pound bank note and handed it to Holly, who shoved it inside the top of her garment without hesitation. The fact that Myfanwy didn't bat an eye at the interaction alarmed Samuel more than the prostitute's behavior. What else did his ward get up to when he wasn't around—or, rather, when he wasn't paying attention? It was safe to admit now that over the past year, he had not been the most observant guardian. He could blame his wrecked eye or his busy schedule, but those were paltry excuses at best. Samuel had avoided Myfanwy for self-preservation reasons, pure and simple. And the effects of all her alone time were…disconcerting.

Myfanwy stuck out her hand, and the young woman shook it. "I know you'll love it," Holly said with a pretty smile. "Remember, you have to rub it in long and hard. I find the more you do that, the better it works. Don't be afraid to really work it in there."

Myfanwy nodded, and only when Holly believed that the lady was going to truly take her advice did she retire back into the gaming hall.

Myfanwy watched her go for long seconds, her face open and wistful.

Samuel couldn't help but ask, "What is it?"

"I was just thinking," she said thoughtfully, "about cricketers."

Samuel hadn't been expecting that response. "Cricketers?"

"Yes." Myfanwy turned to the carriage and offered her hand

so he could help her inside. But she hesitated before climbing in, a perturbed expression behind the gauzy veil. "Our clothes aren't made for our jobs. It seems sportswomen have more in common with ladies of the night than I thought."

Chapter Fourteen

"**Y**OU'RE NOT WEARING that, by the way."

Myfanwy blinked, dragging her attention from the window. They'd been in the carriage for over ten minutes, and she'd given up on waiting for Samuel to speak. She'd expected his bluster to begin the moment the carriage door slammed behind them. But he'd been quiet, morosely so, letting the lanterns lining the streets cast shadows over his face as they lumbered by.

"Not wearing what?" she asked.

He tipped his forehead to the sack in her hands. "Whatever face paint Holmes's strumpet"—he grimaced—"*Holly*—gave you. You're not wearing that nonsense on your face."

Myfanwy clawed at the brown cotton sack. "Do you really think Holly is Holmes's…" Her mouth felt impossibly sticky, like she'd just eaten a bowlful of caramel.

Samuel grunted, crossing his arms. His thighs splayed wide. He swallowed the entire seat, filling the area as a liquid would fill any container it was poured into. He tried to hide it, but there was ownership and pride in his behavior, and it amused her. Alongside her father, Myfanwy had sat in a great many carriages with a great many peers, and the difference was evident. Those men never filled a space like Samuel; they expected their surroundings to fill something in them. It was a small distinction, albeit a heavy one, like the handful of coins Holly didn't want tinkling in her skirts.

"I doubt it," Samuel answered, still eyeing the package in her hand as if it were brimming with poison. "Holmes might be a bastard of the first order, but I've never known him to be uncommonly sleazy. He leaves the merchandise for the paying customers."

Myfanwy frowned, shifting in her seat. "Don't call her that."

A long pause permeated the space. "My apologies." Samuel sighed. "I don't know why I said that. It was ungentlemanly of me—" He threw up his hands between them. "Strike that. As you said before, I'm not a gentleman."

His voice was bitter, and Myfanwy thought back to what she'd said to Holly. She hadn't been making a point; she'd pointed out a fact. A positive one. Myfanwy had a feeling that Holly's opinion of gentlemen wasn't the best.

Samuel continued. "Nevertheless, you still aren't putting that shite on your face."

It dawned on her that he thought Holly had given her pastes and powders for her visage. She reined in a chuckle. She thought Samuel knew her better than that. Myfanwy barely tolerated the corsets and petticoats Society forced her to coat herself in; brushing an extra layer over her face was a burden too far.

"Ladies don't paint their faces," she returned.

He nodded. "Exactly."

She cocked her head, annoyed by how certain he sounded. "However," she said, imbuing a thoughtful lilt to her tone, "adding a little rouge wouldn't hurt. People would hardly notice."

"No."

Myfanwy sucked in air through her nose, pressing her tongue harshly into the back of her teeth. "No?" She laughed. "You can't tell me what to do or wear."

Samuel's eyes narrowed, but that was all he gave her. He could have been encased in plaster for how still he became. Then, slowly, he unwrapped his arms and leaned forward, heavy and skulking like a lion just waking up in the morning. He positioned his elbows over his knees. "Do you want to make a bet on that?"

It was an apt question, especially since they'd just left a gaming hall; however, despite the influences of the Lucky Fish, Myfanwy's night wasn't feeling entirely auspicious any longer. She tossed him a question of her own.

"Why are you so against it?" she asked. "You've never struck me as a stickler for convention."

Her query pushed him back against the seat. His big, deep-set eyes lost their connection with hers and latched on the window. "I'm not," he said, rather cagey.

Good. Let him be on the back foot for a change.

"You sound like a real spinster to me," Myfanwy goaded him. "Like a soul-crushing grande dame."

He *humphed*. "I'm nothing of the sort."

Myfanwy's laugh was genuine now. "Oh, come now. I'm only teasing." She attempted to sober herself. "Tell me."

Samuel rolled his eyes, still avoiding her gaze. "Because," he said, shrugging, "women like you don't need it."

"Women like me?"

"You know what I mean," he rasped.

No, Myfanwy most definitely did not. "I'm going to badger you until you finish explaining," she said. "And we both know how aggravating I can be."

The put-upon grimace Samuel gave her almost hurt her feelings. Surely she wasn't *that* aggravating.

He mumbled something under his breath.

"What was that?"

"You're too pretty for it," he said.

Myfanwy straightened away, as if the force of his words blew her off axis. Now, she was the one who couldn't quite meet his eyes, and he was the one intent on continuing.

"Some women can handle a little more," Samuel went on, waving his palm over his face awkwardly. "But you...wearing all that color would only detract from your"—he coughed into his fist—"beauty. Inside."

Myfanwy couldn't understand it, but tears were pooling in her eyes. As she started to wipe them away, Samuel noticed the emotion, and his two-toned gaze grew large and frightened. "Besides," he added with a shaky laugh. "If you wear that trash on your face when you play, you'll risk it running into your eyes from all the sweat, and you won't see the ball properly. And then where will we be?"

Myfanwy didn't laugh with him, not when she knew that his last comment was made in fear. His fear. Of her.

"Women don't sweat," she whispered.

"Horseshit. Everyone sweats."

From under her lashes, Myfanwy watched Samuel come to terms with everything he'd just divulged. They'd kissed at night under the cover of darkness, and yet this small admission seemed to point an even greater flame toward his soul. She knew he lusted for her, knew he found her desirable, but hearing that he found her greatest, truest beauty on the inside rather than the outside was a revelation of honesty she'd never hoped for from the taciturn sportsman. She should have pretended to buy face paint much earlier.

Samuel wasn't filling the carriage anymore. He shoved himself in the corner so completely, it was like he was trying to blend in with the crimson upholstery. Myfanwy didn't like seeing him like this, but she'd be lying if she told herself she wasn't a little entertained. She was so used to his acting disgruntled and angry with her that she almost preferred him that way. That was the only explanation for what she did next.

Myfanwy tipped a glance at the sack before placing it on the seat next to her with a heavy sigh. "What would you do?" she asked.

Samuel's eyebrows knitted together in a fierce seam.

"If I came to you with my face all colored like a doll?" Myfanwy scooted to the edge of her seat, cupping the edge as she veered forward. They were still too far apart for her liking, but she resolved to only meet him halfway. She wanted another kiss, but she wasn't going to jump on the man to get it.

Samuel's damaged eye glowed in the darkness, as unnerving and exciting as seeing luminous eyes in the dark forest, always aware that they were watching your every movement. It felt like being stalked, and there was nothing unappealing about the sensation.

"I would take it off you," he said. It was a plain, succinct statement; nevertheless, it still caused her stomach to flip-flop like she was falling from a great height. *More.* Myfanwy wanted more.

She stretched further across the divide of the carriage. "And if I run? If I won't let you catch me?"

It seemed like her words had to fight through the tension in the air to reach him, because she had to wait for a response. Finally, Samuel's lips curled up and he peeled himself away from the seat. Blinking slowly, he bowed forward, setting his forearms on his knees again. Still too far away, though. "I would catch you."

Myfanwy's laugh was completely void of breath or sound. She lowered her lashes—intending to stare at his bad leg—but her focus got stuck on his...well...his manhood, which looked much, *much* healthier.

Samuel's laughter didn't have the same problem as hers. There was nothing stuck about it.

Myfanwy licked her lips, compelling herself to continue with the game. Because that's what this was, wasn't it? Just a game? With a kiss for the winner?

The need was pure in her voice, so bright it was almost translucent. "You couldn't catch me if you tried."

Samuel's mouth closed. His jaw was tight when he leaned over even further and said, "What makes you more upset, Myfanwy? The fact that I could catch you or the fact that I've never tried?"

Oh, she deserved that. Nevertheless, knowing that didn't make it sting less. Myfanwy almost retreated to her corner of the carriage. She might have, too, if Samuel hadn't reached out and taken her hand. Painstakingly, he cupped it in both of his and slid her thin glove off, dropping it on the floor. He turned her hand palm side up. With callused, rough fingers that knew a life so different than hers, he used his time thoughtfully, tracing the lines top to bottom, side to side.

Recounting her past or reading her future?

Whatever the information he gathered, it didn't make him content. On the contrary, Myfanwy noticed his frown grow deeper as he studied her.

She tried to break the heady moment. "You remind me of an old gypsy woman." She chuckled. "Are you going to tell me my fortune?"

His studious brow didn't relent. Samuel shook his head as he continued to caress her. He wasn't following the lines of her palms anymore; he was tracing her scars. Myfanwy didn't have many—certainly not as many as him—however, she'd attained her fair share with the cricket bat in her hand these last few years. She never noticed them because she never found a reason to dislike them as other ladies might.

"Your hands shouldn't look like this," he said. The words came out part wounded animal, as if all the pain in the scars bit and stabbed and scraped into his own skin.

Utterly self-conscious, Myfanwy attempted to pull away, but he wouldn't release her. Samuel continued to hold her—and astonish her.

Her voice wobbled when she replied, "I like my hands."

He tore his gaze away from her palms to grant her a baleful look. "These are not the hands of a lady."

"They are my hands," she said airily, "and I am a lady. Ergo, these *are* the hands of a lady. Besides, it's none of your concern."

She felt his breath on her skin as he lifted her hand closer to his face. "Everything about you is my concern."

"Yes…because of your promise to my father."

Samuel's chuckle was plaintive and short. There and gone

like a drop of rain lost in the earth. "It has nothing to do with your father."

Her pulse hammered, and she desperately hoped he couldn't feel it. From the slight smile on his face, Myfanwy realized it was a losing battle. She tried again. "Because you want to beat Cremly?"

He shook his head again, only slower this time, hypnotic and almost sensual. Myfanwy leaned in further. She was more than halfway across the carriage now, but at least she wasn't on his lap. She wouldn't go that far!

"It has nothing to do with Cremly," Samuel answered.

"Then why?"

Samuel didn't answer. And it didn't matter anyway, because soon, Myfanwy forgot the question. Because it was then that he lifted her hand to his mouth and, one by one, took his precious time kissing the tips of her fingers. He pressed them to his full lips and gave each a benediction, a blessing. There was nothing lascivious, and yet there was nothing innocent about the act either. Myfanwy's breath lodged in her throat as she watched him touch her in this intimate way.

He ended the exchange by placing his mouth on the flesh of her palm, his nostrils flaring, his eyes open and daring as they fixed on hers, almost begging her not to speak, not to give voice to this erotic act unfolding between them.

So, Myfanwy didn't. She jumped on his lap instead.

Samuel was ready for her.

Myfanwy locked her arms and thighs around him, leaving no safe place for the man to hide. He didn't seem to want to. Samuel's lips found hers in an instant, and he pillaged her swiftly and ruthlessly, finally giving words to all the unsung emotions that had bumped alongside them in the carriage. His mouth laid claim to her, sweeping and filling her with undiluted passion.

This is it, Myfanwy thought. This was finally the moment when they would go from friends to lovers—even though they weren't truly friends, and she hadn't the faintest idea what made lovers. It didn't matter. This act was as purposeful and defining as pulling Excalibur from the stone. Samuel was the rock—he was always the hard place—but Myfanwy knew that all he needed to do was relinquish his hold. Then, and only then, would greatness envelop them both.

Myfanwy lifted on her knees, plastering her chest against his, adoring the way he pressed his hands into her back, pushing her even harder on him. They traveled higher, and Samuel placed one hand on the back of her neck, guiding her head where he needed it, canting her to the right angle so he could plunder the depths of her mouth more. He tasted like fire, all fervor and intensity, so electric in his need that his touch pulsed and shocked her all the way to her core.

Samuel was like gravity to her, always pulling her in his direction, always making her fall into his arms.

Myfanwy tugged at his necktie. "We should probably stop," she whispered into his mouth, defying her actions. "We're almost home."

Samuel kissed the mutiny from her lips. "This carriage will run for as long as I tell it to," he growled, sliding a hand down her thigh. With an impatient flick, he whipped her skirts up, baring a thigh. His hand latched on like a barnacle to a ship and gripped tight. "I fucking love your legs." His voice ached with pure need. "So fucking strong."

Myfanwy would have laughed—out of shyness—more than anything, but she stopped herself. Because he made her think about his legs and how he couldn't use them as he once could. And that made her mind go back to the package on her seat. He was perfectly amiable enough at the present. Would he let her use the tincture on him now? Not wanting to ask the question— her lips were already in the middle of something—she reached behind her. When her hands came up with only air, she forced herself to break away from the kiss to glance back at the cushion.

And then she saw it. A slight, familiar form just outside the carriage.

"The boy!" Myfanwy shrieked, slamming down harshly on Samuel's *rather* turgid lap.

"Fuck!" he yelled, shutting his eyes in a brutal hold, grabbing her hips and readjusting her into a better position.

Myfanwy didn't have time to apologize. She was already rapping on the ceiling of the carriage, yelling for the driver to stop. "It's him," she yelled in Samuel's face. "It's the boy from the other day. The one who dropped off Annabelle!"

She didn't wait for recognition to come to Samuel—the poor man still hadn't even opened his eyes. The minute the carriage came to a halt, she whipped open the door and hopped out onto the street, frightening the dickens out of the poor child.

Not enough to freeze him, though. After a moment's shock, the boy, as was his habit, took off like a shot. He scrambled down the street, but Myfanwy wasn't about to let him win this time. Neither was Samuel. She heard him shout from the carriage; however, it didn't work on her or the boy. Neither of them stopped. If anything, the boy was incited to panic even more.

He had youth on his side, but Myfanwy had her long legs. They ate into the pavement, and within seconds she was right behind the child. She only had to reach out and she could grab the back of his shirt. Only, for once, she was beaten to it. Samuel's arm snaked into her periphery as he snatched the back of the boy's threadbare collar. Releasing a nasty expletive, he yanked hard, and the boy snapped backward, landing on his behind on the sidewalk.

The abrupt motion proved to be too much for Samuel. His leg went out underneath him like the damaged foundation of a house, flimsy and shattering, and he crumpled next to the boy. He closed a grimace over his yelp, but Myfanwy could see the toll the effort took on him. His face was marred with anguish, and a heavy layer of sweat coated his forehead. Like her, his chest pumped from the run; however, every breath he expelled seemed to be riddled in agony, like the pain was tattooed into his very core, with nothing there to abate it.

Slithering like eels, the boy's limbs struck out as if he was ready to make another run for it, but Myfanwy plopped down next to him, pinning his shoulders with her hands. "You're not going anywhere—"

"I didn't steal anything, I swear," the boy cut in, his youthful eyes bobbing frantically.

Myfanwy glanced at Samuel, but his frown was set squarely on the boy. No help there. "Stealing...?"

He was close to crying now. He'd seemed so much older the first time she encountered him. Maybe that was because he'd been standing so close to Annabelle. Now, on his own, Myfanwy saw him for what he was—a young child himself, a terribly frightened one. Close to hysterics.

The boy's bottom lip trembled as his words flowed like a river. "I promise. I just wanted to see her. I didn't take anything from the lord's house."

Myfanwy could sense Samuel's shoulders straightening at the mention of his being a lord. They didn't have time for all that. "Who did you want to see? The little girl you deserted on our doorstep before you ran away?"

The boy's expression completely changed at the mention of Annabelle. The tears could no longer wait. He broke like a dam. "I didn't desert her," he sobbed. "I would never do that to my sister!"

Chapter Fifteen

S AMUEL WOULDN'T SIT. Even though his leg throbbed like it had just been kicked by a twenty-hand Clydesdale, he would not show weakness in front of the street urchin. The time to be heavy-handed was now—especially as the deceitful bugger was hunkered in his kitchen, eating him out of house and home.

"Whenever you're ready," Samuel prodded dryly as the boy took yet another gargantuan spoonful of beef and onion pie that had been left over from dinner. His mouth was so stuffed that the boy could only nod and close his eyes in heavenly rapture. The pie was good—Samuel could attest to that. He'd been planning on finishing it before bed. That notion was now spoiled.

"Let him eat," Myfanwy admonished him, sidling next to the boy at the cook's table, her head in her hand as she watched him attack his food. Samuel couldn't stop himself from meandering into the prurient, dark corners of his mind while he waited. Just minutes before, he'd been kissing the fingers that tapped so delicately along her jaw. He'd also been licking the long lines of that creamy jaw and sucking on the insistent tongue inside of it.

He limped to the far end of the table, making sure his nether regions were covered. He wanted the boy to believe he was the director of this inquisition, not some deviant. A massive cock-stand would do a lot to counter that notion.

Time was not on his side. "All right now, that's enough," Samuel announced, stretching across the table and swiping the plate away. The boy's spoon hung in the air. Slowly, with great intention and regret, he placed it on the wood counter.

"Where do you want me to start?" the boy asked, folding his hands in front of him like he was kneeling in the confessional box. He better hope that he had the kind of answers that would make Samuel want to absolve him of his sins.

Samuel pinned him with a sardonic look. "How about we start with 'sister'—"

Myfanwy reached out and rubbed the child's arm. "After you tell us your name."

Samuel released an annoyed breath and scowled at the pots and pans hanging from the ceiling. It was like he wasn't even in the room.

For his part, the boy gave him a nervous glance before fixing his attention solely on Myfanwy. "Aaron," he said. "And Annabelle is my sister."

"We gathered that part," Samuel said. "Why did you dump her at my home and run off to heaven knows where a week ago?"

If the boy had a shell, he would have climbed into it and never come out. His ruddy face bloomed so red that the myriad freckles covering it were blotted out. Samuel chastised himself again for failing to notice the resemblance. Although Annabelle's auburn hair was a picture-perfect image of Myfanwy's, her galaxy of freckles was pure Aaron. And though the boy carried a sooty mop of hair on his head, the children shared round faces and blunt little limbs, as well as eyes that appeared more feline than human. The word came to him instantly. *Savage.* The boy looked positively savage.

Hit with an unfamiliar dose of pity, Samuel slid the plate back in Aaron's direction.

Aaron wrapped his arms around it, though didn't tuck in as he had before. "Our mum died last month," he said slowly, the words fighting their way out of his mouth. "The money is gone.

It's been gone for a while. Ever since…" He stole a bashful look at Myfanwy. "Ever since the lord died. Mum found work on the boards, as she always had, but when she got sick…" His head fell, just barely missing the pie.

"Your mother was an actress?" Myfanwy asked gently. "What was her name?"

Pride filled his young voice. "Victoire Ruby."

Myfanwy's brows knitted together, and Samuel found himself speaking up before he could stop himself. "I saw her once. She was…good." *Praise indeed,* he thought, perturbed by his pathetic lack of loquaciousness; however, it worked. Aaron scooped his spoon into the pie once more and took a comforting bite. He didn't seem to notice that Samuel was lying for his benefit.

Myfanwy did, though. She regarded him like he was a puzzle with no chance of solving.

"She was bloody brilliant," Aaron said in between chews. "But…"

"She got sick," Myfanwy filled in.

Aaron nodded meekly. "Consumption. When she died, I tried to take care of Annabelle as best I could, but Mum's friends traveled a lot, and we had no family to speak of." His ears glowed so red they almost looked purple. Samuel recognized shame easily, and his heart bled for the boy who carried it like a shroud. Aaron's voice wilted like a cut plant left out in the sun. "It was hard."

"How old are you?" Samuel asked.

"Eleven."

Myfanwy's hand went to her mouth, but a small gasp still leaped out. Samuel had spent most of his life alone, and it had not been an easy one; however, when he was eleven, he was safe and fed in the comfort of his parents' small, modest home in Sutton. He had his issues with his father, but he'd have to be completely blind not to see how fortunate he'd been.

"I just needed to know if she was doing well," Aaron went on. His tiny, narrow shoulders bobbed as sobs overtook him. Samuel remembered what those shoulders felt like when he'd hauled the boy into the carriage. His bones had felt horribly small, almost birdlike under his rough-spun clothing. Annabelle's clothing hadn't been so desolate, though she'd only shown up in the one dress. Samuel wondered if Aaron had kept that dress for her to make a good impression on them, or if every coin he managed to earn had gone to the welfare of his little sister.

"Did you know my"—Myfanwy's voice caught, and she swiped her hair away from her face nervously—"the viscount?"

The boy nodded. "My mother made me leave when he came to visit, but I met him a few times. He was nice enough. I'm sorry he died."

In an instant, Myfanwy appeared hungrier than the urchin. "And did he...did he know about Annabelle?"

Aaron nodded again, this time with a wistful smile. "He didn't forsake my mother or Annabelle, if that's what you think. Sometimes I'd hear them talking in the other room. He wanted to marry her. He didn't care where she came from, but my mother... She didn't want that life. She said his people would never accept her. Besides, she loved the theatre, and she didn't want to give that up."

Myfanwy's face softened. "Your mother sounds like an amazing woman."

A slight quiver came upon Aaron's lips. "She was," he replied tightly. "The viscount provided for us, put us in the nicest home I'd ever seen. He'd planned to tell you...about Annabelle." Shyly, he glanced up. "I heard them talk about that too. He was just waiting for the right time. He was afraid that he would disappoint you."

Myfanwy nodded, falling back in her seat, her own lips beginning to quiver.

"He was a good man," Aaron went on. "For a time, I hated him, though. When he stopped coming by... I didn't know he died. We found out in the newspaper."

"That must have been difficult for your mother," Samuel

interjected.

Aaron dropped his gaze to his food, pushing it around with his spoon. "It was."

"Why didn't you find family?" Samuel asked. "I assume you have grandparents. Why didn't you look for them after your mother died?

Aaron gulped. "I suppose I do, but I've never met them. My mother only ever said they weren't good people. She told me where she grew up but said that after she joined a traveling acting troupe, she never looked back. To be honest, I'm not sure if I even want to find them." He flicked his head toward Myfanwy. "I figured if Annabelle needed family, you would be it."

"But what about you?" Myfanwy asked.

"Oh, don't worry about me. I'll be all right," the boy said, puffing out his pathetically small chest. "You're Annabelle's family, not mine."

"You'll stay here."

"You'll stay with us."

Samuel and Myfanwy stared at one another as their voices rang out in unison. He wasn't even irritated that she'd made the decision without consulting him. It was the right one.

Aaron needed to be convinced, though. He placed his spoon down quickly and launched to his feet, grasping the edge of the table to steady himself. The poor thing was ready to topple over. If the bruised crescents under his eyes were any indication, the boy hadn't had proper sleep in days. "I have a place to stay. I don't need your help," he said, backing away from Myfanwy. She let him go, but Samuel could see her forearm muscles tense. She was ready to catch him at any second. Aaron wasn't going anywhere tonight.

The boy slapped his dusty gray cape on his head, covering his greasy hair. "I just wanted to make sure my sister was safe. This doesn't have to be forever, you know. I can take her back once I get settled. I just need to find a proper job, a proper wage, and then we won't bother you anymore."

Myfanwy's eyes were getting misty. "You're only a child—"

"I'm not a child!"

"And you aren't a bother."

"I don't take charity!"

"How about a job, then?" Samuel asked, his smooth tone cutting through all the emotion like a knife through butter. "It's hardly charity if I have a job that I need filled for someone exactly like you."

Both pairs of eyes blinked at him from across the table. Samuel merely smiled, congratulating himself on landing on the solution so quickly. Once it came to him, it made perfect sense.

"What...what is it?" Aaron asked, trying to hide the hope that still bled through every syllable.

Samuel glanced down at this pocket watch. "It's late. We'll get into it tomorrow. For now, you should join your sister. No doubt she'll be overjoyed to wake up next to you. I'll have the maid make up a room for you tomorrow. You work for me, and you'll get room and board and a stipend every week. When you feel like you're finally on your feet, then you can leave, but"— Samuel narrowed his gaze—"not until you prove to me you can take care of your sister and yourself."

"But sir," Aaron said, shaking his head. "That might take months."

Samuel slapped his hand over his chest and pretended to stumble backward. "Oh, thank the Lord. I was assuming it would take years."

⇉⟫⟪⇇

JUST WHEN SAMUEL found a position on his bed that didn't make him want to pass out from the incessant pain, a knock sounded and the door opened a sliver.

For once, he was glad that the person on the other side was rude enough to barge in without waiting.

Samuel knew who it was anyway. It didn't matter where, but he could always tell where Myfanwy was in the house. In the past, he'd told himself it was because he could avoid her. Now he attributed his keen senses to the simple fact that knowing where she was calmed him. Knowing she was close calmed him even more.

Myfanwy slipped through like a secret. She was still wearing the black dress he'd found her in earlier at the Lucky Fish, but she'd taken the ridiculous veil off. *Good,* he thought. The damn alluring netting highlighted her face in a way that made him want things. Desperate things.

Myfanwy leaned against the door, her hands tucked behind her back. Her eyes flitted about the room, jumping from corner to corner, obviously trying not to land on his bare chest. Samuel's legs were spread out over the covers, and, thank the Lord for small mercies, he hadn't taken his trousers off yet. He liked to believe that he might have yelled for her not to come in if that was the case, though he couldn't be sure.

Self-consciously, he propped himself higher on the pillows against the headboard. He attempted to keep his expression stoic and contained, but he could feel the cold sweat gather at his forehead. His leg was pulsing like a hot iron, and it felt odd to unclench his jaw from its habitual response.

"Did you need something?" he asked blandly when she continued to stand there. Why did it feel like she was trying to make her mind up about something?

Myfanwy straightened away from the door. "Oh, yes," she said, her voice unusually high. "I wanted to thank you for what you did tonight. What you did for Aaron."

Samuel's chest almost dropped through the bed to the floor. He'd wanted her to say something else. Something about their time in the carriage. Something to do with just them.

Myfanwy ambled to the bed, and the closer she came, the more Samuel's hair stood on its end like he were a cat in the middle of a scare. A *thank you* could be made from across the room, he thought.

Her hands came around to her front, and he noticed she was carrying that ridiculous sack that the prostitute had given her. Samuel wanted to bang his head back against the headboard. *This again?* He wasn't in the mood for a fight.

"You don't need to thank me," he said sourly. "The boy needed a place to stay. I have two brothers. As much as I detest the nosy bastards on the best of days, nothing could keep me from them if I thought they were in trouble."

A lovely smile curled onto her face. "So, this is a habit for you? Playing the hero?"

Samuel huffed. "You know as well as I that I'm no hero."

"Aaron thinks you are. When I tucked him into bed, he practically had stars in his eyes. 'I will do anything the lord needs of me,' he said. 'I will be the best worker he's ever had.'" Myfanwy reached the edge of his bed. All the air inside Samuel's body seemed to vanish as he waited to see what she would do next.

He licked his lips. "I did it for Annabelle."

She nodded, glancing down at the package. "You took me in for my father, you took Annabelle in for me, and now you are helping Aaron for Annabelle." Her brown eyes gleamed. "Do you want to know a secret?"

Samuel gulped.

"I think you didn't do any of those things for other people. I think you did them because they were the right thing to do, and you are a good person. What do you think about that?"

Finally, goddamn *finally*, she lifted her knee and climbed onto the bed. Samuel didn't move an inch, afraid he might scare her away. He didn't know what she was doing there, only that he didn't want her to leave anytime soon.

"It's a good theory," he said.

She raised an eyebrow. "Only a theory?"

He nodded.

"But a good one?"

He nodded again.

Myfanwy crawled further onto the mattress, sitting on her feet at his side. He could grab her. It would take less than a second to haul her into his arms and kiss her until she came. Only Samuel didn't. He stayed where he was, barely flinching a muscle. There was something going on in that head of hers; the gears were shifting with intention. He'd stared down enough bowlers to know when it was best to swing and when it was advantageous to let the ball fly past.

The apples of her cheeks filled with mischievous life, and Myfanwy shyly played with the sack in her hands, rolling it around and around as if it were a crystal ball ready to announce their future. "I have another theory," she whispered. "You're in a tremendous amount of pain..." She looked up at him from beneath her heavy, sultry lids. "And I think I have something that can help."

Samuel's cock almost jumped out of his pants for joy. Swiftly, he shifted, hoping Myfanwy didn't notice. All of a sudden, he loved her theories; his entire body was in rapt attention for more. The room hummed with the possibilities.

Ordinarily, Samuel would have been embarrassed by how breathless his next words came out, but he didn't give one damn. "What do you have in mind?" he asked.

She angled her head to his legs, and there was absolutely nothing Samuel could do to stop his cock from dancing at this point. His fingers itched. He was in a losing battle. All the explanations and nonsense words he'd used before about not wanting to ruin Myfanwy or destroy her old admiration for him flew out the window without so much as a by-your-leave. Nothing was more important than her hands on him.

Samuel was determined to hold her soon, engulf her; all this stalling was making his leg pain seem as slight as a silly itch. What was Myfanwy waiting for? Couldn't she see he was ready? Didn't she know that all she needed to do was snap her fingers and he would submit to her? That it had always been so between them?

Deliberately, Myfanwy placed the sack on his belly. His sensitive muscles bobbed underneath the cotton like a slow-rolling sea.

Her teeth emerged as her smile grew bigger. She reached inside the sack and pulled out a plain amber bottle. "I'm going to need you to take off your pants now."

Chapter Sixteen

I F IT TOOK Myfanwy forever just to work up the nerve to join Samuel on the bed, she made up for it by getting his trousers off in a hurry. He was incredibly helpful in that endeavor. The order wasn't even fully out of her mouth and his hands were already working on his front buttons. She wanted to help him glide the fabric down his legs, but Samuel completed the task in no time. However, the end result left something to be desired.

For some reason, Myfanwy assumed his undergarments would be short, cut off before the knee, but they were sadly long and white and covering the entire area she needed to massage. They were essentially trousers underneath his trousers.

They both stared entirely too long at his nether regions. Myfanwy made a clicking sound with her tongue, feeling panic begin to bubble in her chest. She didn't know how much longer her cavalier act would hold. Kissing him would solve all of this. Samuel didn't think as much when he was busy kissing her, and she was less anxious. But Myfanwy hadn't intended to storm into his room and debauch him—not at first, anyway. A selfless act was her goal. And Samuel's layers were getting in the way.

"You weren't supposed to be wearing those," she remarked.

"I wasn't?" Myfanwy could hear the amusement in Samuel's voice.

She plucked at his undergarments. "The fabric is thin, but I don't think the tincture will absorb into your skin unless you're...um... Well, you're..." Myfanwy cast a hopeless look at the hearth, thinking it must be blazing for her to feel so uncomfortable, only to realize that Samuel hadn't bothered to light a fire that night.

"Naked?" he finished.

"Quite."

Samuel shifted further up the bed. She couldn't look at him. Her embarrassment was as cloying and sticky as toffee pudding. "Myfanwy," he said gently over her head. "I don't need you to massage my leg. It hurts, yes, but I just have to deal with it. Nothing ever helps, so I've found it's always best to just get through it."

Not good enough! Thoughts jumbled together in her mind. Samuel took care of so much, and yet he was so alone. Whoever took care of him? Whoever put *him* first?

The bed sank lower as he tried to inch away from her, but Myfanwy slapped her hand on his chest—his very naked chest. "No," she stated firmly—as firm as the muscles under her fingers. He hadn't played proper cricket in a few years, but one couldn't tell from his upper half. Well-formed and lithe, Samuel's body had the sculpted, chiseled look of something cut from rock, all angles and sharp points, shaped expertly and pulled tight against the bone. He didn't have much hair on his chest, and what he did have was so light in color that it barely registered. Myfanwy held her fingers firmly against his skin, so she didn't play with the small curls.

"I will look away while you take off your undergarments," she said officiously. "Then you can cover your... Well, you know, your..."

"Cock."

"Lap."

What did he just say? Myfanwy's eyes almost jumped out of her head. But if she was expecting an apology from the incorrigible man, she was mightily mistaken. She buried her face in her hands and shook her head. "I can't believe you just used that word."

Samuel's laughter was thick and guttural as he worked to do her bidding. "Don't be such an innocent," he said, shifting the bed as he did what she asked. "I know you've heard worse on the cricket pitch."

"That's the cricket pitch," Myfanwy squeaked from under the darkness of her hand. "This is the—" She stopped. Feeling no more movement on his end, she peeked out from between her fingers and saw him naked—but still covered—with the bed-clothes draped around his hips. Her mouth dried as she took in his long legs, much hairier than his chest. Even bruised and scarred, they brought to mind pure power. The ability to run and run until your lungs couldn't take any more and threatened to burst out of your chest. Samuel could tear down the pitch faster than anyone Myfanwy had ever seen—like Zeus blowing a ship across the sea with the power of his lips. He'd been so beautiful. And yet, she realized, nothing had changed. Here he sat before her...still beautiful, maybe even more so now that she knew him as a person and no longer an idol.

"What are you really doing here?" Samuel asked gently, low-ering his head to catch her bashful gaze. His eyes were wide, his expression open. *Honesty.* Simple honesty poured out of him. And...hope? "What is this, Myfanwy? Tell me. Because you sit here all timid in front of me, but this is *my* room you're in in the middle of the night. *My* skin you've asked to touch. *My* body you've made bare. I've done it all, and now it's your turn."

Myfanwy had always considered herself forthright, but being that way and being treated that way were two different things. Samuel was asking for her truth, and he deserved it. She wanted him, but again, that was not why she'd knocked on his bedroom door. "This night is not about me; it's about you. I don't want to talk about me or my father, please... I just can't right now. I'm not here to answer questions."

With a desperate, pleading look, she unscrewed the bottle and poured a little of the oil into her hands. The room was immediately infused with wintergreen, making it seem as fresh and light as a forest at daybreak. She rubbed her hands together, pleased at how tingly and stimulated her skin became by the simple action. When she laid her hands on Samuel's thigh, he flinched as if she'd burned him.

"Stay still," she warned, gently working into his flesh, not wanting to knead too deeply, too quickly. She had no basis to test any of her theories, though it made sense to her that one must wake up the muscles before one really exercised them.

The room ebbed and flowed, at first feeling impossibly small, as if any major move would throw them together. But as Myfanwy began to work, the air swelled with emotions and questions, shy glances and shallow breaths.

Soon she got the hang of her exertions, learning the way Samuel's body responded to her touch. Much like she'd seen the cooks manipulate dough in the kitchen, the longer she pushed and pulled, the more the tension in Samuel's leg eventually gave way and a softer, suppler muscle emerged underneath her hands.

She heard him groan and lay his head back against the head-board, closing his eyes, wincing at times, sighing at others. Myfanwy was helping him, and that knowledge spurred her on. If he was opening to her in body, then maybe she could get him to open in spirit.

"What did Holmes mean earlier," she began, watching his eyebrows rise, "when he talked about professionals and how they are the only ones who understand winning? I don't understand."

Samuel's chest expanded as he took a massive breath. Myfanwy wanted to place her hand there again and massage the space over his heart. Could this magic tincture stimulate that unyielding space?

"No, you wouldn't understand that, would you?" Samuel replied lazily, almost sleepily. "But it's not much different than what Cremly was spouting off about before."

"Cremly?"

He nodded. The lines of his face softened, but he couldn't fool her hands. Just saying the marquis's name caused his muscles to turn to steel under her ministrations. "The professionals-versus-amateurs nonsense," he began. "The idea that professionals ruin the sport by demanding to be paid. The amateurs—*the gentlemen*," he sneered, "never take into account that the professionals cannot afford *not* to be paid. These men don't come from much. If they choose to play instead of spending the day working, then they miss out on wages for their family. And most of the professionals are the better players. The crowds pay to come to see them. Why should they be ashamed to have a cut of that?"

"They shouldn't—"

"And if they want to make a little more by betting on the game, why shouldn't they? They're betting on themselves, for Christ's sake."

Myfanwy wove her hands around Samuel's knee, the one that gave him such a difficult time. He hissed between his teeth as she manipulated the area, giving it the attention it so desperately deserved. "Did you bet on yourself?" she asked with a heavy dose of trepidation. "Is that what Harry meant by 'winning'?"

Samuel finally opened his eyes, and the blue orbs appeared oppressively tired. "Of course. I was always told to bet on myself to make extra money. It was the surest bet I'd ever make. I'm afraid I'm a jaded beast. I have little to no faith in others, only in myself."

Myfanwy snorted. "Did my father tell you that?"

"No," he said wistfully. "No, it was someone else."

When Samuel didn't explain further, Myfanwy let it drop. There was no sense in pushing; he would tell her if he wanted to.

"Did you know the amateurs don't even get ready in the same pavilion as the professionals?" he went on, his tone gaining strength. "They think it's below them. They travel in different trains—hell, they even enter the pavilions in different areas than professionals on their own teams. But they still deign to hire us professionals to bowl to their sons while they attend Eton and provide labor on the grounds of their clubs that would never accept us as members. It has nothing to do with the money. If you look closely, you'll notice that men like Lord Cremly always seem to walk away from a cricket match with a heavier pocket than they came in with. No...it's just another way to stigmatize those who grew up poor, because we are *better* than them. Professional cricketers are the best of the best, but that can't be allowed, so they try to swipe us down any way they can. One sneer, one joke, one slight at a time, until men like Joe Danvers and Benny Hardcastle are no longer gods of the pitch, but old drunkards to be laughed at."

"I can't imagine anyone laughing at you."

"Because I don't give them a reason to." Samuel made a ragged sound in the base of his throat. "Your father taught me everything. He taught me to behave like a gentleman, even though I was far from it. He taught me to wring as much money out of the game as I could so that I could leave on my own terms and was never beholden to anyone."

"But you didn't leave on your own terms." She tapped lightly on top of his knee. "I thought this was the reason why you retired, and the injury to your eye."

Samuel glared at the offending limb as if it were a best friend who had stabbed him in the back. "After a time, the eye healed, or healed enough that I could still find a way to play. It was the leg that kept me down. It refused to move the way I needed it to. It slowed me, and hurt so much that I found it difficult to think of anything else. I've seen a few doctors. Some said I was done for; others said ice baths would help and that I'd be on the mend in no time. But it never felt right." His cheeks glowed red, like he was in the confessional telling Myfanwy a terrible secret. "I didn't see the point in trying to return. If I couldn't play at my old level, what would be the point?"

Myfanwy frowned, caressing his rough calf, digging her

thumb in so hard that his foot trembled. His words angered her. "It's still a game," she replied. "Do you have to be the best? I'm sure at one time you enjoyed it just for sake of playing. Can't that happen again? Isn't that enough?"

Samuel snorted, crossing his arms. "Says the woman who hates losing so much that she cast all her ego aside to ask me to coach her team."

Myfanwy laughed despite herself. "I suppose you have a point."

She settled back on her feet, admiring her handiwork. Half of Samuel glistened like a god before her, drenched in her oils, lacquered to a relaxed shine. With the content smile on his lips and the lethargic way he was situated on the bed, she could almost believe she'd cured him. But if their talk had taught her anything, it was that some of Samuel's injuries weren't anywhere near the surface—and potentially out of her reach.

"There," she said, rubbing her hands together, absorbing the last of the oil. "How does that feel?"

Samuel flexed his leg, twisting it back and forth and bending it a few times. She watched him closely and didn't detect a single grimace. On the contrary, he rewarded her with a grin. "It feels... Damn, it feels better. Much better."

"Holly told me it was a magic cure."

Samuel arched a brow at the bottle on the table. "Do I want to know what the prostitutes use this oil for?"

Myfanwy shrugged. "I don't see why not. Holly said she uses it for her legs when they're sore after work."

Samuel's grin turned tight. "Jesus Christ," he muttered.

"Oh, don't be such a snob. If it's good enough for them, it's good enough for you."

"Is that why you went to the Lucky Fish tonight? To find this oil?" His voice lowered. "Or to find me?"

"I told you, I'm not answering questions tonight." She turned to place the bottle back in the sack. She was almost off the bed when Samuel's hand stopped her.

"So, that's it, then?"

Myfanwy wasn't sure what to make of this man. She was so used to the curmudgeonly brute; he looked every bit the rascal now, with his loose, dark blond curls swept off his forehead, his crooked nose pointing at her as best it could. His lips quirked up at the ends like he was laughing at a joke that only he had heard.

She couldn't help but play along. "What more did you expect?"

Samuel's mouth curled devilishly to the side. "Honestly...I thought you would kiss my leg and make it better."

Myfanwy stoned him with a wry look. "I'm not your mother."

"My mother never did that...and I'm well aware of what you are and what you aren't."

The words were out of her before she could stop them. "What am I, Samuel? What am I to you? Because every time I try to be something, you push me away."

His grin deepened, cutting into the frown lines. Myfanwy's heart hurt when he looked at her this way, so youthful and buoyant, as if anything was possible, as if his best years were still in front of him. *With her.*

With a grace that startled her, Samuel shifted from his spot, languidly moving toward her. His actions were slow, hypnotic, like he was wading through water to find her. When he reached her, he pressed her back onto the bed, covering her with his body, his face just above hers, poised and ready. Myfanwy shivered through the intimacy of it, the possession and power he deftly wielded.

Samuel's expression was difficult to read, though she thought she caught an appraising smile as he raised his hand to her chest, tracing his fingers over the lace and seams of her high-necked gown. "What are you to me?" he drawled, keeping his touch as light as his voice. He was like a magnet. Whenever his fingers drifted over her body, Myfanwy could feel her skin beating through her fabric, pulling toward him.

Samuel made his way higher, running his tips along her sharp jaw. "You are a woman who has given me a gift tonight, one that I am more than willing to repay."

So, that's it, then? Myfanwy quickly slammed the door on that vulnerability. Her voice came out like a puff of smoke. "You vowed not to ruin me. Is that still the case?"

Samuel nodded. His gaze was dark and mesmerizing. Myfanwy couldn't shake the feeling that he was a magician weaving a spell over her; her limbs were soft and pliable, ever-ready for him to command. But somewhere in the back reaches of her mind, she told herself to stay strong, make him pay for this…make Samuel give more—give everything—for the right to her body. And it *was* only her body. Despite what she'd told Jennifer, Myfanwy knew her heart had already been given away long ago. The man was so blind that he didn't know he kept it for her. She desperately hoped it was still safe.

Samuel's lips were exquisitely gentle as he replaced his fingers on her jaw. "I have no future to give you, and I won't take away a chance for you to have your own. But I can't stay away from you, either," he said, kissing a path down her neck. "You're a pain in my arse. You're a meddler who never knows when to leave well enough alone. You've bewitched me."

Myfanwy arched her neck to allow him more access, but still, she pinched his shoulder. "You're horrible at wooing!"

Samuel chuckled against her skin. "I'm not wooing, darling. I don't have to woo you; you've already been properly wooed."

"How…how…so?"

He crawled down her body, nuzzling in between the valley of her breasts, against her trembling tummy, taking deep, full breaths like a man starved for air. Myfanwy raked her hands through his hair, holding him against her, afraid she might never let him go.

So caught up was she in the riotous emotions he was drowning her with, Myfanwy didn't notice his hand had wandered to her leg, where he was pulling her skirts up with silky intention. "I remember you watching me on the pitch," he said. "Did you think I didn't know? Did you think I couldn't feel your eyes on me? I tried to ignore it. Ignore you." He sat back and placed both of his hands on her thighs. He massaged them with the same intensity she'd used on him, but Myfanwy didn't feel it in her muscles. The jolt of pleasure traveled straight to the apex between her legs. She dug one heel into the mattress, and Samuel wrapped his hand underneath her thigh, following the lines of her body all the way to her behind. "But it's a hopeless cause; I can always feel you," he purred, kneading her flesh. "You haunt me, woman."

Myfanwy found his gaze. It astonished her, the level of heat and wanting she witnessed. "I haunt you?"

He nodded, fixing his attention back on her long, supple limbs. "Of what could be. You put terrible fantasies in my head of what *I* can be."

"What can you be, Samuel?"

He dipped his head to her thighs, placing his nose at the center that was so very open and so very afraid of what he might do next. He placed a solemn lick at her entrance, causing Myfanwy to curl her toes so hard they cramped.

He lifted his head infinitesimally, and all she could see was his two-toned eyes over the reaches of her belly and pelvis. "Whole," he said.

And then he lowered his chin and proceeded to break her into so many pieces, Myfanwy didn't care if she ever came together again.

Chapter Seventeen

THERE WAS A lightness in his being. Samuel would have assumed he was drunk; his leg only ever felt this relaxed after he'd downed a half a bottle of whatever alcohol he had at hand. But it was the afternoon, and he hadn't touched the stuff. This feeling—this carefree anticipation—was all because of Myfanwy.

And he was doing everything in his power not to hate himself over it.

At least he hadn't ruined her. Although that was just playing with semantics. By touching the viscount's daughter with his working-class hands, he'd ruined her. By speaking to her in his uncouth, vulgar ways, he'd ruined her. And by licking her slit so well that she came in his mouth, Samuel had definitely ruined her. *And* himself, because he'd be damned if he would quit anytime soon.

Stop thinking about it! he chided himself, hanging his head in his hands.

Samuel hunched behind his desk in his office at the tavern, counting down the minutes until the ladies' practice was to begin. He'd left (or fled) his room early that morning—too early—and come straight here. He hadn't wanted to risk Myfanwy waking up in his arms, all delightfully tousled and ready while he sported his morning cockstand. He wouldn't have been able to stop himself. Then her ruination would have taken on a whole other meaning.

He'd barely been able to hold himself back last night. The vision of Myfanwy sprawled out before him, writhing and panting while he massaged her pussy, had made his balls fit to burst. Luckily, she came quickly, splintering in half before he had the chance to give her his finger or pet her pearl. She'd been so fucking ready for him. So ready and willing to ignite.

She'd given him so much last night. Samuel felt like a glutton.

But he'd woken up a happy one, and remarkably clear-eyed, since he hadn't had to drink his pain to sleep.

So, as he sat at his desk, waiting and remembering, ideas flew unbidden into his slightly guilty, remarkably cognizant, and available brain.

Good ideas, too. Very good ideas. And he jotted them all down, determining ways to make them happen.

Which was why when he ambled onto the field five minutes early for practice (though still later than all his players), he wasn't alone. Joe Danvers and Benny Hardcastle were dutifully at his side and, for the most part, standing *mostly* straight by their own power.

Still, even with his newfound confidence, the decrease of pain, and the problems he'd solved so early, it took Samuel far longer than he planned to meet Myfanwy's gaze. Her brown eyes were shielded by her bonnet, but he saw her lips pinch as he came forward, her expression confused and...hurt?

Shit. Why hadn't he left a note this morning? He'd been so worried about keeping her reputation intact that he'd completely disregarded her heart. Samuel would fix it; by hook or by crook, he would make it right.

"And what do you have in store for us today, Mr. Everett?" a lady asked, stepping forward from her teammates. *What was her name again?* Not old by any means, this woman still seemed more mature than the others. Samuel could always spot a fellow world-weary traveler.

In an instant, it came to him. "Thank you for asking the question, Lady Everly. I've brought in some help." He slapped his friends on their backs. "This here is Joe Danvers and Benny Hardcastle, two of the most formidable men I ever played with. They're going to be helping out, bowling and showing you some tactics on the field. This way everyone gets the attention they need. And also…"

Samuel snapped his fingers at Aaron, who was hiding behind Myfanwy's skirts. Before he'd sent the boy to bed the night before, Samuel ordered him to follow her to practice, though he hadn't told him why. Now, it was time for the lad to earn his keep. "You," he said, causing Aaron to hop into view. He was wearing the same filthy, muted clothes, which reminded Samuel about the list he'd made for Annabelle while he killed time this morning. He would have to add more to his shopping excursion.

"You will shag balls. Whenever one goes astray, it's you who has to fetch it. It's not Benny or Joe's job. It's only yours. Do you understand me? Balls aren't cheap. I don't want us losing any."

Aaron nodded, seemingly growing six inches at the instruction.

Good.

Samuel surveyed his motley crew of a team. The women were fast learners. There wasn't one tight sleeve among the group. The sun was shining. His leg was just barely throbbing, and Myfanwy had stopped looking at him like she was ready to gut him, throw him in a pot, and roast him for dinner.

It was a lovely day for cricket.

And for starting over.

SAMUEL YANKED SO hard at his head that he was surprised he didn't pull out a hank of hair. "No. No. No. Goddammit, no!" He pounded over to Benny, who was working with a short spitfire of a girl on her bowling approach. *Anna.* He remembered her name was Anna. "She's not working the dirt, Benny. For fuck's sake! Teach her how to read the ground. And there's not near enough red on her skirts. Make sure she's rubbing the ball harder into her side."

Benny hesitated, sending Samuel a reproachful look. It had been a long day, and Samuel had worked everybody to their limits—especially his new coaches.

"Should you really be speaking like that to the ladies?" Benny asked in a fearful whisper, his poor, dehydrated face melting into a hangdog expression. "It's not proper, like."

Samuel slammed his hands on his hips, scowling at the old bruiser who'd never backed down from a fight in his life and now was afraid of a bunch of Society ladies. "On my pitch, they're not ladies; they're cricketers. *My* cricketers. Now, stop acting like their nursemaid. I hired you to coach, so coach!"

Benny's three chins wobbled glumly as he nodded, returning to the black-haired girl. Samuel didn't retreat until he heard Benny instruct Anna on how she had to use the bumps and divots in the ground when she bowled the ball. If she hit one just right, the ball would bounce up at a dizzying angle, surprising the batter and causing them to make a bad swing. Cricket was all about inches. The team that won always used the most to their advantage.

"What about the red on her skirts?" a soft voice asked behind him.

Samuel twirled to find Myfanwy's friend, Jennifer, at his back. Like Myfanwy, she had found it difficult to make eye contact with him today...though, he suspected, for very different reasons.

"You've never rubbed the ball on your skirts before?"

Jennifer shook her head.

"Toss me the ball," he ordered her, then caught the red leather ball she threw him. He held it up to her, pointing at the seam down the middle. "There are two sides of a cricket ball," he began, twisting it in his hand. "They both start the match perfectly smooth. But a smart bowler doesn't want to just bowl the ball; he—*she*—wants to make it dance."

Samuel fired the ball straight down into the dirt before picking it back up. "You see, a ball takes a lot of damage during a match, and all those dings and scrapes make it rough, but if the bowler can rub one of its halves on her side, she can maintain the smoothness. And that can affect how much the ball swings in the air. If one side is rough, and the other shiny, the ball can dance so much that a batsman will fall on their arse trying to keep up with it."

"So that's why I always see the men with red marks on their trousers," Jennifer said, seemingly to herself.

"We used to say that if a man finished a game with white trousers, then he's no real cricketer." Samuel grunted. "I suppose we'll have to change the saying to include skirts."

He tossed her the ball back, and Jennifer smiled as she caught it.

Samuel rocked on his heels, not sure what else she wanted from him. He'd answered her question well enough, but she continued to stand in front of him with stars in her eyes, acting like he'd just announced free drinks for the rest of the night.

Just when Samuel was about to bark an order to send her back to the others, she surprised him.

"Thank you," she said suddenly, playing with the ball in her hand. "Myfi told me about last night after"—her voice lowered—"the Lucky Fish. I told her it was a bad idea to go, but she rarely listens to me once she makes her mind up."

A sick dose of discomfort nagged at Samuel's core. How *much* had Myfanwy told Jennifer about last night? He glanced over Jennifer's shoulder to his team. Male cricketers talked about everything under the sun—the more unsavory, the better. Were female cricketers the same? Christ, he hoped not.

Jennifer snagged him from his thoughts. "And thank you for not confronting Sir Bramble," she said, her face turning red as she pawed a foot into the ground. "He only escorted us there because

I asked him to. It wasn't his fault. He's… Well, he's a lovely man."

Lovely? Christ, he hoped Myfanwy never described him like that to her friends. *Virile. Strong. Fast.* Hell, he'd even take *handsome* before he'd accept *lovely.*

Did Myfanwy think he was any of those things? After the way he'd left her this morning, he wasn't so sure.

Samuel caught Jennifer waiting for his answer. He cleared his throat, trying to be diplomatic. He couldn't agree with the girl about Sir Bramble's actions, but he appreciated her loyalty and didn't wish to diminish her opinion of the baron. Sir Bramble had his faults—mostly his weakness for the blond chit defending him at present—but he was one of the only decent gentlemen of Samuel's acquaintance, which was saying a lot.

"You're right," he replied sternly. "Myfi is close to impossible to deny. She's stubborn."

"In the best possible way." Jennifer chuckled. She turned to watch her friend across the wide field. "But she's also lovely, isn't she?"

Samuel caught Jennifer spying at him from the corner of her eye, once more eager for his response. He nodded to the group. "Time to get back in line," he ordered her gruffly. Dutifully, Jennifer did as she was told right away.

Not like another woman Samuel couldn't get out of his mind.

Because Myfanwy was extraordinarily stubborn. And a pain in his arse.

And lovely. Yes, she was that indeed.

"Samuel, wait a moment. I have something I need to talk to you about."

Samuel was just about to leave the field and return to the tavern when Joe Danvers called him to a stop. The practice had ended a half-hour before, and Samuel had thought that he and Aaron were the only ones left. Samuel had been taking his time with his new employee, explaining how he expected all the equipment to be organized and stored after the training sessions were complete. The boy had been right to boast about his abilities—although Aaron knew next to nothing about cricket, he did know how to work hard. He was caked in sweat, hands as grimy as a gutter, but he'd earned his coin, and Samuel was only too happy to award it to him.

"Go on inside and get something to eat," he told Aaron as Joe jogged up to him. After his being on it most of the day, Samuel's leg was faring better than expected; however, he couldn't say the same about his old teammate. Joe was moving like a newborn colt, all wobbly and uncoordinated. But that wasn't what alarmed Samuel the most. Joe's pallor was ghoulishly gray, with just enough green peeking through to make him resemble a dead fish. His eyes were bloodshot, and he was wheezing so raggedly that Samuel worried he was about to keel over. He could definitely catch Joe if he fainted, but carrying him anywhere substantial would be beyond the pale.

"You did well today, Joe," Samuel said evenly, hoping his calm demeanor would rub off on his friend.

Poor Joe looked close to weeping. "Don't lie to me, Sam," he replied, setting off a coughing fit that forced him to bend over until it passed. He wiped his mouth and straightened his spine, leveling Samuel with a weighted look. "I know what I was, and I know what I am. I can't believe I let myself get this bad. Remember how fast and skinny I used to be?"

Samuel nodded, mirroring his friend's wistful smile.

"Old man Bauser used to call me Lightning because nothing could stop me." Joe stared off into the distance as if the past was being performed like a play in front of him. "I liked that. I liked that when people talked about me, they only had good things to say, and nothing could stop me..." His expression guttered like a candle left out all night. "Well, the drink can stop me now.

Always does. You know I wake up every morning saying I won't do it. I actually talk to myself and tell myself not to drink one drop. And I can't understand it. Hours, hell, minutes later I find myself walking to your tavern, ordering a drink, filling myself up until I can't remember my own name. It has a hold, I tell you. It's a dark, dark thing."

Samuel slapped him on the back. "I know, Joe. I know. But look at what you did today. You were out all afternoon without taking a drop. Congratulate yourself for that."

Joe shook his head, chucking ruefully. "It's not enough."

"It's a start."

Joe squinted at the faint light streaming in between the clouds, blowing air slowly from his mouth. "I suppose it is. But that's what I wanted to talk to you about. It was hell today, hell on earth, plain and simple, but I want to keep coaching…if you'll have me."

"Of course I'll have you, Joe. We already talked about it. You'll get a wage and everything—"

"No," Joe said firmly, putting his hands up between them. "Don't pay me a thing. Promise me you won't even sneak a couple of coins in my pocket."

There. In the dim glow of the sun, in the sharp determination of Joe's eyes, Samuel finally recognized his old friend.

"You know what I'll do if I have money—I'll just drink it away. I only ask for this job and some food at the end of the night, and…well…" He rubbed at the back of his neck.

"What is it? Anything."

Joe glanced up sheepishly. "You know that sporting goods business you're starting…the one Sir Bramble is investing in?"

Samuel nodded.

"Put my wages toward that. And then…you know, if I get myself straightened out and respectable, maybe I can help you grow it. Cricket is over for me, but maybe I can still be a part of it in some way."

Samuel smiled gently at his friend who had seen such highs

and lows in his life that he couldn't comprehend the beauty of the middle. Then he led them away from the tavern, assuring Joe that there would always be a place for him in cricket.

Later that night, as Samuel made his way back to his home—where he hoped Myfanwy was waiting up for him—he rescinded his thought from earlier. Joe Danvers was a *lovely* man. If Myfanwy ever used that word for Samuel, he would only ever be grateful.

Chapter Eighteen

MYFANWY'S EARS PERKED up at the crash. She knew a cricket ball breaking a flowerpot when she heard one.

She closed the book, not bothering to mark her place. She wasn't really reading it anyway. She was biding time. Treading water to see how the night would proceed.

Myfanwy ventured out to the garden, hiding in the shadows slanted across the brick wall, and noted the familiar voices.

"Good on you, lad," Samuel said, patting a beaming Aaron on the shoulder. "Just like that. People like to think that speed is a bowler's greatest tool, but that's utter shite. It's all about control. Control the ball and you can control the game."

Side by side they ambled to the far side of the garden, locating the ball that Aaron had bowled. Samuel picked it up next to a new pile of rose petals and tossed it to the boy. "Are you certain you've never played before?"

Aaron shook his head in a rush, like he was drying his hair. "Never, sir. I preferred football, myself. Always thought cricket was for nobs and tossers. No offense, sir."

Samuel chuckled, leading him back to the start. "No offense taken. Unfortunately, the game *is* full of nobs and tossers, but also some pretty swell lads as well."

"Like Benny and Joe?"

"Like Benny and Joe."

Samuel positioned the boy toward the bushes once more, kicking at his feet until Aaron's stance was to his liking. "All right now, try it again. Aim for that big, fat red on the right. Let's see if you can take the whole head off."

Aaron heaved a giant breath, squinting at the poor plump flower. He cradled the ball in his hand like it was a baby bunny, twirling it around as he considered his next action.

Myfanwy watched with wonder as he took off down the lane, launching the ball with all his might. The rose had no chance. Samuel had asked. Aaron had delivered. It was that easy.

Samuel whistled in appreciation. "Damn, that's mighty fine. You've got a gift, lad. A real gift."

Aaron stared at the older man as if he'd come down from heaven to relay the words. It didn't matter what Samuel did or said for the rest of his life—he was officially a god to the boy.

It struck Myfanwy that she'd seen that look before. She'd been a young girl but couldn't have forgotten that blatant adoration. It was the same way Samuel used to look at her father—with love and yearning and a little bit of fear. Fear that the boy would ever disappoint the man he respected so much.

"Do you really think I could make a go of it?" Aaron asked shyly. "Can men really make a living from cricket? Obviously, I'm not one of those Eton types."

Samuel grunted. "Neither am I."

"But you have all this."

"I earned all this. From cricket. You can too, if you work hard enough."

"I can work, sir," Aaron said.

"I know you can, lad. I know you can."

Myfanwy had had enough. She was afraid if she listened any more that she might start crying at the beauty of it all. She shoved off from the wall, clearing her throat of all the emotion that threatened to overtake her. "Now, don't think you can go off and join a club anytime soon," she said, smiling at the way the two jumped when they noticed her. "My team still needs your help. It was absolute paradise not having to go running after all our balls today in practice. Having you there is a godsend."

Aaron happily smiled. "I wouldn't think of leaving," he replied. "I got too much to learn."

"Good answer," Samuel said, mussing the boy's black hair. "That's enough for tonight. I've got a full day for you tomorrow. Why don't you go inside now and get ready for bed? Your sister was incredibly upset when Sarah forced her to retire earlier than you."

"Yes, sir," Aaron said right away. No wonder Samuel liked him so much. The boy was the only one in the house who didn't talk back to him. Aaron wished Myfanwy a good night and, after an awkward bow, rushed inside to do his master's bidding.

Samuel stared after him for a long while, an amused expression on his face.

"Something's different about you," Myfanwy said, breaking his tranquil moment. "You're smiling. Dare I say it, you seem almost happy. And you're not even drinking."

Immediately, Samuel's expression veered back to its usual scowl. "I don't need to be drinking to smile." He launched down the path toward the ball. He located it quickly and tossed it up in the air, catching it with a flourish. "Just a little moonlight and cricket, I guess."

Myfanwy gawked at the carefree display. *Moonlight and cricket?* "Now you're almost poetic."

"I'm not poetic," he muttered. "I'm just..." He searched for the words.

Myfanwy leaned over comically, as if she were physically pulling the word from him. "Happy? Go ahead; it won't kill you to say it."

"I'm not happy," he griped over her giggles. "I'm just... I don't know." He swiped a hand over his face. "Did you come out here for a reason? Do you need something?"

Oh. Well, that was putting her on the spot. How did one say:

I was wondering if you wanted me to massage your naked body again tonight. And maybe do...other things?

It turned out that Myfanwy didn't need to say anything. Her awkward body language apparently said it all, because Samuel coughed into his hand and shifted his weight from one foot to the other...without much difficulty.

Samuel caught her interest in his leg. "I used your tincture again today," he said, placing too much emphasis on each word for it to sound remotely casual. "I...ah...feel much better...thanks to you."

Why was this so difficult? The garden was charged with so much electricity, and yet Myfanwy felt sluggish, like her brain was only partly working. The man's tongue had been between her legs last night, and today she couldn't even manage a halfway decent sentence. "Yes, I...ah didn't know if you would need me again tonight."

Samuel's gaze shot up to hers. "Do you...want to help me again tonight? I wasn't sure..."

Myfanwy ambled over to the bench, sticking her nose up in the air. "Well, not if you've already applied it yourself."

"Well, I didn't know!"

"Why didn't you ask sooner?"

"Because I didn't..." Samuel dropped his gaze to the ground sheepishly. Finally, he shrugged. "I didn't want to expect anything from you. We didn't talk about it—"

"Because you left early this morning before I woke up. You didn't even leave a note, and then you barely looked at me during practice." Was she honestly still angry about waking up alone this morning? *Yes. Yes, she was.*

Samuel took a step toward her and then stopped, rethinking that dangerous decision. "I didn't know what to say. Last night was..."

Find a word, Samuel. Find a good word.

"Wonderful," he finished.

Myfanwy's body relaxed *and* sang like a victorious nightingale.

He went on, "But I still don't..." He rubbed the back of his neck. "I mean to say, I know what I want...but I didn't want to assume...and I want to be careful of not...of not..."

The silly man. He'd worked himself into quite a state; his complexion was almost green. Was that what thinking about their time together did to him? Myfanwy almost felt bad for him, the way his need for her seemed to be at direct odds with his devotion to her father. Well, her father wasn't here anymore. And she was.

"Calm yourself, Samuel. There's no need to get so upset." She rose from the bench and sauntered over to him. Myfanwy would never consider herself adept at flirting, but years on the pitch had made her adept at using her body. She moved her hips languidly, like a shark's tail in the water. "You don't need to be scared of us." She reached out and took the ball from his hand. "There is no *us*, anyway," she said with enough conviction to make him swallow audibly. "I already told you. I'm not the marrying kind."

His laughter was weak and thin as his hungry eyes followed her every movement. "And I'm not the marrying type."

A chuckle burst from her chest. "Oh, don't I know it."

Samuel frowned, but she only smiled sweeter. She rubbed the back of her teeth with her tongue, and they felt pointier than usual. "We're both players at heart, right?" She nudged him out of the way, filling up the space. Without another word, she launched into a run and bowled the ball right at a rose, taking everything down in one triumphant *whoosh!* Myfanwy turned back to him with another shrug. "So, let's play."

Desire had completely eclipsed his features. Everything was sharper under the moonlight. There was no hiding. Samuel held out a hand and nodded his head to the windows above them on the second floor of the townhouse. "Should we begin, then?"

Myfanwy let out a mirthless laugh, refusing the hand. "I had something different in mind tonight. A little friendly competition."

"There's no such thing."

My God, they were so similar. "An unfriendly competition, then." When he nodded, Myfanwy continued, "Let's bowl. Whoever kills the most roses wins."

Samuel *tsked*. "Those poor roses."

"It's a symbol of our relationship. Don't you see? Roses are for love. What we have is…"

"Lust."

The word was deliciously wicked on his lips, and it made her shudder all the way down to her toes. "Quite."

Samuel cocked his head. "Fine. But it won't be much of a competition. I'll have this thing won in five deliveries."

"Not so fast," Myfanwy said, pulling her hand away when he tried to take the ball from her. "There's more. When I kill a rose, you have to take off a piece of your clothing."

"And if I kill a rose?"

Myfanwy grinned. "I'll obviously do the same for you."

"And the man or woman left standing with the most clothes wins?"

She nodded.

Samuel contemplated her for a long moment. "And people think male cricketers are bad influences on the opposite sex."

Myfanwy laughed. "Maybe this will make men think twice about not allowing women to play with them. Think about how much more fun it would be."

⤜⟫⟩✕⟨⟪⤛

THE BALL WHISTLED through the air, clipping—but not chopping—another crimson rose.

Samuel's crestfallen look was priceless. Myfanwy clicked her tongue. "Ooh, so sorry. You just missed that one—again. Looks like I can win it all with this last bowl."

Samuel rolled his eyes, but dutifully trudged out of the way. He'd had every right to go into the game confident. As he'd remarked to Aaron, control was everything in cricket and he had expert control—*when Myfanwy had all her clothing on.*

His first three deliveries had been masterful, brilliant really, clipping off full heads as easily as one might pluck off a dandelion top with one's thumb. But then his concentration started to mysteriously waver. He blamed Myfanwy.

Just like a man, she thought. How was *his* lack of concentration *her* fault? Yes, she could have removed smaller, less conspicuous articles of clothing. And yes, *maybe* she was pushing matters when she argued that all three of her petticoats counted as one item. But she was the woman and therefore the expert in female attire. Did she try to manage Samuel when he took off his coat, waistcoat, and trousers? It wasn't her fault that his undergarments were just another layer of trousers!

As Myfanwy was just down to her chemise, it was quite evident that *she* wasn't wearing undergarments other than her stockings. It made life easier that way—especially in matters of seduction.

"How can you expect me to focus when you're flittering around like that?" Samuel complained as Myfanwy was preparing for her wind-up.

She cast him a noxious look over her shoulder. "I'm hardly flittering."

"You know I can see right through that gown…slip…whatever it is?"

Myfanwy was positively giddy, though she brushed him off. "It's not like you haven't seen it before." She squinted at her target rose, raising her arm, and—

"I haven't."

Her arm fell to her side, and she turned to face him. "What do you mean? You got quite the eyeful last night." Myfanwy went back to her rose. She locked in on the flower, twirling the ball around in her hand until she got just the right grip on the seam.

"It was dark in my room, and you were fully clothed, if you remember."

Why was he talking so much? Was he trying to distract her? *Ha! Nice try!* "My memory is perfect," she remarked matter-of-factly. "I distinctly recall your being able to push fabric to the side when it was in your way."

"Ahh, yes," Samuel said as if he'd just indulged in a succulent piece of pie, "but under all that fabric, in the dead of night, I still couldn't appreciate the scene as fully as I would have liked."

Myfanwy's breath was unsteady. She began to twirl the ball again, feeling that something wasn't right. "How..." She chewed on her bottom lip, annoyed that she was too weak *not* to ask the question. "How *would* you have liked to...appreciate it...*me?*"

She could practically hear the damned man grinning. "Oh, I don't know," he drawled. "You came so fast. I wanted to admire that pussy of yours more. I can't wait to see if it's the same color as your nipples, all soft and petal-like, virginal pink. Did you know your pussy mimics a rose? Most women don't, but it's plain as day with all its lovely, silky folds and the way it blossoms when a man touches it right."

Myfanwy's legs almost went out from under her. She was perfectly aware of what he was doing, and now she couldn't even follow her target without seeing an entire bush of puss—*ladies' private areas*—winking back at her. *Damnation!*

"That's all very well and good," she seethed, "but it's time for you to be quiet now so I can win."

"What?" he asked innocently. "I was merely answering your question. I thought you might find it interesting."

"Quite."

"Yes. Quite."

Myfanwy lowered her chin and attempted to block the infuriatingly alluring man from her mind. But it was easier said than done. Even though her consciousness was directed toward her aim, even though her focus and mind were single in their want, her body cried for something different. All her senses were seizing on the man behind her. The hairs on her arms were raised, her stomach was in knots, and a buzzing was in between her ears.

Nevertheless, Myfanwy was determined to win. How could she look him in the face otherwise? She'd started this game to prove a point—she couldn't quite remember what that point was at the moment, but it didn't matter. She had to finish as the victor.

Myfanwy started slow, but once her feet picked up speed, the rest of her fell into place. It was harmonious, so simple, the way her body could just remember when everything else felt cloudy and discombobulated. The wind hit her face and her arm wound up behind her, swinging viciously from her side, releasing the ball at the exact right time, at the exact right angle. Nothing matched it, this exquisite mixture of pace and accuracy, this earth-shattering blast of preparedness and opportunity. When hard work paid off and one could finally rest on the laurels of achievement.

As the ball barreled down the lane, skipping in the battered grass, Myfanwy wanted to turn away. She knew where it was headed. Watching it smack the rose seemed extravagant. But, try as she might, she couldn't tear her eyes from the bushes. Which was a good thing.

Because if she hadn't seen that damn ball sail left of the rose and bounce off the brick wall, she wouldn't have believed it.

Myfanwy's vision blurred. She'd missed? She'd *missed*. The bastard *made* her miss.

Her arm fell. Her knees wobbled. Her ego shattered.

Samuel didn't laugh, which made everything even more frustrating. There was nothing worse than bragging about oneself and not being able to deliver on those promises. Humble pie had never tasted so disappointing.

"I missed—"

Samuel grabbed her arm and twirled her around to face him. "Who the fuck cares?" he asked before slamming his mouth against hers.

For a few seconds, Myfanwy struggled. Her mind and her body, again, were not in concert. *Who cares?* she railed as his tongue plundered her mouth. *Who bloody cares? I care!*

But then Samuel ran his hand up her torso, resting it on the side of her face. Gently, so very gently, he held her cheek in his palm as if she was a priceless work of art. And all reservations about the game—the silly game—fled her mind.

There was only this. There was only him.

This had been the point of it all. Finding her way back into his arms.

Myfanwy's body clicked and everything began to take shape.

Samuel walked her back to the bench. Without unlocking their lips, he rearranged their bodies, taking a seat and swiftly bringing her down on top of him. Through her thin chemise, Myfanwy's knees skimmed against the stone as she straddled his legs, but she felt no pain. She only felt his arousal, large and engorged, snug in the home of her inner thighs.

Myfanwy squeezed them, and just that action was enough to create a zap of energy she could savor. It tasted like moonlight and honey, the first winter snow, and freshly whipped cream.

For a time, they were just content to drink from one another, sharing breaths and tongues, their hands roving free and unhindered. Myfanwy's hands seemed to have a mind of their own whenever Samuel's chest was near. Strong and so well shaped, his form was not popular among the men of the *ton*. In Society, men were applauded for their grace and slender limbs, their appearance showcasing the ease of their lives and their matching temperaments.

But Samuel was stone underneath her. A piece of armor with all the chinks and scrapes to show that he'd been in battle. He was not made to show. He was made to serve.

"Is this what you wanted?" he panted, finally tearing his mouth away. It took Myfanwy a beat to comprehend his words. He palmed her breast and massaged her with a force that made her arch into him for more.

Her brain was awash with sensations. There were too many and yet not enough. And sitting on Samuel, cuddling his manhood, feeling his lips sear into her skin terrified her...because she couldn't understand what was missing. Myfanwy always knew what she wanted and, more importantly, how to attain it. Here she was lost to her baser self, relying on instincts that weren't as nimble in this new field.

"Y-yes," she stammered. "I think so."

Samuel chuckled, leaning her away from him. He pulled down the neck of her chemise, exposing her breast to the chilly air. When his mouth swallowed her nipple, she gasped at the explosion of heat. Myfanwy wrapped her arms around his neck and stared at the night sky, clouded black and dull from the smokestacks over London. And yet with his mouth on her, with his tongue lapping her sensitive skin, it seemed like all the stars in the sky had come out to light his way.

Samuel let the nipple drop from his mouth and blew on it gently as if it was an ember needing to be fed. "I know so. This, is, is what you want. And it fucking scares you."

Myfanwy opened her mouth to protest, but he caught her too readily, kissing the words and her protestation away.

"It scares me too," Samuel said into her mouth. "It's terrifying, this thing that we bring out in each other."

Samuel directed his attention to her other breast, providing the same exquisite torture. "Then why do you do it?" Myfanwy asked.

He bit her nipple and glanced up at her impishly. "Because it's the best, most thrilling thing I've ever experienced in my life."

Myfanwy didn't know if he'd planned it, if he was managing her now as he had during their game, but his words imbued her with much-needed assurance. *Her*, Myfanwy Wright, was the source of this otherworldly pleasure? She didn't know much about the sexual act but was pretty certain she hadn't even skimmed the surface yet.

She unwound her arm from his neck and worked a hand

down his body. Samuel's small bursts of breath egged her on as she toyed with his chest through his shirt, circling her fingers around his nipples, tracing the lines of his pronounced ribs that reminded her so much of a birdcage. His muscles ebbed and flowed with her movements, hiding at times, while demanding to be touched at others.

When she found her way to the buttons of his undergarments, his breath stopped completely. He didn't move. He was waiting for her.

Myfanwy unlatched the buttons slowly, working up the nerve. Control—she wanted control back in her own hands, and this was her way of attaining it.

"Show me," she said softly, pointedly, allowing his hand to cover hers and escort her under the wool. Samuel positioned her fingers around his shaft, and he took his time, running her hand up and down his length. Her mind desperately tried to bring up another experience that was similar to reassure her nervous self, but nothing came to the forefront. Because nothing in her life had prepared her for this. He was at once soft and hard, smooth and rough, wanting her to go faster and then pulling back, cherishing her slowness. But he was also at her mercy. And Myfanwy liked that.

Getting a feel for the act, she picked up speed, reading his breaths, translating the tension in his body. Samuel was always so staid, so calm, so collected, but here in her arms, in her capable hands, he let himself go. He bucked his pelvis into her, goading her on to grip him harder, stronger.

"Ah, fuck, that's it. Just like that," he gritted out, one hand at the top of her spine. He rested his head on hers, and she watched a rainbow of emotions play across his face. Pain. Excitement. Desire. And then fear.

"I want you to come with me, sweetheart," he panted, sliding a hand between them. He flicked up her chemise and petted across her seam, almost making Myfanwy jump out of her skin.

"No," she said, trying to nudge him away with her hips. She

frowned at his rod in her hand. "I can't think when you do that."

His laughter was thin, on edge. "I don't want you to think, wench. I want you to feel my finger in you. I want you to come as I burst in your fucking hand. Now."

Myfanwy's stomach flopped. She didn't think she'd be able to. Not like this. Not when he'd ordered it. And yet the moment his thumb found that special place at the top of her core, she was filled with the telltale signs that it was only a matter of time. His rod grew even thicker in her hand. Something was primed to happen. Their slick bodies bobbed and weaved around each other like tree limbs fighting for the sun's rays. The end seemed as far as the horizon, but it came on them in an instant. The second he pressed his finger inside her, Myfanwy's spirit cried out in relief. She keened in fulfillment and was followed seconds later by Samuel, who muffled his scream in her hair, burrowing his face into her neck.

It was thrilling and, as Samuel had said, equally terrifying.

As he picked her up and brought her inside to his room, Myfanwy couldn't even remember who'd won the game. She fell asleep as her head hit the pillow, concluding it must have been a tie.

Chapter Nineteen

"**B**ENNY HARDCASTLE," MYFANWY said the following night while her hands were busy massaging Samuel's thigh. This time around it hadn't taken her nearly as long to get to the matter at hand, since Samuel had been incredibly helpful before she even knocked on his door. Naturally, the man had already been in bed—naked, with the tincture on the table next to him.

Myfanwy still didn't know what game they were playing, though she wasn't of a mind to stop anytime soon. In all honesty, she didn't see the problem in becoming lovers by night and coach and player by day. It worked. *For now.* And now was all she had. Soon, she would reach her majority and move out, starting her new life. She would have her club and Samuel would have...Samuel.

She'd arranged this entire liaison, and it was all going as she'd planned. Myfanwy told herself that questioning it would only use up time neither of them had and also dredge up words like *ruin* and *responsibility* and *ward*, which only served to depress the romance. Their lives had been difficult enough these past years— why create drama and confusion that threatened to steal the joy they were experiencing with each other?

"Benny Hardcastle?" Samuel repeated, his eyes closed, his expression blissful as he rested against his headboard. "Why the hell are you thinking of that old bastard when this magnificent specimen is before you?"

He meant it as a joke, but Myfanwy's laugh was paltry at best. It took everything for her to actually perform the massage and not throw herself on his mouth. It had been thrilling to discover that Samuel Everett was good at so many things other than cricket.

A fire burned in the hearth, and Myfanwy wiped away sweat from her temples. She was always so hot around him. His body was dewy and shining against the backdrop of the flames, his pale skin, tight but fluid, not nearly as knotted as it had been previously. She smiled to herself. Myfanwy should tell Holly to bottle this miracle tincture and make a fortune.

"I've actually been thinking about him a lot today."

"You have?" His voice was soft but dangerous.

"I have."

Suddenly, Samuel moved. As agile as a cat, he threw Myfanwy down on the bed and loomed over her, his arm muscles bulging at her sides, framing her.

"Tell me," he said, placing a light kiss on the side of her neck. Myfanwy had also come prepared that night, wearing a robe—and only a robe. The belt was doing its job at the moment, but there was no telling how long it would last. "What is so special about Benny Hardcastle that has made him stick in that head of yours?"

Even with the crispness in his voice, Samuel couldn't hide his playful nature. Myfanwy wondered if he even noticed that he didn't duck his head with her anymore. His milky eye was no longer a concern; she could look her fill at the exotic blue ring and he didn't seem to mind. *Trust.* He was beginning to trust her.

"We need a practice game before we meet the matrons on the pitch," she replied, running her hands up his arms, delighting in the rough-hewn nature. The bumps and bruises, the scrapes and scars, only added to his appeal. This was no peacock, no corset-wearing dandy.

Samuel frowned against her neck, stopping mid-kiss. "I'm lost. Now we're talking about a practice game?"

Myfanwy smiled cheekily, bending her legs on either side of him, cupping his pelvis. Samuel's abdominal muscles flexed in response. He liked that indeed.

"You're the one who told me about Benny's benefit match, the one that Lord Cremly ruined, correct?"

Samuel's good mood soured. "Correct."

Reaching up, Myfanwy kissed the frown off his face. "I think he deserves another. Can you find old friends and players who would want to play us? Really play us, not humiliate us with arms tied behind their backs?"

"I don't know," Samuel said, toying with the knot of her belt. "Many of the old lads are lost now, drunkards or dead or beating out a living in factories." He eyed her warily. "And the rest might not want to play women."

"You can convince them," Myfanwy urged. For extra measure, she ground her pelvis along him in invitation, watching as he licked his lips. "You're the great Samuel Everett. They'll do anything you say. Tell them the women always get a good crowd and that they're playing for Benny. They'll do it. I know they will."

"All this for Benny, huh?"

Myfanwy twisted her lips impishly. "And us, of course. We need the practice. And you know I want to win."

Samuel went back to his kissing. With his tongue, he traced a path to her ear, where he whispered seductively, "Yes, I know you want to win. So do I."

"Then let's win," Myfanwy breathed. "Together."

SAMUEL FOUGHT A grin. He couldn't have been more pleased with himself if he tried. It had only taken him a couple of weeks, but he'd managed to do as Myfanwy asked. He'd scrounged up all the best ex-players he could find and announced Benny's benefit match to all the papers.

The turnout astounded even him. Myfanwy had been right—some might consider female cricket players a spectacle, but it was one they didn't want to miss. He'd sold tickets to the event out of the tavern, and in the end, five hundred had been bought.

Five hundred people! To watch a bunch of ladies smack the ball around with a load of dried-up, has-been cricketers. It boggled the mind. And it also put a salve on the spirit. It was commendable for Myfanwy's team, that was true, but it also signified that his men weren't all down and out. England still remembered their old favorites. His friends' bodies might be hoary, but they weren't forgotten.

Samuel wasn't naïve. He understood that this one event wouldn't change much for the retired cricketers, but maybe—just maybe—playing for Benny's benefit would revive something inside them. Maybe they wouldn't drink themselves to sleep tonight. Maybe they would feel less like failures when they found their beds. Maybe they would recall that they used to be great, and nothing, not age nor neglect, could take that away from them.

Although, to be fair…they weren't the best-looking bunch.

Minutes before the match was set to begin, Lady Everly marched up to him on the pitch, a pinched expression on her genteel face. "That is who you found? But there's only nine of…*them*," she said, adding so much weight to the last word that Samuel was surprised he didn't sink into the grass.

He held his grin, nodding at the men limbering up on the other side of the field. Nine men he'd known since he was Aaron's age; nine men who'd played with him and against him in the most vicious battles of his life; nine men who were on the wrong side of thirty and had gained more weight than muscle.

"They'll give you a match. You just worry about your grip," he said, morphing into the coach once more.

Lady Everly blanched at his tone. "My grip is fine."

"It's not fine," Samuel countered. "You see Bucky Walton over there, scratching his head?"

She squinted against the sun. "You mean the man who looks like he hasn't seen a bath in three years?"

"He doesn't look that bad." In fact, he *did* look that bad. Samuel reminded himself to offer Bucky a free room at the inn tonight with one of the biggest tubs he had. "If you choke your grip with Bucky, he'll break your hands. He bowls so fast that you'll drop the bat the moment it makes contact. *If* it even makes contact."

Lady Everly flicked him a dismissive glance from the side of her eye, never taking her focus off Bucky. "I'll score runs off him."

Samuel snorted. "Not with that grip. You have to loosen it, Jane. You're playing too tight, like you don't want to lose."

She snorted right back. "I *don't* want to lose, *coach*. I assume you don't want to either."

"No," Samuel answered, folding his arms, moving to block her line of vision. "I want to win more than I don't want to lose. There's a difference there, and I'm not sure you've found it yet." He sighed when she turned on him and began walking away. "Look, Jane. I know I don't know much about you."

"You can start by learning my name. It's Jo, not Jane," she said over her shoulder.

Fuck. He knew that. "Yes, my apologies. *Jo.* I know your name. I do. And I know you played for the matrons. Myfi told me what they did to you."

Jo's skirts flared when she twirled back around. Her face, usually so placid and refined, was mottled with raw emotion. "You don't know the half of it."

Samuel retreated, balancing on his heels. "You're right. I don't. But I know what it's like to want revenge. I know that murderous feeling you get when you see the others who've wronged you. It's like your whole body gears up to strike, builds to such a crescendo that nothing will start again in life until you right all your goddamn wrongs. But even when you do, even when you beat them or punch them in the face, it doesn't change anything. They'll always be bastards who treated you badly. And I'm sorry to tell you this, but no matter how good it feels to win, for some reason, that feeling will never be as strong as the nasty way they made you feel."

Jo sniffed, shielding her face from his. "So?" She shrugged. "What do you do if beating them doesn't solve anything? You want me to just not care?"

"Fuck no," Samuel spat with a sneer. Jo flinched at his coarse words, and then she laughed. "I want you to loosen the fuck up. Forget about what those slags did, so that when you beat the pulp out of them, you'll be able to bloody enjoy it. Christ, what the hell did you think I was going to say? Now stop standing around, speculating on the cleaning habits of the other team, and get ready."

Samuel stomped off, leaving an amused but inspired Lady Everly in his wake. The pleased feeling came back to him. Yes, he was mighty proud of himself today. No one had told him coaching would be this difficult, but he was quite sure he was getting the right of it.

"But there's only nine. You didn't find enough men," she called after.

Samuel didn't answer. She'd get her answer soon enough.

Chapter Twenty

J OE DANVERS CLOMPED his mud-stained boots on top of the table and raised his pint glass (full of apple cider) in the air. "Three cheers for Benny Hardcastle! The best brick who ever chucked the ball. This wasn't the swan song I had in mind for you, friend, but it was the best I could have hoped for. To Benny!"

"To Benny!" the crowd roared inside the Flying Batsman.

Samuel raised his glass and, once more, had to elbow someone out of the way before he could get it to his mouth. The tavern was fit to burst. He'd only invited the teams back for a celebratory drink after the game ended an hour ago, but most of the crowd had decided that they should come along for the ride as well. Naturally, one drink had turned into two, and then too many.

Although, Samuel had to admit, he was enjoying himself. His girls had played their hearts out and came away with a win. It was a close one—too close for Samuel's liking—but they managed to squeak by the men by seventeen runs, in no small part because of Lady Everly. She hit a fifty. Samuel had a feeling she wouldn't be letting him forget that pertinent fact anytime soon. Just as he wouldn't let her forget that her grip had been noticeably looser.

Yes, it was a good day, and only getting better with Myfanwy at his side. She'd found Samuel in the tavern the moment she entered and hadn't ventured away from him once. Not even when he'd had to help Tim behind the bar, and not even now, when a few of her teammates were mimicking Joe's horrible behavior and standing on Samuel's respectable tabletops, belting out a song.

No, Myfanwy was just where she was supposed to be—next to him. Samuel told himself not to get used to it. He knew better than most that nothing lasted forever, but for this one brief afternoon, he hushed that rational part of his brain. Maybe it was because he was surrounded by some of the friends of his past, and childish laughter and hoppy beer hugged him in this space, making him feel safe, but he allowed himself to feel young. Hopeful. Like he was at the beginning of a journey rather than at the end. He let himself contemplate a future rather than resigning himself to one. Like he'd told Jo, he focused on winning instead of not losing. What a magical way to regard the world. When he was young, it used to be the only way he saw it. How would life be different if he let himself think that way now?

"Uh-oh," Myfanwy said, stealing Samuel from his thoughts. "There's that look again. It can't possibly be happiness, can it?"

Samuel snaked his arm around her middle, pulling her closer. There were so many people squished into the room; no one would notice the covert embrace. And would it matter if they did?

Samuel issued a disgruntled huff between a barely there smile. "I might be slightly pleased, but that's only because you lot didn't embarrass me out there today."

Myfanwy laughed, and the way her brown eyes sparkled at him made him feel like the only man left on Earth. Lucky. Blessed. Chosen. "I took six wickets."

"I know that, Miss Myfanwy."

"And I hit for forty-eight runs. Two sixes!"

"I know that as well, Miss Myfanwy." Samuel couldn't feel the pain in his leg. When she smiled up at him like that, all he felt was the magnetism pulling him to her. God, he wanted to kiss her right now. He had his office in the back. Maybe she wouldn't mind getting lost for a little while…

"*You* only scored forty-seven," she added smartly, dousing his ardor quickly and efficiently.

Samuel reached deep within himself not to let that comment sting. She was only ribbing him as players did; however, he was upset that he hadn't scored a fifty. But it had been a while since he'd played a proper match, and he was still rusty and worried about how much stress to put on his leg. The fact that he could do more than he'd anticipated had thrown him, oddly enough, making him play less aggressively. It would take time, he told himself. Not only did he have to rebuild his strength in the limb, but he also had to build back his trust in his ability.

After three years on the sidelines, he was almost afraid to consider that he still had something left in him, that he could still make the crowds chant his name by the power of his swing…but he did. It was there. Just out of reach, but it was there.

Samuel lowered his head, sliding his lips just a breath away from her ear. "I want you."

Myfanwy snapped her neck up to meet his gaze. She was shocked, but just as hungry as he was. "I want you too," she said boldly.

Samuel's cock jumped. He glanced over her head at the door to his office. "We could hide away for a few minutes."

She grinned. "Have our own celebration?"

He nodded, taking her by the waist and nudging her through the crowd. "That's exactly what I was thinking."

Samuel loved Myfanwy like this, so carefree and up for anything. Mischievous and cocksure. She reminded him so much of his old self, and that didn't hurt as acutely as it once had. If anything, it made him want to be that optimistic man again. For her. That man could make love to her, provide the future that she deserved. That man would have the power to create a life that was strong enough to stand up to all the discourse and gossip an unlikely pair like them would create. That man would be proud of who he was and the name he would gift his wife.

Wife.

Did he dare? The old Samuel would have dared anything.

Samuel saw that man. Clearly. Effortlessly. Could feel him reanimating his body.

They were steps from the door. Already, Samuel could taste her silky skin on his tongue, hear her scream out in climax against his neck—but then he felt a tap on his shoulder. "What is it now?" he griped, half turning.

"Oh, so sorry, Mr. Everett. I didn't mean to disturb."

Sir Bramble. Good, decent, unoffending Sir Bramble. He was the last man in the establishment who deserved ire of any kind. Samuel put a damper on his desire and gave the gentleman as pleasant a greeting as he could muster.

"Sir Bramble," he returned, shoving Myfanwy behind his back. "I'm happy you could make it out today to see that match. I'm sure the ladies, and Benny, appreciated it."

Sir Bramble nodded warmly. "Indeed. Is it right that I heard Mr. Hardcastle is taking home one thousand pounds from the event? You did a good thing today, Sam. You and your team. And…" His smile held an undercurrent of embarrassment. "You should also be applauded for your play. You're not at one hundred percent yet, but I'm positive you'll get there soon. I don't know what you're doing at home, but it's working."

Samuel jerked when *someone* pinched him in the back. *Ha!* If Sir Bramble only knew.

The baron went on. "I'm sure the ladies will miss you when you return to playing full-time, but they'll always appreciate what you did for them. I know my Jennifer…um, I mean Miss Jennifer, can't speak highly enough about you."

Sir Bramble's words stunned him, not because Samuel hadn't thought about playing again—it was always on his mind—but because he'd never heard anyone else say it out loud until now. For years, it had been a secret just for himself, but now it was like Sir Bramble had breathed life into clay.

Samuel twisted around, and, sure enough, Myfanwy was right there listening to their entire conversation. His woman wouldn't lower herself to pretending like she wasn't eavesdropping. "I haven't decided anything yet," he told Sir Bramble. "Everything is still new. I'm just thinking about my team."

"Naturally," Sir Bramble agreed amiably. "I suppose it's just wishful thinking on my part. The sporting goods business will be even more of a gold mine with you actually playing." He slapped Samuel on the shoulder. "Ah, let's not talk any more of it. This is a day for celebrating, not talking business."

"As you say," Samuel replied. "Good day to you—"

"I hope to do my own celebrating, soon. I can't help but think a lot of it has to do with you," the baron rambled on, casting an obvious and ebullient smile toward the ladies dancing on the table. There in the thick of it was Jennifer, her arms around Jo and Anna, singing—*badly*—at the top of her lungs. Not for the first time, Samuel wondered what their parents thought these paragons of virtue got up to when they spent time at the cricket club.

Samuel scowled at Jennifer, ignoring the odd note in Sir Bramble's voice. He should yell at her to get down. He couldn't have her falling and twisting her leg. She was one of their fastest runners. "I didn't do anything," he muttered.

"You've done a lot," Sir Bramble insisted. "You're a real friend, Sam. We will never be able to thank you enough."

He extended his hand, and Samuel shook it before the man eventually meandered back into the merriment, his attention returning to Jennifer, who caught it effortlessly.

"What was that about?"

Samuel had known the question was coming, but that didn't mean he was in the mood to answer it. He faced Myfanwy's condemning expression, wondering if he could get her to pause her inquisition until after they were done celebrating in his office.

The muscles around her eyes tightened. By the arch of her brow—which was sharp enough to slice a man (Sir Bramble, most likely)—Samuel understood he would get no such concession.

"It was nothing," he remarked easily. Beggar that he was, he tried nudging Myfanwy toward the room once more, but she stuck to her place like concrete.

"It wasn't nothing," she replied stubbornly, fingering the buttons of his coat idly. "What was Sir Bramble going on about? I never would have taken you to be 'real friends.' I thought you were only business partners."

Myfanwy's tone started off innocently enough but became more accusatory, with every word like it was a snowball cascading down a mountain, gaining in speed and threat level.

Samuel didn't understand her dislike for the easygoing baron. Myfanwy had never said anything negative about Sir Bramble, but she also never said anything remotely positive about him. She merely ignored him, which was the most cutting thing a woman like Myfanwy could do.

Samuel chose his words wisely, still hoping to get her into that office. He kept his countenance relaxed, spreading his fingers wide on her hips, trying to remind her that there were more important things to be *talking* about. "Oh, the man is in a tough spot, that's all. Every once in a while, he asks me to relay a letter to Jennifer, and she does the same. It seems it's the only way they can converse without her mother reading their correspondence."

Myfanwy stepped out of his grasp, bumping into two men behind her, who bumped her right back. She didn't even bat an eye; she was too busy regarding Samuel as if he'd just kicked two kittens and was on the prowl for more.

"She does *what*?"

"I know!" Samuel replied. "I couldn't believe her mother reads the letters either—"

Myfanwy waved an impatient hand. "No, I already know that about Jennifer's mother. The nosy woman always reads Jennifer's letters first. She used to read mine before we realized it, and that's why she hates me so much. What do you mean Jennifer asked you to carry his letters? And why would you agree to it?"

Samuel's fragile mind was running a mile a minute, and yet still too slow. Most of his blood had already rushed to his cock, and his ill-equipped brain had been left to fend for itself. First, he wanted to ask Myfanwy what she could possibly write to Jennifer that would make Mrs. Hallett so offended, but he decided that story was for another time. Samuel wasn't one to tell people what they wanted to hear, but he desperately wanted to find the perfect explanation that landed him in that office with his head in between Myfanwy's plummy thighs.

Unfortunately, the more Myfanwy glared at him, the further that dream floated away. In the end, he told the truth. "You know that they have feelings for one another. They wanted privacy for their courting." He shrugged. "I wanted to keep my player happy and thought it was innocent enough."

"You thought it was innocent?"

Was that a question?

"There's nothing innocent about it!" she continued, searching through the horde. "Just look at him! Sir Bramble watches her like a lovesick hawk. He's always near her, staring, hoping, waiting for her to notice him. And when he's not near her, he's sending countless bouquets and now letters! It's not normal."

Samuel really should stop while he was ahead, but that idea was as foreign to him as Greek. "It sounds perfectly normal for a man in love...and Jennifer doesn't seem to mind."

"Are we looking at the same woman?" Myfanwy cried, throwing her arms at the couple in question. "Of course she minds!"

Samuel followed her eyeline toward Jennifer, who appeared the very definition of infatuated. London Bridge couldn't have crossed her smile, it was so wide, as she shared amorous glances with the baron. "I'm looking at your friend and I see a cheerful girl who won a match and is enjoying the attentions of a fine young man. How can you pretend otherwise?"

"I'm not pretending," Myfanwy replied, becoming cagey under his scrutiny. She pulled away from him even more. Samuel had to admit defeat; the office was definitely not in the cards that afternoon. "I just want her to keep her attention on the upcoming match. Sir Bramble is distracting her."

"Horseshit," Samuel scoffed.

Myfanwy's lips thinned into a dangerously straight line. "Since you are her *coach*, I thought you would agree with me. Now isn't the time for emotions and liaisons. She can go back to…dealing with him after the match. We only have a few more weeks, for heaven's sake. How could that man just make her forget herself?" She tossed a fallen lock of hair over her shoulder, squirming as Samuel remained quiet.

Her voice was noticeably weaker when she added, "I thought we'd be on the same team on this."

The same team. That was Samuel's problem. He saw it now. They would never be on the same team, no matter how much he wanted it. And he did want it. Stupid man. He'd allowed himself to want Myfanwy *and* cricket, to hope for a trajectory so different than the one he was on.

Like Icarus before him, Samuel had flown too high. For a moment there—for one brief respite in his piss-poor life—he'd actually believed that he could touch the sun, could recapture everything that he'd lost. Falling to earth had a way of sobering a man.

Jennifer didn't forget herself—Samuel did.

"Is that what you're doing, Myfanwy?" he asked softly, the swirl of optimism buzzing around him biting into his skin like vengeful hornets. "Dealing with me until you get everything you need and can move on?"

Myfanwy's features almost convinced him otherwise. The way she balked, the effort she employed to make him feel insane for asking the insensitive question. "How can you say that?" she asked, wounded, hurt, like he was kicking *her* now.

She reached out, poised to touch him—and then she paused, hesitating before finally laying her palm over his heart. Wary. Uncertain.

"We…we're…different," Myfanwy stammered. "We're not like them. I thought… We never talk about us…our situation." She looked up at him, her brow creased in confusion, her eyes turbulent. "We agreed it was just a game. That's what you wanted… I thought…"

Samuel's heart was beating too fast. He wasn't sure what he'd wanted her to say, but it hadn't been that. His fingers stretched. He could wrap her hands around her waist again. But he didn't. He was bumped from behind by a reveler, and yet he still held his ground.

Myfanwy's gaze narrowed. She saw it. She always saw everything. But she couldn't see him. What she was doing to him. Maybe what they were doing to each other, balancing in this constant state of limbo.

"You're right," he said carelessly. His lips wouldn't open; his smile was closed. "We are different. It was always just a game, correct? A game we both chose to play. A friendly game."

And games always end.

That seemed to appease her. Myfanwy nodded slowly, but Samuel could still view hints of trepidation behind her assured veneer, a sense that she'd lost something that could never again be found.

And Samuel, even with his bad eye, could see what she wanted to say next. The words that were on the tip of her tongue, but she was too much of a coward to release. The same words that he'd said to her not so long ago when they'd both been sanguine and optimistic in the present.

There was no such thing as a friendly game.

Not when there would always be winners and losers.

Chapter Twenty-One

MYFANWY WAS BESIDE herself when her aunt called, asking if she would like to go for a drive. Myfanwy jumped at the chance; she needed the fresh air. More importantly, she needed an escape from that townhouse.

A week on from the benefit match, Samuel and she weren't necessarily fighting, but they weren't speaking either. To make things even more awkward, they maneuvered around the rooms, avoiding one another with polite indifference, plastering smiles on their faces in front of Annabelle and Aaron and dropping them the moment the children were gone. Exhausting, it was, and confusing. Discussing their unusual relationship wasn't something she or Samuel were particularly good at, and now that deficiency was even more pronounced.

It was like they were stuck in a dance neither of them knew and were determined not to stomp on the other's toes. But the more they clammed up, pretended to read the other's mind, stepped ever so lightly, the more they lost any sense of rhythm and hurt one another. Myfanwy didn't know how to stop the music.

She didn't return until late in the afternoon, but it still felt too soon. Maybe it was because she never let her mind travel far from Samuel these days.

"Here we are, my dear. I'm not dropping you off at an empty house, am I?" Aunt Abigail asked, craning her head out the window as the carriage slowed to a halt. "Do you think Mr. Everett is in for the night?"

Myfanwy hid her smile as she climbed out of the conveyance. Her aunt had also been extremely inquisitive over Samuel's whereabouts when she picked Myfanwy up for their leisurely drive. The man had made an impact on her. "I'm not sure, Aunt, but it is no bother. I don't mind eating alone."

"Oh no, that won't do." The older woman followed her out of the carriage. "I simply must walk you inside. You know, if you lived with me, you wouldn't have this problem," she remarked in her loving *but* know-it-all manner.

Myfanwy turned to her aunt with a ready smile. "But if I lived with you, I wouldn't look forward to our drives as much."

That comment did much to placate Aunt Abigail, though she played it off with a disgruntled chuckle. "You're just pleased because I said I would ask about that cottage we saw for sale."

Myfanwy's stomach leaped at the mention of the sweet little house they'd found on the outskirts of town—and the beautiful field that accompanied it. "It was perfect, wasn't it?"

Aunt Abigail *humphed*. "Perfectly small."

"I don't need a large home."

"Well, you certainly won't get it in that cottage."

Myfanwy rolled her eyes amiably and started up the stairs. "The land was perfect too."

Aunt Abigail's boots slapped on the stone steps. "What would you even use all that land for? I hate to inform you, my girl, but you're not exactly heralded for your green thumb."

That was true. And her aunt hadn't even witnessed the bedraggled roses in the garden.

Myfanwy reached for the doorknob. "You know exactly what I would use it for."

"I know, dearest," Aunt Abigail answered morosely. "I was just hoping you'd changed your mind."

"Ha! You should know better than that!" Myfanwy laughed as she swept open the front door to a deserted foyer.

"Where's Benjamin?" Aunt Abigail asked, twirling in a circle as if the butler was trying to sneak up on her.

"I'm not sure. He must be busy."

"This place," Aunt Abigail grumbled, taking off her cape and handing it to Myfanwy as if she were the new Benjamin. "You went from a viscount's house to a madhouse. I truly never know what to expect when I come here—"

High-pitched giggles bounced into the foyer, cutting off the tirade. The older woman froze as more peals of childish laughter struck them. Her impenetrable scowl deepened, as if the cheerful sounds were the noises one usually heard in a productive slaughterhouse.

More gaiety skipped over to them, only this time it included a masculine element that Myfanwy detected easily. Was Samuel *laughing*? How was the world still spinning?

"Who is making all that…" Aunt Abigail began, gliding toward the drawing room.

"Wait, Aunt! I have to tell you—"

But Abigail avoided Myfanwy's outstretched hand, sailing right past her as if she were nothing more than a pesky fly. The cat was out of the bag now. Myfanwy had planned to tell her aunt about Annabelle during the drive; however, the right time never came. Myfanwy had ultimately concluded that there might never be one, and that she would ponder another time next year to break the joyful—and unforeseen—news. The busy woman wasn't supposed to follow her into the house and ruin Myfanwy's carefully planned procrastination.

"What in the world is going on here?" Aunt Abigail boomed.

The laughter immediately died.

Myfanwy winced. She didn't want to go into that room. No one could make her. Maybe she could just pretend she hadn't heard anything. She could tiptoe right up the stairs and hide under her covers while Samuel explained her father's furtive double life and long-lost love child to his only sister, who had lived the majority of her adulthood as chaste and faithful to her dead husband's memory.

Yes. That was what she would do. Heartened by her decision, she picked up her skirts and took her first step up the staircase—

"Myfanwy! Come in here. *Now!*"

She blew out a defeated breath and spun right around. Apparently, she wasn't getting off that easy. She lumbered to the drawing room, her head so heavy it felt like it was sinking into her ribcage.

But the image she found as she entered the room picked her spine up so swiftly that it was as if someone had stretched her from end to end.

Dolls. So many dolls. And toys. So many toys of all kinds and shapes and colors littered the drawing room so that there were no seats to be found, and those that could be were already being used by uppity dolls. And in the middle of this whirlwind of childhood delight sat Annabelle and Aaron on the floor...with Samuel, red-faced and carefree right next to them.

On. The. Floor.

Myfanwy stalled next to her aunt, who grabbed her wrist as if her life depended on it. The woman's voice wavered when she finally spoke again. "Myfanwy, dearest. Please tell me that all these dolls belong to you."

AN HOUR LATER, Aunt Abigail's hands were still shaking in her lap, though at least her mind had settled—slightly. "So, again," she said, her expression telling everyone that she wished she could be anywhere but in the claustrophobic drawing room of dead doll eyes. "You are basing all this—my brother's reputation—on a child's hair color?"

The child in question had been whisked upstairs by Sarah soon after Myfanwy and her aunt entered the domestic scene. It was clear to everyone that playtime was over. Samuel and Aaron now sat across from the women—in proper chairs—looking like they were readying for a firing squad.

"It is an unusual color, you have to admit," Samuel replied. His voice was hoarse and unused, since this was one of the few times that he'd been able to interject in the past hour. "And the boy filled us in on the rest. He can account for the viscount's...interest in the mother."

Aunt Abigail squinted at Aaron, who wilted under the scrutiny. "So, you're running a bloody orphanage now?"

Samuel's jaw firmed. "Hardly."

Abigail hopped up from her chair, pacing the little open space that she could.

Had Samuel truly bought all these toys for Annabelle? Myfanwy wondered. And it wasn't all for the girl—Myfanwy noticed that Aaron's clothes were clean and new, and there was a smattering of boys' toys included in the heap. Toy soldiers and a train set were scattered among the laces and tea sets. When did Samuel have the time? And why hadn't he asked Myfanwy to help?

Aunt Abigail's frantic mumblings soon blotted out all of Myfanwy's tumbling thoughts. "But my brother wouldn't do this. He loved his wife. And he would *never* have a child out of wedlock, and then abandon it."

"He was providing for the child and the mother," Samuel explained, nodding to Aaron. "He wanted to marry the actress, but..." His words trailed off. Apparently, he didn't have the heart to finish the sentence. *The viscount died.*

Abigail's skirts fanned furiously as she turned on him. "But how do you *know* for sure? This could all be some story, some fiction to steal the money from your pockets."

Men much older and distinguished than Samuel had melted under Abigail's inquisition before, but he held his ground. "I know," he said. "I believe the boy."

Those plain words knocked the steam out of the older woman. Aunt Abigail slumped next to Myfanwy on the settee once more, seemingly down, but not out.

"What will you do?" she said, her fire doused. "You can't keep all these children under your roof, Samuel. It's not right. You're never home. You're not...fit."

Aaron found his backbone and came to his feet. "Who says he's not fit?"

Myfanwy smiled at the poor lad, who swiftly lost his nerve and glued himself to Samuel's side again after another of Abigail's annihilating looks.

Samuel patted the boy on the knee and broke the stalemate. "You're right," he answered diplomatically. "I'm not fit. But what would you have me do? I hired an investigator, and he informed me that the mother's parents are still alive and live a few hours north of here. I plan on visiting them in the coming days."

Myfanwy was thrown. When had he hired an investigator, and why hadn't he told her? A feeling of loneliness—*otherness*—swept over her, as if she was on the outside looking in. She hadn't truly had that feeling in years. It made her want to hide in a broom closet, closing herself off from everything.

"Good," Aunt Abigail replied. "And if the grandparents don't want them, then you can put them in an orphanage. A *nice* orphanage," she amended quickly. "One where they can find respectable, God-fearing parents to take care of them. People who need and want them. People who will do a decent job of it."

Samuel stared down at his hands as he rubbed his fingers. "I could do a decent job of it," he said softly. He flicked his head toward Myfanwy. "I've kept her alive, haven't I?"

Abigail swiveled her neck back and forth around the room, wide-eyed, like a deranged parrot. "Are you trying to be funny? Please, dear boy, please tell me you are joking. My niece might still be alive, but her reputation is dead in the water. She never attends *ton* events unless I force her, she plays cricket more than she answers calls, and she still plans on eschewing marriage to live alone in the bloody country. Under your watch, she's become positively feral. And you think you should be *praised* for that?"

Abigail placed a hand on her bountiful chest as if attempting to settle her wild and disappointed heart. She closed her eyes and inhaled dramatically. "Samuel," she started again, minutely calmer. "I do not say these things to hurt you, but you need to know you are out of your depth. You are a cricketer. An entrepreneur. A"—she tapped her teeth together—"tavern owner, but you are not a guardian. I'm sorry. I know you had a relationship with my brother, and he made you promise things..." Her voice wandered off before she fixed on Myfanwy, her countenance increasingly impotent. "I'm so out of joint right now I think I just might allow you to buy that house we saw today. If you don't want to live with me, fine, but you cannot stay here. People will talk. They'll say he's housing his bastards—"

"What house?" Samuel asked, the words coming out of him like a shot.

That lovely feeling that Myfanwy experienced earlier in response to her quaint cottage didn't return. "It's nothing," she replied, her gaze in her lap.

"It's not nothing," Abigail interjected. "It might just be the answer we need. You can't stay here. What will people *think?*"

Samuel rose to his feet. The action was so smooth and unhindered that Myfanwy was instantly reminded of their massaging sessions, and finally her stomach made an appearance, fluttering in that delicious, nervous way.

"She's not going anywhere," Samuel stated firmly. His bad eye glowed like a pearl, and Myfanwy heard Aunt Abigail let out a rare squeak. "You talk about being proper and then in the same sentence allow your only niece to live alone God knows where. That is not happening. I promised your brother I would watch over her, keep her hale and content, and dammit, that's what I'm doing. Look at her, for Christ's sake," he said, throwing an arm Myfanwy's way. "She's damn near perfect. She's healthy and strong and so smart it makes me want to beat my head against the wall half the time. So, she doesn't want to marry any of those imbecilic idiots in the *ton*? She should be applauded for that, frankly. She sees the world in her own way and wants to change it instead of allowing it to change her. She's not settling for a future; she's taking the one she wants no matter what stands in her way—" Samuel's voice caught, and he pinched his lips together, almost as if he was upset that he'd let himself go this far, this long. His eyes were wide, unblinking, like his speech was as much of a revelation to him as it was to her.

Myfanwy was on the edge of her seat. She wanted him to go longer and farther. Did he truly think those things about her? Did he think her perfect? After a week of silence between them, she was greedy for any sign—any sense of clarity—that he still felt something for her. Wanted something more from her.

Samuel breathed heavily out of his nose and tore at his wavy hair before letting his arm fall to his side. "She's bloody lovely," he said, his ragged voice just above a whisper. "And I know I didn't have anything to do with that, but I didn't get in her way either. I can do the same for the others."

"You mean you'd keep us?" Aaron asked, his freckled young face open with pure, unadulterated hope. "Forever?"

"Christ, not forever, but...yes, until you're ready to leave." Samuel sighed. "*But* I have to speak to your grandparents first."

Myfanwy's entire body burned with admiration like a thousand torches had been sparked inside her. "Yes, Aaron. Forever," she told him. The boy ducked his head immediately, flicking away something from his eyes.

Aunt Abigail *tsked*. "Forever is a long time, Mr. Everett."

Samuel's smile was weak, but it was still there when he looked at Myfanwy. "Not when you're happy."

Chapter Twenty-Two

THE FOLLOWING MORNING, Samuel came upon Myfanwy and the children in the dining room for breakfast and immediately stifled a curse. She was ripe for him. On Sunday. Of all days.

"Oh good, you're ready," she said, patting her mouth with her napkin and rising from the table. Myfanwy sported a soft yellow day dress that covered her from stem to stern, and yet Samuel's mouth still went dry at the sight. She was like a gift, delicately packaged, inviting him to unwrap.

With herculean effort, he tried to rid the unhelpful thoughts from his head. It was only because she hadn't come to him in recent days that he was so…parched. And yet the way she stood at the table, her shoulders pulled back, her eyes daring him to argue, made it plain that the woman could be covered in burlap and Samuel would still think her beautiful.

He gave the children a smile, attempting to appear unrattled despite the trap he'd just walked into. "Of course I'm ready," he replied evenly. "It's—"

"Sunday, yes, I know," Myfanwy said, walking around the table toward him. "And I'm also aware that you do whatever it is you do today." She smiled like she was ready to say *checkmate*. "But you also told my aunt that you were going to meet with the children's grandparents, so I assumed you would add it to your trip." Her lashes flickered impishly as she surveyed his body up and down. "You seem like the kind of man who likes to kill two birds with one stone."

Samuel's mouth was open before his rebuke could be formulated. But he would deny her. Allowing Myfanwy to join him on this day would add to its hellishness. There was a reason he'd kept it secret. It was only his burden to bear.

However, yet again, she was ready for him. "I will not be denied," Myfanwy said. Lightly, she placed her palm against his chest, and Samuel would have thought her a witch. With that barely there touch it felt like she was pulling the breath, and the refusal, from his lungs.

And she knew it. Her smile grew wider the longer he stayed silent. "I'll get my things," she said, leaving Samuel in her wake with absolutely no room for argument.

THE JOURNEY TOOK a miserable two hours. Not that it was his companion's fault. In Myfanwy's defense, she was the ideal travel partner—she stayed quiet and took up very little room. Samuel's wandering mind and anxiety were the true problem. Scenario after scenario spun in his head of the upcoming day, and not one ended in a pleasant experience. In the end, he merely wished to protect her, which was difficult, because most of his energy for Sundays was applied to safeguarding his own sanity.

"Are we here?" Myfanwy asked, jamming her face against the window when the carriage veered from the main road onto a dirt path just west of Sutton's main square.

"Don't make yourself cross-eyed," Samuel answered wearily. "There's nothing to see. More houses, more fields, always more of the same."

Myfanwy retreated from the window, casting him a dubious frown. "I think it looks lovely," she said. Samuel barked out a laugh, but sobered quickly when he realized she wasn't joking.

"Lovely?" he choked out. "It's provincial at best."

She searched out the window again. Even with Myfanwy blocking his view, Samuel knew what she was looking at—the Phillips' farm...the Shackletons' farm...the Mosleys' ramshackle home that perpetually seemed like it was one rainy day away from collapsing in a heap.

"It's quaint," Myfanwy said, fogging up the glass with her breath. "It looks just as charming as any other small town in England."

"Small, yes." Samuel chuckled. "Sutton is indeed small."

"Sutton?" she said, excitement evident in her voice. Samuel didn't think he'd ever heard anyone say the word in such a cheerful way before. It felt wrong, like writing his name with his left hand. "Are we going to your home? That's what you do on Sundays? Visit family?" A shadow fell over her face, and Myfanwy surveyed her expensive gown, patting at the muslin with erratic hands. "I wish you would have told me. I would have worn something different. I would have..."

Samuel reached out and clasped her hand. She wasn't playing; her pulse hammered nervously against his fingertips. "You have nothing to worry about," he said sincerely. "They'll like you just fine."

The carriage lurched to a stop. With a drawn-out sigh, Samuel forced himself to release her, but his body couldn't be tempted to do much else.

Myfanwy's lips curled up at the sides. "What are you waiting for? If there is nothing to worry about, shouldn't we go inside?"

It felt like four elephants were sitting on Samuel's chest. Eventually, he nodded and dragged himself to open the door, knowing that Myfanwy would probably never look at him the same way again.

"OH, YOU HAVE quite the appetite, don't you?" Samuel's mother clucked as she bobbed and weaved around the dining table, adding more food whenever any serving platter dipped below her level of hospitable approval. "You're a devil, Samuel, for not telling us you were bringing a guest. I would have made more!"

Samuel grimaced and eyed the dozen or so scones on the rough-hewn table. The woman had raised three sons; it was her habit to cook as if an army was visiting. Though, he had to admit, Myfanwy was doing her bit to make sure she downed everything on her plate. And then some.

"I don't think it's polite to talk about a lady's eating habits, Mother," he answered, winking at her so that she understood he was only jesting.

She laughed, a great big belly laugh that was anything but ladylike, and fell into her chair, wiping away the gray wisps of hair that curled around her forehead like a nest. "Oh, you're right," she agreed. "I'm sorry, dear. That was bad of me, wasn't it?"

Myfanwy's spoon stalled halfway to her mouth. Samuel wondered if she'd even heard any of the conversation, so fixed on her stew she was. "Oh, I don't mind," she replied, surprising him. "Samuel's cook is very good, but it's not every day I get food as wonderful as this. I'm sorry if I'm appreciating it too much."

His mother beamed with the intensity of Zeus's thunderbolt. Samuel had been wrong. His mother didn't like Myfanwy. She *loved* her and would until her dying breath.

A grunt came from the other end of the table, and Samuel sighed.

His father, on the other hand... Well, his father was his father.

Samuel had almost forgotten the old man was there; the last hour had been so blessedly uneventful. Samuel knew his mother would be welcoming. The moment Myfanwy stepped inside the tiny cottage, his mother had flitted around her like a demented butterfly, showing off the home and garden for a surprisingly drawn-out period despite the fact there wasn't much to it. The abode was a basic thatched-roof cottage with the dining room, kitchen, and drawing room effectively splitting one open space between them. It boasted of two bedrooms, one of which Samuel had had to share with his brothers. A far cry from what Samuel lived in now, it still held a soft spot in his heart, which had everything to do with his mother's gift for decorating, needlework, and cooking skills. The house was cramped, but far from unpleasant, and always smelled delicious.

The only unpleasant aspect was the man who continued to make chuffing noises in the back of his throat like a spoiled child just waiting for everyone to ask what was wrong. Samuel wouldn't be asking that question anytime soon. From experience, he was more than aware that the answer was never worth the fight that ensued.

However, he should have recognized that ignoring him wouldn't stop his father. If the curmudgeon wasn't given the attention he wanted, then he would simply take it.

"So...you're the viscount's famous daughter, are you?" Samuel's father asked, sitting straight in his ladder-back chair like a king on his throne. Samuel hated to admit how in awe he always was of his father, who had the supreme ability to appear both imperious and pathetic at the same time. At least he wasn't drunk. The old man usually saved that for the evening's festivities.

"You know she is," Samuel said.

Even with the warning in Samuel's tone, Daniel Everett didn't take his gimlet eye off his guest. "And you live with my son?"

Myfanwy turned to Samuel with a questioning look before starting to speak, but he cut her off. "Again, you already know this. I'm her guardian. She lives under my roof *as my ward.*"

Finally, Daniel fixed on his son, his mouth morphing into a deceivingly warm smile. But, once more, Samuel was reminded of his father's duplicity. The man, once known for his handsomeness and strength in his youth, still harbored vestiges of thick blond hair and clear, piercing blue eyes. His large, solid body filled every space it entered, and the town still talked about the time he'd wrestled three men on a dare and won—without resorting to biting a single one. But time had a way of trampling on a man's spirit, and Daniel had had his fair share of misfortune.

Ten years ago, he'd been laying brick like any normal day when his attention was diverted from a friend telling an amusing story. That second would haunt him, and his family, for the rest of his life. At that vulnerable moment, the wall he'd been working on collapsed. Most of his fellow workers got away unharmed, but Daniel—who'd always been touted for his speed and agility—had been slow to react. In the end, he'd managed to save the majority of his body, but one hand had been caught under the rubble. Smashed and broken beyond repair, it now lay useless at his side, causing the man daily pain as well as daily bitterness. Because that wall hadn't only taken Daniel's hand, but his ability to earn a living.

Samuel squared his shoulders at his father's frank perusal of him. One would think it would get easier through the years, but something about the threshold of his childhood home held dark magic. The second he entered, Samuel felt like a child again, afraid and disappointing.

"Don't act like you aren't ecstatic about having one of them under your roof," Daniel said through his chews of beef. "Isn't that why you latched on to that viscount so fast? It was always your goal to be like them."

This diatribe was nothing new. Samuel had heard it countless times before, only this time Myfanwy could also hear it, and his blood began to simmer. "I don't know who put those tales into your head, Father. Certainly, it wasn't me."

"You didn't have to tell me," Daniel replied, slamming his good hand on the table, flicking stew off his spoon. "You showed me when you ran from home as quickly as you could. And you came back, acting like a peacock with your clothes and your carriage, throwing it in our faces. So much more refined, you were. But now look at you. You're hiding your limp, but I know it's there, and everyone can see how you ruined your damn eye."

Ha! A peacock? The only colors in Samuel's wardrobe were brown, black, and blue. He was hardly a rainbow.

"Father," Samuel said stiffly, sending a weighted look in Myfanwy's direction. "Now isn't the time. I didn't come here to fight."

"Fight!" Daniel spat. "Of course you didn't. Because that's not what gentlemen do, is it? God forbid they dirty their hands." Not waiting for a response, he turned his aggression back to Myfanwy. "Has he told you about the Gentlemen vs. Players match yet? Well, you're a smart girl. I'm sure you know that every year at Lord's they play that special match. It's even in the papers all the way out here. The Players always won. Professionals are always so much better than the amateurs. But then the amateurs started getting smarter and 'borrowing' a few professionals to help keep the matches competitive." He grimaced as if pulling the next words from himself were like pulling a thorn from his side. "My son…my son wanted to be chosen so badly. No, Samuel never told me, but I would hear him whining to his mother. For some reason, even though he was the best, they would always overlook him. Even with all his efforts, they never considered him an equal. And they never will…especially not now." Daniel fell back in his seat, seemingly exhausted by his son's failures. "I told you." His voice had thinned to a hoarse whisper. "I told you…"

Samuel's knuckles turned white as he gripped the edge of the table. "You told me nothing. You taught me nothing."

"I taught you to be better!" his father sneered, lurching at Samuel like a cobra ready to strike. "I told you not to be like me, a laborer, a man who is only as good as the body he's blessed with. And what do you do? You go out and play cricket. Ha! Cricket! A sport for nobs and fancy lords. I told you they'd take everything from you. I told you they'd take and take until your body broke like an old mule." His smile was impossibly cruel as he focused on Samuel's eye. "And I was right. Now where are your lords? Where are those highborn friends of yours? They aren't beatin' down your door anymore, are they? Your life is over. Congratulations."

The room was unbearably dense, stiff, like no one could move for fear of snapping in half. Three sets of eyes burned into Samuel, but he couldn't think of what to say. How could he make his father accept that the shame and embarrassment he felt crippled him more than anything that happened on the cricket pitch? And that the joy and freedom he'd found after he left his home to begin his career was the stuff that men dreamed about their entire lives. But he couldn't say those things, because his father would never understand his son's point of view. In Daniel Everett's eyes, despite everything Samuel had done in his life, he was a failure because, in the end, he'd ended up as lame as his father.

And that sick way of thinking made Samuel furious. Because he was nothing like the old man. His knees might crack when he stood, his nose might not be anywhere near straight, and he might not be able to detect a punch coming from his left side as quickly as from his right, but Samuel still had fight left in him. *He* could provide for his family, and that family was the whole reason why his life wasn't yet over.

Daniel still had a family after he'd lost his hand, but he'd chosen to kneel down at the altar of self-pity, near-comatose with resentment, instead of living and fighting for them.

A slow, patronizing smile came onto Samuel's face as he matched his father's severe gaze. "If I'm such a failure, how is it that you're still living in this house?" he asked. "Who brings you money each week to pay your food and any other necessities you might need?"

"Samuel, no!" his mother cried out in a broken sob. "You mustn't." The lines of her face sagged in despair, and the ache it caused almost made him stop.

Almost.

"What?" Samuel asked, leaning his forearms on the table, twisting his neck back to his father. "You mean he doesn't know? He thinks *you've* been the one keeping the family afloat these past ten years with your sewing and knitting?" He *tsked*, staring into his father's dark blue eyes that were so much like his own. "No," he said, lengthening the word until it struck a dismal tune. "No...don't fool yourself, Mother. *He knows*. He's a bastard, but he isn't stupid. He knows I'm the reason he has a roof over his head, and he hates me for it." Samuel reached for one of the scones and rolled it around in his hand as if it were a cricket ball. "I'm the son that did everything wrong. I'm the son who never listened, and yet I'm the one who puts food on your table. Week after week. Month after month. Year after year." He took a large bite of the scone, making a show of chewing and swallowing it before he continued. "You say we are so alike...and you're right, Father. I'm not a gentleman and I'll never be. But answer me this. How does it feel to eat another man's food? Because I wouldn't know."

Chapter Twenty-Three

S AMUEL DIDN'T SAY one word as they collected their things. The goodbyes were dismal, with even his mother suffering from a momentary lapse of politeness, allowing Myfanwy and Samuel to leave the cottage without a proper farewell. It was for the best. Myfanwy didn't know what she would have said anyway. *Thank you for this lovely afternoon* didn't seem appropriate under the current, acrid circumstances.

As they walked out to the carriage, Samuel kept his distance, but even the few steps he lagged behind Myfanwy felt like a schism that might never be bridged. His chin down, his eyes heavy and downcast, Samuel was a shadow of himself. His body continued to move, but his soul, the happiness that Myfanwy had begun to see these last several weeks, was missing. He was pale and bloodless, as if being here had drained it all from him.

Was this truly what he did every Sunday? Travel to his family home and withstand his father's jealousy and abuse in order to gift his mother money? Couldn't he just send the money with a messenger? Anything seemed preferable to having to sit at the same table as that cruel man. A man who looked so much like Samuel but was so very different.

Nevertheless, the answer came swiftly to Myfanwy. The joy his mother had for his presence was telling. Samuel would never take that away from her; he couldn't hide in London knowing it would cause his mother pain, even if visiting created fresh cuts into his skin each week. On this one day, Samuel would always lose. He was damned if he did and damned if he didn't.

He stopped outside the carriage, lifting his hand to help Myfanwy inside. Still, he kept his gaze averted as if he was Medusa and afraid he might turn her to stone with one glance. Her heart wept at the pink spots highlighting his cheeks, at the red rims lining his eyes. Samuel wouldn't cry in front of her, but the effort it took to remain impassive was making its mark.

She placed her hand on the top of his shoulder. "Samuel—"

"Not now," he said. The words were blunt and harsh, and he softened them with a wan smile. "Please? Not now, Myfi. I just want to go."

She dropped her hand. "Of course," she said, allowing him to tuck her into the conveyance. "I understand."

However, the longer they sat together, bumping from the road, their thoughts clouding the atmosphere like a fireplace with a broken flue, the more Myfanwy did *not* understand. Samuel had no reason to be mistreated so. He hadn't failed. And he had absolutely no reason to be disappointed in himself.

Samuel was…well, Samuel was Samuel.

And the love of her life.

And Myfanwy would not let him live one more second on this Earth believing he was anything less than remarkable.

She was on him before Samuel had a chance to blink. Crossing the divide of the carriage, straddling his lap, Myfanwy locked herself in place with her thighs. If he thought he was going to throw her off, he was in for a fight.

Samuel's eyes went wide, and his mouth opened, and Myfanwy cut him off the only way she knew how. Placing her hands on his cheeks, she brought him toward her, crushing him with a kiss that would leave no questions. Myfanwy swept her tongue between his teeth, conquering any resistance she felt, canting her head so that she could envelop him totally and completely.

Samuel was safe in her arms; he was whole and admired and loved.

And he was...unresponsive.

For a moment, Myfanwy felt his arm lift behind her. She could sense it hanging at her back, not touching her, as if he were judging whether he should continue this dance or sit it out. That was no good. Yet again, she couldn't allow him to think.

Still holding his face, Myfanwy leaned back, meeting his eyes, which were bright but also stunned.

"I am going to make love to you right now, Samuel Everett," she stated firmly. "And before you say it, you have to know that you are not capable of ruining me. You are the finest man I have ever known. Nothing you could ever do would change that or lessen my feelings for you. Do you understand?"

Myfanwy was certain they were both holding their breath. She waited, fighting the bashfulness and unease that threatened to force her back to her side of the carriage, pretending this whole burst of emotion had never happened.

The ring around Samuel's damaged eye became deeper, blazing like blue flames. The intensity scared her, as did his continued quiet, but his next movement saved him. Cautiously, almost timidly, Samuel stretched toward her, placing a sweet, languid kiss on her lips. It lingered there, rekindling their breathing and the passion that was stirring between them. And then his hand behind her finally landed, gently palming the back of her head, shifting her so that his kiss could gain more purchase, gain more of *her*.

And that was all it took.

Myfanwy's pulse hammered between her ears, creating a thumping, savage rhythm of pure need. Samuel fixed his other hand on her hip and intensified his grip, rocking and swirling his pelvis against hers in pace with their kisses.

The atmosphere was charged and muggy, and in no time, Myfanwy was tearing at her clothes, begging Samuel to help release her from the confines of her tight muslin sleeves.

"I don't want to—"

"Don't you dare say you don't want to do this...that you don't think *we* should do this," she cut in ferociously.

Samuel regarded her curiously, his smile crooked. "I wasn't going to say that. We definitely should do this. Over and over again. Forever and forever." As if putting a period on that statement, he bit at the rose-petal curve of her earlobe. His hands trembled as he reached behind her to work on her buttons. "I was going to say that I don't want to hurt you. I should go slow, but I don't think I can."

"Then don't," Myfanwy replied with a franticness to her voice that excited her. "I'm not asking you to. Just give me what I want. You."

Samuel grunted in response, and together they fought through the layers of fabric they could. Myfanwy bounced and twisted on his lap, ever mindful that the more she wiggled, the harder he became under her. Whenever she would shift too far away, Samuel would pull her back down, grinding his pelvis into the cradle of her thighs, rubbing her until she was panting with the thrill of what was to come. Having never made love before, Myfanwy was in the dark on how it would work in a carriage. To be honest, she hadn't thought that far ahead. But, as usual, putting her trust in Samuel was a safe bet.

He had no issue with the confined space. Samuel wrapped his arms around her torso and hugged her with a hint of vulnerability. The act almost stole all the breath from her lungs, but Myfanwy swiftly concluded that breathing was not as important as hearing his heart beat erratically against her sensitive skin.

"My God, I love your smell," he said, his soft voice at odds with the tension in his body.

Myfanwy giggled. "What do I smell like?" She dipped her head to his neck and licked his skin, delighting in the way he jerked at the sensation. He tasted salty and clean, and she had to do it again.

Samuel lifted his head from her hair and kissed a trail down her neck, pushing the neckline of her dress down and out of his way. Awkwardly, Myfanwy tried to help him and rearranged her gown so that her arms were finally free, and it pooled at her hips. Her corset still shielded her body from him, but at least she could hold him without being so restrained. Freedom was what she needed, utter abandon.

Languidly, like dew drifting down a flower stem, Samuel caressed her clavicle with his nose and forehead. He only stopped to kiss her at the base of her neck, before continuing his journey. Overheated and piqued, Myfanwy shivered from the attention.

"You smell like lavender and sex," he said with a hoarse chuckle. He ducked lower and reached inside her corset to lift out her breasts, which were firm and puckered from the frenzy. Samuel blew on the nipples, a wicked smile on his face as the rosy points stood proudly under his amorous onslaught.

He caught her eye and held it as he dipped his head to a nipple, rolling his tongue around it like it was melting candy, catching every last bit, before finally capturing it between his teeth. Myfanwy's mouth dropped open at the intimacy, but nothing came out, and nor could she look away. It was a confusing, heart-pounding effect having him touch her in that way while also making love to her with his gaze. She felt weightless and raw, prime for ravishment.

When Samuel turned to the other nipple, Myfanwy attempted to remember what they were speaking about. She licked her lips. "I…I don't even know what sex smells like," she replied. In response, Samuel grinned around her flushed nipple. "But I'm sure I don't smell like it."

It was if she'd dared him to do it, because in an instant, Samuel's hands were underneath her skirts. Without taking his lips from her breast, he repositioned Myfanwy in his lap so his knuckles could sweep across the heavenly schism between her legs…once, twice…three lazy passes, which were enough to make her close her eyes and mew in pleasure.

"You always get so wet for me," Samuel purred against her

skin. "Sopping wet."

Myfanwy's eyes shot open. "I'm...sorry?" she said, although she couldn't understand why.

Samuel nipped at her nipple. "Never apologize. You're perfect. I want you wet. Because when you're wet, I can do this."

He sank two fingers into Myfanwy, and a fullness overtook her. It was still slightly uncomfortable, and her muscles tensed from the invasion. Samuel leaned toward her, taking her mouth once more, exploring her ecstasy as he pumped into her, stretching her walls, milking her sex until the discomfort was completely lost. "Breathe," he said, resting his bottom lip on hers, sweeping his tongue along her teeth. "I'm getting you ready, sweetheart. I think we both know I'm much bigger than my fingers."

Myfanwy answered with a broken laugh. He was showing her too much at the moment for her to focus on everything he said. When he added another finger, she winced, but didn't pull away, not when his thumb had found the little bundle of nerves that somehow made it all work. He petted her gently, and then more insistently, undulating his hand in a way that made her dig her hands into his hair and hold on for dear life. Myfanwy bounced on his lap, recognizing the bursting stars that were beginning to build inside her lower belly, stretching all the way to the soles of her feet.

She held him against her chest in a shocking grip, but suddenly, everything was too tense. She was pulled so tight and waiting, waiting, waiting, for the tinder to spark inside her.

"Relax, my love" she heard Samuel say, but Myfanwy couldn't. She needed something and she needed it now. Nothing could happen, nothing could move forward, until that need was assuaged.

She was bucking against his hand with abandon, and the explosion seemed to sneak up on her. One second, she was mindless, and the next she was keening, arching her back to a degree that had her head hanging halfway to her seat.

In a rush Myfanwy couldn't contemplate, Samuel moved, and soon she was back on her side of the carriage, boneless and dreamy. He shifted between her legs and pushed up her skirts while his other hand worked impatiently at the buttons of his trousers. The blue-green vein in the middle of his forehead pulsed as he finally released his manhood and massaged it in his hand, pumping himself with the savage grace and care with which he'd just touched her.

Myfanwy watched the performance with avid curiosity, in a fever over what he was about to do to her next.

Samuel glanced at her, and the intensity of his face softened. "Don't be afraid," he said. "You'll be able to take me."

"I know," Myfanwy replied. "I'm not afraid."

"You were the one that asked for this," he went on, his voice hitching as his rod appeared to jump in his hand. A small spurt of liquid sat on the head, and he coated the rest of himself with the glistening substance. He slanted over her, placing one hand on the cushion at her side.

Myfanwy wiggled her bottom closer to him so that her thigh rubbed up against his swollen appendage. Samuel groaned, and she did it again. "Don't pretend that I was the only one," she whispered. "You wanted this too."

Samuel closed his eyes, his forehead furrowed as he placed himself at her entrance, pushing inside one blessed inch at a time. "Open for me, baby," he urged. Myfanwy grasped his arm and could feel the power he was using to go slow for her benefit. She took a deep breath and allowed her legs to relax as much as they could, begging her resistance to fade.

"That's good, so good," Samuel said, sinking halfway inside her. The pain was there. As ready as he'd made her, it hadn't been enough, yet Myfanwy found that watching the emotions play out on his face helped her. Despite his gruff exterior, Samuel was only ever gentle with her, and her making love for the first time was just another example of that sensitivity.

But Myfanwy wasn't a doll or made of glass. She was a woman.

She reached for his chest and began to unbutton his waistcoat and the linen shirt underneath. When she'd created enough room, she seized on his bare skin, rubbing her hands up and down his torso with the same energetic pressure she'd used for his leg. "Samuel? Samuel, look at me."

It took a moment, but he eventually opened his glossy eyes to find her.

"Kiss me." Without hesitation, he curved down, capturing Myfanwy's mouth. Wrapping her arms around his neck, she kept him near her, whispering on his lips, "I won't break."

Samuel tried to rise away from her, but she wouldn't let him. Taking advantage of his internal confusion, she flexed her pelvis, pulling more of him inside her. The difference was startling. Actively participating in the act alleviated most of the discomfort, at least in her mind. It was like playing a match versus standing on the outside, merely watching.

She did it again, and Samuel gave up, dropping his head with a groan. "I know you won't break," he said, his voice strained. "But I don't want to hurt you."

"I won't let you hurt me," she replied readily.

And it was the perfect thing to say. Samuel stared at her for a long pause before letting out a soundless laugh. He nodded, coming to terms with the rightness of that one little statement. Myfanwy was strong and sure of herself. She would not let him hurt her. Though perhaps the reason she loved Samuel so much was because he would rather die than ever do so.

"Now stop thinking and ride me," she said, experimentally rolling her hips. *Yesss.* That was rather nice.

Samuel definitely agreed, because with one smooth motion, he surged into her, filling Myfanwy until she felt ready to burst. He didn't stay there, allowing her to acclimate to their situation. Samuel's blood was high, and she *had* asked for it.

There was no time to think about the consequences of the action or the minor tinge of burning that was quickly turning into a distant memory. There was only Samuel as he laid claim to her.

Like dealing with an unbroken stallion, Myfanwy kept her hands securely on the reins, matching his thrusts with little ones of her own. They pounded into one another, without finesse or poise, only lust and greedy fervor.

Samuel's mouth was never far away. He went back and forth between her lips and her nipples, never sure which he wanted more. Myfanwy felt like her entire body was held hostage by him and his whims, and the more he doted on her, the more he coveted.

His tempo swiftly turned inelegant, and it was that zealous eagerness that pitched her over the edge. Her sex began to tighten and reach for the friction it needed. She cried out from the helpless want of it all, and Samuel answered with a cry of his own, thrusting harder and harder, faster and faster, until they were brutish and heedless for that one thing that would split them apart but also make them whole.

It came upon them in a rush. Samuel grew impossibly large, brushing her inner walls at just the right angle to make her combust, spasming and jerking inside her with shallow dives until he called out her name in a growling benediction.

"Fuck. Fuck. Fuck," Samuel whispered as he collapsed on top of her. It was a lovely prayer, though one Myfanwy wouldn't be repeating in public anytime soon. She would save it for the bedroom.

She held the back of his head, tickling his damp neck with her shaking fingers. "I agree," she said.

Samuel didn't respond. He didn't even chuckle. For the rest of the drive, he stayed in her arms, sleeping peacefully against her inviting skin.

Myfanwy did not do the same.

Now that she knew what sex smelled like, she was content to enjoy the idyllic fragrance as long as she could.

Chapter Twenty-Four

"SAMUEL… SAMUEL, WAKE up. We're home."

Samuel opened his eyes to darkness. As if he'd slept for the first time in years, it took him much too long to summon to mind where he was. Nevertheless, the moment he nuzzled the soft, succulent mound of skin, he remembered every blessed thing—including the fact that he'd fallen asleep right after it.

What an ass.

"I'm sorry. I'm so sorry, sweetheart," he said, reluctantly picking himself up from Myfanwy's chest. He scrambled back to his side of the carriage, but not without taking her with him. Samuel situated her on his lap, placing her legs across his own as if he were holding a child. However, there was nothing childlike about Myfanwy's expression. She seemed incredibly pleased with herself.

"Shouldn't we go inside?" she said, chuckling while he ran his hands all over her, making sure she wasn't irreparably damaged by his wicked salacity. Yes, Myfanwy had asked him to let go of his restraint, but a virgin had no idea what she was asking for. It was Samuel's responsibility to ensure her first experience was memorable, and he had slept through it.

"What are you doing?" Myfanwy asked, slapping his hands away.

Samuel took a long, steadying breath. "I'm making sure you're all right."

"I'm all right."

"How do you know?"

"Samuel, I think I know if I'm all right or not. What's wrong with you?"

"I feel asleep!" he cried, dragging a hand through his hair. His wavy locks were already plastered in funny angles all over his head, and his nervous hands weren't helping matters. He was positively befuddled, and the crazy woman was loving it! Samuel had heard of skittish virgins before the act, but not skittish men after. He couldn't contain the thumping of his heart. If he didn't know any better, he'd assume an attack was imminent.

One by one, with peculiar thoroughness, Myfanwy fastened the buttons of his shirt. It was ridiculously comforting. "You were tired. After the afternoon you had, you needed your rest."

"Who cares about what I needed? *You* needed *me*."

Myfanwy scrunched up her nose. "Samuel, I got you... I got exactly what I needed."

Well, there was that. His ego was slightly assuaged. Not that Samuel needed her to say it; his cock was still coated in her scent, and he would be dead and buried before he forgot the clench of her lovely release.

"But..." he began, folding her hands on her lap. It was damned difficult to think with Myfanwy sprawled all over him. Though the thought of placing her on the other side of the carriage put him in even more of a panic. "I should have thanked you—"

"*Thanked* me? Samuel, this wasn't a cricket match. You don't have to thank me for participating."

He scowled. Why was she making it so difficult? He was trying to tell her that this wasn't just another sexual act, that he'd never experienced anything as profound as what he'd shared with her—in a goddamn moving vehicle, no less. But Samuel couldn't get the words out. Not with the aroma of her pussy still on his fingers and the carriage dark and overheated by their stamina.

Yes…stamina. Samuel had never thought of it before, but it made perfect sense now. Of course making love to a sportswoman would be otherworldly. Myfanwy's strength and energy harmonized with his own. They were a perfect match for this act. And probably more, if he ever let his poor heart dote on it…which he couldn't at the present. One step at a time.

Samuel tried again. With his finger under her jaw, he directed Myfanwy to meet his gaze. She was solemn, astonishingly so, as she waited for him to speak.

And yet, once more, the words eluded him. "I just wanted to make sure that you knew that I… That we…" He blew out an exhale and shrugged.

Myfanwy's smile widened. "You want to make sure that I know we can do it again? Yes, good idea. How about now?"

⇥⟫⟫⟩⟨⟨⟪⇤

SAMUEL COULDN'T GET them into the house fast enough. Myfanwy shrieked when he lifted her in his arms and erupted into squeals of laughter as he ran up the steps and pounded on the door with his boot. Nighttime had fallen on the swank neighborhood, and although it was a prime time for couples enjoying their evening strolls, thankfully, there was no one to gape as Samuel made a lovesick fool out of himself.

How Benjamin managed to let them in without breaking that stern look of his, Samuel would never know; nevertheless, discretion was one of the butler's strengths, and Samuel paid him a king's ransom for it.

He bounced Myfanwy higher in his grasp and was just about to charge up the stairs when familiar and perplexing voices stopped him in his tracks. Myfanwy and he exchanged curious glances as he slowly—and reluctantly—set her feet on the ground. She smoothed her dress in front of her before taking short, intrepid steps to the drawing room, only pausing to sneak a peek at the mirror on the wall, no doubt making sure the word *sex* wasn't written on her forehead in black ink.

The conversation increased in volume, and Samuel couldn't place the odd mixture of voices he heard. He was sure he could identify them one by one, but together they made no sense at all.

Together they halted at the entrance to the room, stretching their necks inside to inspect the activity. Nothing could have prepared Samuel for what awaited him.

Normally, Sarah would have whisked the children to the nursery by this hour, and *normally* Aunt Abigail would have been comfortably situated in her own home, and *normally* Joe Danvers and Benny Hardcastle would have been glued to their seats at the Flying Batsman.

However, Samuel surmised, nothing about this day had been normal, so why would it start now?

Catching sight of the duo in the doorway, Benny lifted his tiny teacup in salute, one gnarled pinky finger raised imperiously in the air. "'Allo, coach," he said jovially, sitting prim and proper in one of the room's dainty Queen Anne chairs. It squeaked tremulously as he shifted toward Samuel. "Joe and I were in the neighborhood and wanted to stop by and discuss the lineup for the big match next week. No rest for the wicked and all that, you know."

Samuel thought he nodded, but he couldn't be sure. Seeing was believing, but he couldn't be positive that he was truly witnessing his two old teammates sitting demurely in his drawing room, sipping pretend tea from a little girl's miniscule tea set with Aunt Abigail and Aaron across from them.

"Mr. Hardcastle, I already told you," Aunt Abigail said with a remonstrating frown. "You don't just lift your pinky finger when drinking the tea. You use it to balance your cup, so you don't spill." She sighed, giving Samuel a put-upon look. "So, you're back, then? Did you speak to the children's grandparents?"

Samuel shook his head, rubbing his temple, attempting to get his brain to catch up on this situation. He was supposed to be upstairs making love to Myfanwy. How had everything been turned upside down?

"Why are you here?" he asked, ignoring her question. Out of the corner of his eye, he noticed blood rush to Myfanwy's cheeks. She must have been thinking the same thing he was. Because fuck it all, they'd forgotten that they were supposed to stop at the grandparents' village before returning that night. They'd been... Well, they'd been preoccupied.

Abigail placed her little teacup and saucer on the end table, arching a pointed brow, clearly annoyed Samuel didn't answer her query. "If you must know, I came by to apologize." She pursed her lips in distaste, as if she'd never apologized to anyone before. "I was harsh yesterday...about the children. Some of the things I said were rather...abrupt. But, in my defense, I was shocked and unsure of how to handle myself. I came here because I wanted"—she closed her eyes, swallowing—"my little niece to know that none of this is her fault and that I welcome her to the family. Wholeheartedly."

Myfanwy trod further into the space. "Oh, Aunt Abigail, of course we know that. You don't have to apologize—"

Her aunt held up a hand, stopping Myfanwy cold. "No. It needed to be said. But when I arrived, I found your nanny or servant or governess... Who is she, exactly?"

"My barman's oldest daughter," Samuel piped in.

Abigail's eyes landed dull and flat on him. "Ah," she said, running her tongue over her teeth. "I think I'll have to remedy that and find a proper governess for the children because—"

"Sarah is doing a wonderful job," Myfanwy replied.

"Hardly wonderful," her aunt argued. "When I walked in the door, they were playing tea right here, of all places, and *Sarah* didn't have the first inkling on how to do it correctly! For heaven's sake, there were no napkins on laps, and she advised Belle to pick the teacup up and leave the saucer on the table." Her face was mottled, her brows drawn all the way to her hairline in utter confusion. "I told you, Mr. Everett. I told you that you weren't fit for this—"

"He is!" Myfanwy broke in, but up came her aunt's hand again. The woman would make a formidable cricket umpire.

"No, he isn't," Abigail said. "But I am."

The room fell silent. The only sound that could be heard was Aaron as he munched on a biscuit that Samuel hoped was real and not a part of the pretend tea set.

"I will help you," Abigail said, rising from her seat. "She is my niece, after all. Belle and Aaron need my help if they're going to have any chance of getting out of this house knowing which fork to use at dinner."

Samuel was about to tell the woman that he never had any clue which fork to use and that he was navigating the world fine enough, but Aaron stopped him.

"Me?" he squeaked. "You want to help Annabelle...and me?"

Samuel's heart cracked for the boy, who clearly couldn't restrain himself from asking the question. Aaron, who had already seen the harsh realities of this world and knew they didn't lessen for children, stared at the older woman, his emotions bare and exposed.

"Of course, dear boy," Abigail returned, her expression softening. "You're family now too, aren't you?

Aaron couldn't find the words, and Samuel completely understood, considering he'd had that very same problem only minutes before. The boy could only nod, lowering his head and swatting at his eyes before anyone could see his tears.

"Now that that's settled," Abigail said, clapping her hands together, "tell me about the grandparents. I will have to talk to them if they expect the children to live with them. I will have to explain that we have just as much a right to them as they do, and that they would be better off here in civilized London and not out"—her lips curled away from her teeth—"in the country."

Myfanwy sighed, and Samuel saw her roll her eyes. He rubbed a hand over the back of his neck. "Um, we didn't... Ah...

There wasn't…"

"Aaron was right," Myfanwy said. She walked over to his side and furtively pinched his back. "They weren't good people."

Abigail nodded approvingly. "So that's it, then?"

Myfanwy turned to Samuel, and he met her gaze. He stared at those big brown eyes feeling everything she was wordlessly telling him. And he agreed with it all.

A gentle smile came to his face, and she gave one in turn. "That's it," he said.

Aaron picked up his little sister and smacked a kiss to her chubby cheek. "We're yours now?"

Samuel grinned at the boy and was about to respond when Benny decided his commentary was needed. "What about us?" he said, throwing a biscuit into his great maw and flicking his head to Joe. "Can we stay too?"

Samuel's grin immediately evaporated. "You two can get out now. I'll see you tomorrow." He shared a look with Myfanwy. "I've got more important things to do than discuss cricket."

Chapter Twenty-Five

MYFANWY YAWNED, STRETCHING her arms over her head. Or she tried to. Something was wrapped around her middle, making any movement next to impossible. She opened her eyes— and was staring straight into Samuel Everett's slumbering face.

"Go back to sleep," he grumbled, tightening his grasp on her hips.

Myfanwy felt impossibly warm—and confused—as Samuel covered her like a blanket, intertwining their legs like a Celtic knot underneath the sheets.

She felt his groan all the way to her bones. "You're thinking too loud," he muttered.

"What... I don't..." Myfanwy stammered. "What are you doing here?"

"This is my bedroom."

"I know that, but you usually aren't in it...at this time," Myfanwy added awkwardly. They'd spent many nights together in this bed, but she'd never woken up next to him. Samuel always made such a point to leave bright and early, avoiding her.

Samuel's two-toned eyes finally opened, and they searched her as if she had gone insane. "Can't a man sleep late in his bed with a beautiful woman?"

Myfanwy was annoyed by how those little words managed to

make her chest flutter. And by how the lazy way his hands roved around her hips made it so difficult to follow the conversation.

Samuel shifted, pressing his pelvis into hers in a snug embrace that left very little to the imagination. "We didn't get to sleep until late, if you'll remember. You kept me rather busy."

Myfanwy's cheeks felt positively scorched. She dipped her head under his chin, inhaling the warm, musky scent of his body. "I don't recall you complaining."

His laugh rumbled against her cheek. "I didn't, and I'm not now."

Samuel's hand wove a path down her side, riding the crest of her thigh until it landed between her legs. Myfanwy's face could not possibly get any hotter. She could feel *and hear* how wet she still was from their lovemaking.

Samuel placed light kisses on her neck as he played with her folds, sleepily, dreamily. "I've never had a woman wake up next to me before," he said, his voice impossibly low. "I like it."

His petting became more insistent, and Myfanwy gripped his shoulder, not able to control the undulations of her lower half. "Do you like it, or do you like me?"

His grin was pure wolf. "Both?" He chuckled gruffly. "What about you?"

The tips of his fingers skipped over the small button of nerves of her sex, and she let out a faint mew. "I like both too," she panted, curving her pelvis insistently toward him, trying to gain more friction.

Without preamble, Samuel pressed two fingers into her. Immediately, Myfanwy's breath hitched, and she jerked away.

"Fuck," Samuel said, lifting his head, scowling. "It's too much. Too soon. We should let your body rest."

Should they? Myfanwy wondered. Because it hadn't hurt *that* much—she'd just been caught off guard by the pinch. And...she didn't want to stop. Now that her seduction had ended, she only wanted to reap the benefits.

Her expression must have been telling, because Samuel's grin came back, just as lustful as it had been before. "I have an idea," he said, sliding from the mattress.

"I don't like any ideas that have you leaving the bed," she grumbled. But Samuel only laughed, walking across the room as naked as the day he was born to the chest of drawers against the far wall.

This was nothing to complain about. The view was entirely to Myfanwy's liking. There would never come a time when Samuel's body didn't astound her...or make her mouth water. He was godlike to her with his long, sinuous limbs and bulging muscles. Just holding him felt like she held all the power in the world. And to make Myfanwy feel even more potent, she noticed that his gait was natural and even, with nary a limp in sight. She wondered if she'd just met him whether she would be able to notice one at all.

And that was because of her. If Myfanwy was being fanciful, she might conclude that it was her love that fixed him; however, it was probably more her lust. If the man could inspire anything, it was that.

Samuel plucked the familiar cotton sack from the drawers and returned to the bed, a devilish expression on his face. "It's your turn," he said, sliding in next to her, throwing the sheets off.

Myfanwy shivered when the wave of cold hit her. Samuel shivered as well, but for very different reasons.

For a moment, they both stared at her naked body, at her nipples instantly growing turgid and puckered from the temperature *and* attention.

Samuel placed his hand over her stomach, stretching his fingers to encompass the entire plane. "You are magnificent," he said, his voice a heady mixture of awe and longing.

"So are you."

"No." He shook his head, moving his hand in circles. "You tell me that you won't break, but I have a hard time understanding that. Priceless things are supposed to be more delicate." He released a ragged breath. "But this—you are the single most precious thing in the world to me."

Two pink spots formed on his cheeks, and Myfanwy wondered if Samuel knew what he was telling her. He loved her. For how long, she wasn't sure, but he was as madly in love with her as she was him. Which made her next move much less intimidating.

Lifting her arm, Myfanwy reached for Samuel's manhood, which stood thick and tumescent next to her. She heard him hiss and squeezed her fist around the base, just holding him, watching as he appeared to grow even more under her grasp.

"Up and down," he whispered hoarsely. "Slowly at first. You pump me up and down. Yes, just like that, sweetheart. Fuck." Samuel's head fell back, and he stared at the ceiling, his Adam's apple popping from his throat.

Myfanwy loved the feel of him, all silky and sleek, glossy and heated, totally at her mercy. But something felt like it was missing, even with all his erotic moans and panted breaths that were making her rather inflamed.

She turned on her side and leaned over, deciding her next move before she could think twice. Myfanwy licked the top of his staff like it was dollop of cream, startling Samuel out of his moment of pleasure.

"Christ!" he cried, planting his hand at the back of her head. Myfanwy glanced up. His golden chest was heaving like he'd just run up a mountain. His eyes were round with shock.

"Too much?" she asked, already knowing the answer.

Samuel moved his hand to the front of her face and swept his thumb across her lower lip. She bit into it, and the tendons of his neck pulsed. "Never," he said.

"Good." Myfanwy went back to him, working his staff while she figured out what to do with her mouth. Samuel gave her no coaching on this part of the act, allowing her imagination and curiosity to inform her. When she'd coated his tip in kisses and licks, she ran her tongue down the side of him, tasting from the base all the way to the top. Samuel trembled uncontrollably, muttering barely coherent words as he bucked in her grasp.

Myfanwy had worried that she wouldn't like the taste of him but was pleasantly surprised. Samuel's flavor was exotic and salty, spicy and masculine, and she decided she would enjoy him even more in her mouth. On an inhale, she swallowed him and took him as deep down her throat as she could, hearing a slew of curses on the outside of her concentration.

"Suck me, sweetheart," Samuel groaned, bucking into her mouth, and instantly Myfanwy understood what he needed. She tightened her lips around him, sucking in her breath as her mouth replaced her hand and she moved up and down his manhood. She remembered her tongue, and when she swirled it around his thickness, Samuel grabbed her shoulders and quickly released himself from her hold.

When he was free, he threw her back on the bed and covered her, locking their mouths in a frenzied kiss that told her that he very much appreciated her little experiment.

Samuel was frantic, palming her breasts, massaging them with his calloused hands. Myfanwy's body was beyond control. She surged underneath him like a wave, rolling and swelling from all the sensation coursing through her. "Let me keep going," she whined as Samuel latched on to her breast, sucking with the same intensity she'd bestowed on him.

"No," he choked out, kissing a trail to the other nipple, laving the mound, cupping it in his hand. "This was supposed to be about you."

"It is about me."

"No," he repeated, leaning back to reclaim the brown sack. His fingers shook as he took out the oil and poured some in his hands. He rubbed them together as she had done before in their massage sessions and placed them on the tops of her thighs, caressing her tender skin in a calm, meandering way that belied his ragged breaths.

Samuel's head was low, and it tracked his hands closely like a sculptor admiring his own work. "It's about time we used this tincture the way it was meant to be used."

Myfanwy climbed up on her forearms; however, the effort cost. Seeing how happy and content Samuel looked as he explored her body almost made her combust then and there. "What do you mean? How is it supposed to be used?"

He laughed near her skin, causing goosebumps to form. His hands traveled further and further toward the apex between her legs. "You aren't so innocent as that still? You know what the girl, Holly, does for a living?"

"Of course."

"Well..." Samuel focused on her inner thighs, moving his hands higher, inch by inch, until he was just below her sex. He kneaded her there, his grip hard and unrelenting as he forced the ache in the muscles to relent. "Now that you're well versed in the art of making love, I'm sure you have a greater appreciation for those that do it on a nightly—sometimes hourly—basis."

Was he still talking? Myfanwy wasn't sure. Her mind had to choose between listening to his words or feeling the blessed sensations he was showering her with. It was an easy choice.

"They use this tincture so they can repair their body, be supple and ready for another customer."

Myfanwy's smile widened. "Are you my customer, then?"

"The only one you'll ever have."

Samuel wasn't looking at her when he said it, but his cheeks flushed once more, divulging more of his heart than he knew.

It was all too much for Myfanwy. She needed him. Now.

She closed her legs and shifted up to sitting. Samuel opened his mouth in protest, and she stopped him with one finger over his lips. She maneuvered him until he was back on his heels, and she situated herself on top of him, her legs on either side of his.

Face to face, nose to nose, they contemplated one another for long seconds. Every time Samuel tried to kiss her, she jerked just out of his reach. Then, just when she couldn't take his adorable scowl any longer, Myfanwy lifted on her knees, centering his rod at her entrance. Slowly, oh so slowly, she impaled herself on him, allowing her body to acclimate once more to his overwhelming force. This time when Samuel's mouth opened, she placed her lips on him, not kissing, only exchanging hiccups of breaths; they fed each other their souls as they shared the riotous sensations.

Eventually, Myfanwy rested on his thighs, taking him fully. Samuel closed his eyes with a groan, and he didn't budge, content to pulse and be sheathed by her. He gripped the flesh of her thighs, waiting...waiting, waiting, for Myfanwy to move.

It was a small development, a flutter and flex of muscles, really. Then Myfanwy arched her back, grinding into Samuel's lap, feeling him massage her inner muscles as proficiently as he had her outside ones. She let her head fall back, and her breasts pushed against his chest, proving too much for him. Samuel lapped and supped on her as she began to undulate, moving up and down, little by little. If cricket was truly a game of inches, so was lovemaking. The tiniest movement could create an avalanche of skin-tingling reactions.

But soon, even that was not enough. Samuel took charge, lifting and lowering her on him; the sound of skin slapping on skin filled the room as erotically as Samuel filled her. Myfanwy clutched the back of his neck, riding him with punishing strokes.

She felt him flicker inside her, knowing that he was close to finishing. Myfanwy wanted them to end this carnal journey together. She arched her pelvis even more, finding a new angle. Their bodies were slick with sweat, bright and gleaming in the morning light. Samuel was her angel—her guardian angel.

That thought tipped her over the cliff. They cried out at the same time, stretching and grinding their bodies even more against each other to sop up every last drop of euphoria from the act. Eventually, they flopped together onto the bed, still twined in each other's arms, still enchanted by what had just overtaken them.

"I suppose we should get up," Myfanwy said when she confirmed that she could speak again. "I'm sure you have a busy day ahead of you."

"I suppose," Samuel said, burrowing his head into her chest like a little boy who thought he could hide from the daylight. "You as well?"

Myfanwy played with his hair, twirling his wavy curls around her fingers. "Naturally. There are always calls to be made. Things to do."

Samuel pulled away, a wry smile on his lips. "We could also stay in."

She gnawed at her lower lip. "Stay in?"

"There are plenty of people here to keep us busy."

"That's true," she replied slowly. "But what would we do?"

"Play."

Chapter Twenty-Six

SAMUEL BOUNDED DOWN the stairs, an idiotic smile on his face. It was always there. Over the past two days while he and Myfanwy had been "playing," he couldn't get the damn thing off—not that he was trying, or even had the energy to. Myfanwy had been taking care of that.

Though, to be fair, her notion of playing and his were at different ends of the spectrum. Samuel had been more than willing to spend most of their nights—and days—in his bedroom, but alas, his sprightly woman had other ideas in her head.

Which was precisely why he found her now in the library, skirts dirty and hair bedraggled as she pleaded with her little sister. Samuel could barely contain his glee at the scene. Myfanwy looked as tired and lifeless as one of the dolls that she'd never wanted to play with.

"Again?" she asked Annabelle, who never seemed to run out of energy or stop asking her older sister to play.

It had taken longer than Myfanwy expected, but Annabelle had finally come around to her. And it was a classic case of *be careful what you wish for*, because now that Myfanwy was a favorite, she had to handle all that came along with it.

"Don't you want to go into the kitchens and see if Cook has baked some new biscuits?"

Annabelle twisted her lips to the side, squishing her adorable cheeks in thought. This ploy had worked the day before, and the moment Annabelle had retreated to the kitchen, Myfanwy took off for a long walk with Samuel to clear her mind.

Annabelle shook her head. "No. You left when I ate the cookie. Play now, Myfi!"

Myfi. Even after Myfanwy explained to the child that they were sisters, Annabelle only called her by her name. Myfanwy never said as much, but Samuel knew it upset her, and hoped that sometime soon Annabelle would make the change.

Myfanwy sighed in defeat. It seemed her cookie ploy would not be successful. Her little sister was a smart one. And not the least interested in cricket. Samuel hoped that changed as well, for Myfanwy's sake.

"Can I play?" he asked, walking into the room.

Annabelle clapped her hands, jumping up and down in her little pink slippers. Abigail had already chided him about them. Apparently, everything he'd bought for the little girl was pink; the older woman explained that a little variety wouldn't hurt.

"Yes. Yes. Yes. Yes," she squealed. "Sam play. Sam play. Sam and Myfi play!"

"Fine!" Myfanwy grumbled, sitting up straight on the chaise to make room for Samuel. He took it readily, loving the way she fell into him when his weight sank into the cushion. "I've hid something in the house, and you have to find it. Do you think you can do that?"

Annabelle's countenance sobered with a nod, and her eyes grew as big as dinner plates.

"I'm not sure," Myfanwy drawled. "I hid my special blue ribbon, and it could be anywhere. *Anywhere* in the entire house."

"Anywhere?"

Myfanwy nodded. "Anywhere. If you find it, then I'll have Cook make a special dessert tonight." She leaned over to the girl, her nose skimming Annabelle's. "With cherries."

Annabelle was back to jumping and clapping, and instantly

became a blur of pink and red as she dashed from the room, searching for the hidden ribbon.

Grabbing the opportunity, Samuel stole a quick kiss from Myfanwy and lay down on the chaise, using her lap for a pillow. "You're such a good older sister." He might have purred when she threaded her fingers through his hair, loving the feel of her nails grazing across his scalp. "Where did you hide it?"

"Hide what?"

"The ribbon."

"I didn't hide a ribbon."

Samuel surveyed her critically and deduced that she was serious. "So, are you telling me that you just sent your sweet, young, naïve—and did I mention sweet—little sister on a wild goose chase through my three-story townhouse?"

Myfanwy threw him a bemused expression, pulling at the ends of his hair. "People don't care about the end result; the search is the most important part, the thrill."

"Yes," Samuel replied dryly, "I'm sure Galahad concluded the same thing when he came upon the Holy Grail."

"Oh stop," she said, slapping his stomach. "I just needed a reprieve. I'll get her soon. Besides, that child is like a bloodhound with a scent. I wouldn't be surprised if she really did find a blue ribbon somewhere."

Samuel reached up for one of her loose tendrils, fanning it against his palm. "She's at a fun age. You know, I don't think you were that much older the first time I met you."

Myfanwy's nose crinkled. "I don't remember."

"You mean you don't remember the exact day you first saw me?" Samuel huffed, pretending to be offended. "I'm shocked. Especially since you became so obsessed with me later. I chiefly recall feeling you undressing me with your eyes during my last year playing."

"What? Are you..." Myfanwy's mouth slackened, but nothing sputtered out. Her face turned the same shade as Annabelle's slippers, and she shook her head as if contemplating whether to speak more or stab him in the heart with her shoe.

Instead, with a flick of her wrist, she rolled him off her lap, dumping him on the floor. "I never undressed you with my eyes," she retorted sharply, trying not to smile as Samuel cackled at her.

"Well, then I stand corrected, although I'm sure you wanted to," he replied with a wink. "Although…it didn't look like your father was dragging you to my matches by your braids. You seemed *thoroughly* engrossed."

"You fiend!" Myfanwy laughed as Samuel crawled back on the couch, tentatively retaking his place on her lap. "Did anyone check your brain when that ball smacked you in the eye? Because sometimes I wonder."

Samuel knocked on his head with his knuckles. "Right as rain."

Myfanwy snorted, sticking her chin in the air. "Maybe I was engrossed, but it didn't have anything to do with you. Well…it didn't have *everything* to do with you."

Damn. Samuel's smile *really* wouldn't go away. "Go on."

"I know my father took me to some games when I was Annabelle's age, but I don't recall them," she explained, gazing off to where the little girl had fled. "I do remember when he began to take me more after my mother passed away." Samuel held her hand, and she smiled, albeit sadly. "I was so transfixed by the green field, the way the sun hit the blades of grass, making everything seem new and sparkly. I remember—"

"Me in my little cap."

"No!" Myfanwy chuckled. "I mean, yes, a little. But—please don't take this the wrong way—it was more than that. Our house was so large and quiet. I never had cousins or friends or siblings to play with. It was just him and me. And then he took me to the cricket grounds. And this whole world opened up. You and all your teammates seemed so close, like best friends. And the easy way you dealt with each, the laughter, and little jokes… It was a revelation. A real family. Right then and there I wanted it, and I vowed that I would have something similar one day. A community of people so I would never be lonely again."

Samuel brought one of her tendrils up to her nose, tickling the somberness away. "So, you weren't infatuated with me. It really *was* the sport that caught you from the beginning."

"Oh no, I *was* infatuated with you." Myfanwy giggled, bending over for a quick kiss. "But that came a little later. Cricket drew me in first. The fellowship and fraternity of it all. People don't understand how important sport is. And not just for men, but for women too."

Samuel palmed the back of her neck and brought her down to him once more, answering her with another kiss. A longer one this time, one that lingered and said *I love you* in every language known to man. When he released her, her lips were swollen and glossy.

"You're exactly right. Thank you for telling me this," he said. "But I still think you were undressing me with your eyes."

IT WAS ONLY right that the sole thing with the power to yank the couple out of the safety and serenity of their home was cricket. With the game against the matrons set for the coming weekend, the team only had one more practice to prepare themselves and—more importantly—calm their nerves.

Samuel put the ladies through their paces, lengthening their practice by an hour that Wednesday afternoon, forcing them through each and every drill he could think of—from balancing while batting to the mundane catch-and-throw techniques that the women always whined about. Samuel ignored their eye rolls and curt asides. Practice wasn't supposed to be fun. One practiced and practiced, doing the same motions over and over again so that muscle memory took root. Thinking could be dangerous on the pitch. Too much of it could lead to overanalyzing and second-guessing. Samuel didn't need his players to think; that was *his* job.

He just needed them to play the way he knew they could. Practice—however mundane—was a necessary evil.

Besides, without those punishing three hours, the ladies wouldn't have had the privilege of standing in a half-circle around him now, flushed and wind-swept, eyes shining and expectant, bodies strong but exhausted.

And exhilarated. So very exhilarated.

"That wasn't too horrible," Samuel concluded, locking his hands behind his back. "Be at the pitch early on Saturday. A good thirty minutes before the match begins so you can warm up." He nodded to the two men standing proud next to him. "Joe and Benny will be there to bowl a few if you want to heat up the bat. So…other than that… Good job. Thank you for coming today."

Samuel nodded again, punctuating the end of his little speech. He thought to move on toward the tavern, but the blank looks he received from the ladies kept his feet firmly in place.

"That's it?" Lady Everly remarked with her familiar bluntness. "That's all you have to say to us?"

"Go on, Sam," Joe added, a shy smile hovering on his face. "You got more than that."

Did he? Samuel wasn't sure what they were asking of him. He'd been on countless teams and had more coaches than stars in the sky, and he couldn't recall one of them being particularly encouraging before a big match.

However, that was them. That was the way things used to be, and it used to work for him. But Samuel was different now.

"Um, right," he said gruffly, then cleared his throat. He caught Myfanwy staring at him with a wry grin, naturally understanding his inner bafflement. "Well…"

Joe saved him. "Ladies," he said austerely, taking off his cap like he was about to kneel and propose. "I… Well, me and Benny here," he said, getting a reassuring gesture from his friend. "We can't thank you enough for letting us be a part of your team—"

Joe broke off as a telltale wobble came to his voice, and he lowered his head. All of a sudden, it struck Samuel how much Joe had changed this past month. One could say it was the booze—and no doubt that *had* played a large role in his transformation—but Samuel knew it was more than that. His complexion had lost its ruddy, greasy shine, and Joe resembled the man he used to be, the one whose legs were as valued and applauded as any great stallion's. His countenance was also altered. Joe's neck might be bowed now, but Samuel was certain that once he lifted his head, his shoulders would be pulled wide, his back straight. Joe Danvers was a man who'd regained some confidence in who he was and who he could be.

Joe blew out a long breath and raised his head. His eyes were noticeably red. "I...ah... I don't know where I'd be if I didn't have this, so... Ah...you know..." He put a hand over his mouth. Benny came up to his side and threw an arm around his shoulder, whispering something indecipherable into the man's ear. Joe's chest shuddered from the emotion of it all.

Slowly, a trickle of sound filled the precarious silence, and Samuel noticed the ladies had begun clapping. Soon, the soft, polite claps morphed into something greater, something akin to the crowds that once cheered Joe and Benny's names not so long ago.

Their heads angled together, the two men responded with bashful grins, shoving their caps back on, allowing the ladies to applaud them in their own special way.

And yet, when it was over, his team still stayed in its place, waiting for more from him.

Samuel's chest was tight, as if something was growing inside him, begging to be released. He took his time, contemplating his players, giving each one a hard stare before moving on to the next. Mimicking Joe, he snatched his cap from his head, rolling it around in his hands.

"I'm not great with words," he began. "It's difficult to know the right thing to say."

"You don't seem to have that problem when you're yelling at us," Anna remarked, causing the others to snicker.

"You provide wonderful inspiration for that," Samuel snapped jovially. His chuckle faded, and he squinted up at the sun, sore that addressing the ladies was proving to be so difficult. Thoughts of what Myfanwy had told him earlier, about how she'd yearned for the camaraderie of a team, came back to him.

He looked back to her. Myfanwy's grin was no longer teasing. Her tanned face was as safe and loving as her arms whenever she held him, and equally freeing.

"The life I was living before you all came into it wasn't much of a life at all," Samuel began steadily. "I spent my hours just putting one foot in front of the other, trying to get through to the next day. I thought my best years were behind me. I was wrong." His voice became high at the last moment as he attempted to keep his emotions in check. Myfanwy, true to her nature, didn't bottle anything inside. The sun glinted off her tears as they trailed down her cheeks. "Even with all that I've accomplished on the pitch, I can say now that these few weeks with you have been some of the best I've ever experienced." Samuel willed Myfanwy to keep looking at him. "And that's because of you."

"Um…" Lady Everly said, her tone cutting through the heightened atmosphere. "Are you speaking to Myfanwy or all of us?"

Samuel blinked. And climbed out of his daze. He raised his brow at Lady Everly. "Myfanwy—and you!" he hurried to add, raising his arms at his sides. "Everyone. All of you, obviously!"

The team chuckled at his befuddlement, and Samuel could feel his cheeks blazing to high heaven. He shook his head at his sorry state and decided to wrap up his awkward speech. "So, if any of you are lucky enough to still be unmarried next year, I'd love to coach you again. If, that is, you'll have me."

Anna crossed her arms, jutting out her hip. "And what if we *are* married?"

Samuel sighed, slapping his cap back on his head. "Well, Anna, since you'll probably be playing for the other team, I'll most likely exploit your weaknesses to the best of my ability, so we rout you good and proper."

Anna tried to suppress a smile as she exchanged looks with Lady Everly. Then she nodded in approval. "That's a good answer, coach. A very good answer."

➤➤➤◀◀◀

A QUIET KNOCK sounded, and Myfanwy entered his office, closing the door discreetly behind her.

Samuel dropped the paper he was holding on the top of his desk and lazed back in his chair. "I thought you would be on your way home by now."

Myfanwy meandered over to him, a thoughtful crease in the middle of her forehead. He didn't think she was doing it on purpose, but her hips had a special sway to them this afternoon. He'd noticed it at practice as well. He'd had to will his cockstand away countless times over the three hours, mostly by bringing up mental pictures of men playing football. It was a pointless sport. Who wanted to play a game that wouldn't let you use your hands? *Silly.*

"No," Myfanwy replied, that crease getting deeper. "Jennifer wasn't here today. It's not like her to miss a practice, especially such an important one. I hope she isn't ill." She shrugged, perching her bottom on the edge of his desk, one long leg dangling idly in front of him. "It's my fault. I haven't written or called."

"Don't be so hard on yourself," Samuel said, utterly beguiled by the innocent white stocking that peeked out from underneath her skirt. So feminine. So lovely. "You've been busy."

She must have heard the libertine insinuation in his voice, because her cheeks bunched up merrily with a thin smile. "You mean *we've* been busy."

"Oh, I'm always busy," Samuel remarked, sliding his chair toward her, caging her as he placed his hands on her hips. Good

Lord, would his desire for her ever end? Not when she looked at him like that.

"What?" Myfanwy said, cocking her head.

"I hate to tell you this, but you're undressing me with your eyes."

She huffed. "I'm merely looking at you."

"No," Samuel said, inching closer. "You're thinking about me in bed, naked, as beautiful and well-formed as Zeus himself."

She slung her arms over his shoulders. "Oh, so you're a god now."

"I am to you."

Myfanwy rolled her eyes, pushing him away. "Such narcissistic nonsense."

"I can't help it." He laughed, picking her arms up and putting them on his shoulders again. "You feed my ego with your lusty glances."

"They're hardly lusty."

"They give me ideas," he said playfully, ignoring her temper. "So, it's best you leave now and check on Jennifer before I act on them."

Even as Samuel warned Myfanwy, he pressed closer. It couldn't be helped. Their magnetism was pure nature. He was the bee, and she was the most succulent flower.

Her mouth opened, and Samuel could hear her breathing become shallower. Her teeth tapped together as if she were weighing what to say next. Her curiosity won out. "What ideas?"

Goddammit. A rush of sinfully delicious coupling positions attacked his brain. But one...one position held prominence over them all.

"Oh," he drawled, rubbing her thigh. "Let's just say I've had fantasies of getting you into this office for a while now. They involve you and a particular piece of furniture."

"A desk?" A nervous giggle escaped her, and Myfanwy peered down at the large mahogany desk. "What could be so enticing about a desk?"

Working completely of their own accord, Samuel's hands dipped underneath her skirt and began a thorough exploration. They skated along those silk stockings until they reached bare, soft, sizzling skin.

"It's not the desk," he answered wickedly. "It's you on it."

Myfanwy's tone was wary, yet she couldn't hide the tinge of yearning. "I am on it, aren't I?"

Samuel nodded, lifting her skirts up to her hips, exposing the source of *his* yearning. "I had something different in mind," he said, lowering his head to her core, inflating his lungs with the salty, sweet aromas of her need. He felt her lean back on her forearms, knocking a pile of his papers to the floor. "Are you sure you don't want to leave now?" He licked her seam in another warning shot.

Her legs jerked. "I have time. Besides," she added with a halting chuckle, "how can I leave now? You have me so very curious."

Samuel smiled into her mound. He wasn't in the mood to take his time. He went straight for her pearl and flicked it with his tongue in languid strokes. Myfanwy's legs tightened against his ears. "Is that all you are?" he asked. "Curious?"

"Maybe"—she panted—"maybe a little more than curious."

"Maybe aroused?" he said, increasing the tempo of his tongue until her pelvis began to rock in time.

"Maybe," she yelped.

"And maybe, just maybe, you're impatient for my cock," Samuel went on, inserting one finger and curling it inside her delicate walls, "because you spent the afternoon undressing me and dreaming about it inside you, giving you exactly what you want, making you come."

Myfanwy was all deep breaths and shaky limbs now. She flopped flat on the desk, arching her pelvis into his mouth, begging him to release her from her torment. "Fine, fine," she sighed. "Whatever you want me to say, just keep going. I'm almost... Oh God, I'm almost there."

That would not do. That would not do at all.

Samuel snapped his head up from her legs and laughed at her groan.

"What are you—" Myfanwy's tirade was cut off as Samuel rose to his feet. In a flash, he flipped her on the table, situating her belly-down against the top and maneuvering her legs so they hung off the end. Her arse was plump and beautiful as it stared invitingly up at him from the edge.

Samuel's hand went straight to his heart, and he left it there for a few calming breaths, as if to keep it in his chest. Round and creamy, her arse was like a bowl of milk he couldn't wait to drown himself in.

Myfanwy twisted her neck, glancing at him over her shoulder. "Is this how you envisioned me on the desk?" she asked, her voice decidedly saucy. She may even have wiggled that beautiful bottom of hers, but Samuel didn't notice. He was too far gone.

"Yes," he answered weightlessly.

"So, are you going to leave me waiting here? I told you...I have things I have to do. I'm a busy, grand lady."

Her words sparked him back to life. Samuel pawed at her globes, filling his palms with her mouth-watering flesh. He moved into her, lining up his cock at her entrance. "Yes, you are," he said, pumping into her in one swift thrust. "Much too grand for me, but I don't give a damn anymore."

Chapter Twenty-Seven

MYFANWY SPUN BACK to the carriage door, checking her reflection in the window to see if her hair was somewhat respectable. She brushed a few wisps off her face, sticking them in the bun at the base of her head and underneath her bonnet. Samuel had tried to help her recoup her propriety before she left his office; however, when he attempted to convince her to let her hair down for the afternoon, Myfanwy realized they had vastly different ideas on what that meant.

Hair *down*? When she was calling on Jennifer's home? Mrs. Hallett would have a fit at the sight, and no doubt, bar her from entering the respectable abode.

Samuel had also left her with the annoying thought that Mrs. Hallett would be able to smell their signature erotic scent the second she entered the house. Here, Myfanwy was on more solid ground. Mrs. Hallett might have four children, but Myfanwy doubted that the unyielding woman had any idea what lovemaking smelled like. If her husband ever tried to drape her over his desk, the rigid woman would probably break in half.

As the butler ushered Myfanwy into the foyer to wait, she was racked with guilt from the uncharitable thought. And then she felt even worse, because when Mrs. Hallett met her, she was positively glowing with delight at Myfanwy's unexpected appearance.

Myfanwy couldn't remember a time that Mrs. Hallett ever smiled at her before. She was so used to dismissive indifference that it took her a few beats to smile back.

"I'm terribly sorry, my dear, but Jennifer has not been feeling well," the older woman chirped. Myfanwy had never heard anyone speak so glowingly about another's ill health before.

"Oh," she said, becoming cagey under Mrs. Hallett's bright gaze. "Is it bad?"

Mrs. Hallett let out a billowing laugh, waving a thin hand in the air. "Oh, no, no. You mustn't worry yourself. It's just a little cold. She'll be back to her old self in no time."

"Oh," Myfanwy repeated, nibbling on her lip. She glanced at the stairs. "Do you think I could go up and visit her for a few minutes? Nothing too taxing—she just missed our last practice today, and I want to make sure she'll be ready for the match on Saturday."

Mrs. Hallett swept her arm behind Myfanwy's lower back, discreetly ushering her toward the door. "Oh, I don't think so. She's been sleeping all day. Best not to wake her."

Myfanwy resisted the pull. "It sounds worse than a little cold."

The older woman's cheeks flushed, and for the first time, Myfanwy saw her grow flustered. "I told you it's nothing, just a small fever. She'll be—" Mrs. Hallett dropped her arm when Myfanwy refused to take another step. She cocked her head, scrutinizing Myfanwy as if she were a diamond riddled with flaws.

Then, after an interminable pause, a wide grin broke out on the woman's face. She clapped her hands in front of her, hiding her excitement like a sheepish child. "Oh, I just can't lie to you, can I?" she crowed, sweeping Myfanwy into her arms.

Instantly, Myfanwy turned into a board as Mrs. Hallett swallowed her in a hug. She was too flabbergasted to even worry about Samuel's scent, which she was certain still clung to her like redolent vines.

"I...I suppose not," Myfanwy stammered, waiting to be released.

Finally, Mrs. Hallett stepped back, her skinny lips pink with joy. "I'm not supposed to tell anyone, but"—she squinted at Myfanwy playfully—"I have a feeling you already know and you just won't let on. I should be furious with you! All three of you," she said, swatting Myfanwy's arm lightly in jest. "I had such wonderful ideas for the wedding."

Myfanwy gulped. A cricket-sized ball was lodged in her throat. "Wedding?" she peeped.

"Of course!" Mrs. Hallett replied, not noticing Myfanwy's discomfort. She was too busy gazing off into the air in a dreamy trance. "It was going to take place at St. George's, and Jennifer's dress was going to be white like the queen's, and she was going to wear red roses in her hair." Her face dropped in a pout. "It was all going to be so perfect."

"But?"

She pointed her long nose back to Myfanwy and shrugged. "My daughter and Sir Bramble had other ideas. It was all in the letter."

A letter? "I don't understand."

"Stop pretending, Miss Myfanwy. I know you know. You probably put the idea in her head in the first place. I'm not angry at you, truly." She flicked a piece of hair off her face. "Well, to be completely honest, I was angry the first day—furious—but I'm over it now. All that matters is that no one finds out that they eloped. We'll just announce it later, say it was a small, lovely, private wedding, and that will be that. My mother was a seamstress. Now my daughter will be a baroness. Who can ask for anything more?"

Myfanwy was starved for breath. How had this happened? And right under her nose. She and Jennifer told each other everything. And for some inexplicable reason, her best friend had failed to tell her about the most important thing in her life.

Jennifer had run off with Sir Bramble like a thief in the night. The more Myfanwy thought about it, the more it made sense. Jennifer had never wanted a large, ostentatious wedding. She didn't care a fig about the *ton*'s acceptance of her. So she'd fled with Sir Bramble. Away from her overbearing mother, who always made everything about herself...and her best friend, who wasn't much different.

Somewhere a line had been drawn, and Jennifer had seen fit to place Myfanwy on the other side of it.

Myfanwy shut her eyes. Her stomach rolled like she could be sick. "Um..." She cleared her throat. "Did the letter say when she'd be back?"

"Saturday, I think, why? Oh." Mrs. Hallett's eyes settled on her shrewdly. "You're still worried about your little match. Dear girl," she said, ushering Myfanwy, who was in no shape to stop her this time, to the door. "She can't possibly play with you now. She's a wife. She has much more important things to concern herself with."

Myfanwy didn't have the heart to resist her. Mrs. Hallett opened the door and shoved her across the threshold. "But...but..."

Mrs. Hallett's smile was rude and patronizing. "Don't be upset, Miss Myfanwy. You should be commended. Your little club did exactly what I needed it to do. It put my Jennifer in the right circles and helped her pass the time until her real life could start. You will always have my gratitude."

It was like she'd stepped in quicksand, and fighting was useless. Myfanwy felt herself sinking one miserable inch at a time. "But...but..."

"I know you're sad, but don't worry," Mrs. Hallett went on, slowly closing the door. "I'm sure your time will come soon. Every woman deserves a husband, and you're no different."

SOMETHING ODD HAPPENED in the short drive from Jennifer's home back to the Flying Batsman.

The fog lifted from Myfanwy's opaque, insidious grief, and anger replaced it, strengthening and feeding off itself as she came closer to the tavern. It was as if Myfanwy had swallowed the fury, and it thumped and scratched inside her body, threatening to rip out of her unless she released it willingly.

And as she stormed through the busy tavern, whipping Samuel's office door open without knocking, she was more than willing.

He looked up from his desk, a ready smile on his face. "Missed me, did—" His words broke off as he sobered, realizing swiftly that now wasn't the time for teasing. "What's wrong? Is it Jennifer?" he asked, rising from his chair.

With long strides, Samuel came to Myfanwy, attempting to take her in his arms, but she smoothly evaded him. "Yes, it's Jennifer," she spat, holding her middle, closing herself off. "And don't act like you don't know what's happened. Were you ever going to tell me? Or was this always going to be your little secret with your business partner?"

Recognition flickered over his face. "Sir Bramble? What does he have to do with me?"

Myfanwy shook her head, amazed that the anger could roar so unrelentingly inside her. "I told you not to get involved. I told you not to pass their letters. And you didn't listen to me."

His features hardened. He was finally aware of where this argument was heading. Good. The last thing she wanted was for Samuel to grovel or beg her forgiveness. Myfanwy wasn't in the mood to play—she wanted to fight.

Samuel's voice was remarkably calm. "I told you. They asked me to help, and I helped. I thought it was harmless."

"But it wasn't harmless, Samuel!" Myfanwy railed, bent over from the pain of the betrayal. "They ran off to Gretna Green. They're probably exchanging vows as we speak. And we're here. We're...here and can't do anything about it."

"What's there to do, Myfanwy? It's out of your control. They love each other. They want to spend the rest of their lives together. This isn't the catastrophe you think it is."

Myfanwy's eyes narrowed.

Samuel hurried to continue. "You love Jennifer. She's your best friend in the world, and I know you want the best for her. Trust that she knows that Sir Bramble is that. So she won't play in the game on Saturday. You don't have to worry about that; you know we'll still win."

"This isn't about winning," Myfanwy said, annoyed that it came out on a sob. Tears and anguish pulled at her until she was helpless to fend them off. She wiped the mess off her face, but it just kept coming. "It's about staying together. Being in charge of our own lives, doing what pleases us, and not what pleases a husband. We are a unit. A family. We have each other. And now that dream is over. Can you see that? Now can you see what you've done? Everything I've worked for, everything I've ever wanted, is now gone."

Samuel's words were quiet; nevertheless, they still managed to prick at her sensitive skin. "She's not Lilly *fucking* Gladwell. Just because she's married, doesn't mean she'll leave you behind."

"You don't know that."

"Oh, yes I do," he said, taking tentative steps toward her. "And the other girls will get married too. You know it. It's inevitable. You're fooling yourself if you don't see it."

Myfanwy lifted her head. "Then maybe I'm a fool. Because I allowed myself to picture this life years ago, and it only took a couple of men a matter of weeks to ruin it for me."

Ruin. Yes. There was that word again. Samuel had ruined her—only not like she'd thought he would.

She lumbered past him to his seat, flopping down in it, holding her head in her hands. Myfanwy felt like a petulant child, but he couldn't understand. *Of course* she knew Jennifer would get married someday. But she'd always pushed that day off to the far horizon of her mind, always thinking they had more time—and the same with the other women. This was her group. She'd found them. She'd *made* them. And now she had no idea who or what she would be when they left her.

Thoughts of rebuilding the team, year after year, season after season, seemed exhausting. Inviting in new members, investing in them, as others married and moved on, always playing against her old friends, and never with them. As Cremly had told her, Myfanwy would always be looked on as the loser in life, despite what the scorecard read at the end.

A lonely existence spanned out before her, one where meeting new ladies—creating new relationships—would only compound the heartache.

"Have I ever asked you to stop playing cricket?"

Myfanwy lifted her head out of her hands, dashing at her eyes to see Samuel clearly. He hadn't moved from his space. Everything about him, from his voice to his figure, reminded her of stone. Implacable and stagnant, just like her future.

She shook her head. "No."

Samuel nodded, his jaw tight. "That's good. I wanted to make sure you remembered that."

"That's not what this is about—"

"No, let me tell you what this is about," Samuel said. He reached out and pulled Myfanwy up from the seat, clutching her shoulders so she was forced to listen to him. "You built yourself a family from the ground up. You took that vow you made as a little girl, and for years you've been single-minded in making it come to life. But in the process, you've allowed your fears to take over. And I understand. You've been left behind by so many— your mother, your father, your friend, and now Jennifer. But you've become so obsessed with it that you've failed to see what's in front of you. You are a member of a team *and* a family. You have me and Annabelle and Aaron and your aunt. You have us. We're here, and we're not going anywhere."

Myfanwy observed the vulnerability in his features, and she desperately wanted to believe him.

But she didn't.

"Another lie," she said quietly. "You're going to leave too. I heard you talking to Sir Bramble that day. It's only a matter of time before you start playing again. And then it's like I'll be a child once more, watching you from the sidelines."

Samuel shook her, frustrated. "You're not listening to me. I'm yours. I'm here. I wouldn't do anything without knowing that you were behind me. I love you. And you love me—you're just too scared to admit it."

"Don't do that," Myfanwy said, breaking out of his grasp. "Don't tell me how I feel, and don't use those feelings against me. We were playing. You said it yourself. It—*you*—were never meant to eclipse everything in my life."

Samuel's face went white.

But Myfanwy couldn't stop. She couldn't get a hold of the thousands of feelings beating against her breast. Pain and betrayal and bitterness were like ink spilling on a white sheet, forever running and bleeding over everything else. "Bet on yourself, right? It was your father who said it. He's the one that told you to trust yourself and no one else. Well..." Myfanwy shrugged hopelessly. "It's good advice."

She headed to the door. It was stupid to have come here. She should have known it wouldn't help matters. Jennifer was still gone, and now Samuel had just muddied the waters further. Now was not the time to tell her that he loved her. Not with anger and resentment and irritation cracking the foundation beneath their feet. She had to think. She had to plan. She needed to find some semblance of control.

"Don't leave," Samuel barked as she clasped around the handle. He sighed. "I'm sorry I turned your life upside down; I'm sorry that your loving me—and you do love me—changes everything. But that's life, Myfanwy. It's an unrelenting, twisted, malevolently lovely thing that sometimes, just sometimes, gives us what we need instead of what we want."

There was a flutter against her palm. Myfanwy's face crumpled in a sob when she felt Samuel reach out to hold her hand, reach out to stop her, reach out to save her from being alone.

"You need me. You know do. Just as much as I need you."

But she wasn't ready. So much of Myfanwy's young life had been warped by change she hadn't seen coming. She refused to let it dictate her decisions when it was staring her in the face.

"That's the thing about growing up lonely," she said, imbuing her voice with steel. "You learn that you don't really need anybody."

And she unwound her hand from his and left.

Chapter Twenty-Eight

T HE NEXT FEW days drifted by in a blur of self-pity. Somewhere in the back of Myfanwy's disheartened mind, she
understood that Samuel wasn't to blame for Jennifer and Sir
Bramble's elopement. In fact, no one was to blame.

In the sanctuary of her bedroom, she chided herself for not
being as elated for her friend as she should be. Looking back,
Myfanwy had had a front-row seat to the burgeoning relationship. Jennifer hadn't hidden it from her—she'd even tried to tell
Myfanwy about her feelings for the baron from time to time, but
Myfanwy hadn't wanted to listen. If anyone was at fault, it was
her.

For not trusting her friend to know what was best for her. For
holding Jennifer back. For being terribly selfish and myopic.

One would think coming to terms with that realization
would have helped matters, but it only made Myfanwy condemn
herself more.

So, she continued to hide in her room, only leaving when she
was sure she wouldn't bump into anyone and be forced to speak,
or when she heard a messenger come to the door, hoping it was
news from Jennifer. She still held out hope a letter might come
saying Jennifer still wanted to play the match on Saturday, despite
her marital status.

But it wasn't only embarrassment that kept her secluded—it was shame.

For his part, Samuel gave her space. He only attempted to rouse her once, the day after their fight in the tavern. When she refused to open the door, he left her to it, telling her through the thick wood that he would be there to speak when she was ready.

Ready. Everything in her childhood had been done in an effort to make her ready to become the woman she would be. She couldn't help but think that she'd failed.

And so it went.

One early morning, Myfanwy lifted her head from her pillow, hearing a light, tentative knock on the door. *Cautious* was not a word she would ever use to describe Samuel, so she felt safe pulling herself off the bed to answer it.

Aaron appeared on the other side, his face mottled with concern as Myfanwy attempted to greet him as normally as possible.

"Hello, you," she said with a little cough. Her voice had been woefully underused of late. She tried again. "And how are you?"

The boy dug his hands in his pockets, idly toeing the bottom of the doorframe. "Oh, I'm fine, Miss Myfanwy. Real fine," he said, playing his own game of pretend. His restless body and flickering gaze that wandered to everything but her seemed anything but fine.

When the silence lengthened between them, Myfanwy said, "Did you need something, Aaron?"

"Yes, miss," he replied quickly, taking a deep breath as if thankful for the question. "Um... Well... Sam"—his cheeks blossomed red—"Mr. Everett, that is, wanted me to ask if you'd be ready to leave soon. He said it would be best to get there earlier than the rest of them."

"I'm sorry, ready?" Myfanwy glanced at the window, finding the pale sun just beginning to make its ascent, its streaks short and wan against her bedroom floor. "Ready for what?"

Aaron's eyes snapped to hers. "Why, for cricket. It's Saturday, Miss Myfanwy. Day of the match against the matrons."

His words struck her like a punch in the gut. Saturday? How had that happened? She could have sworn it was Friday. Had she truly been wallowing for three days? How utterly pathetic!

Myfanwy rubbed at her temple, giving the boy a contrite smile. "I apologize, Aaron. Yes, you're right. I should have known. Um... Please tell Mr. Everett that I'll be down within the hour."

As she went to close the door, Aaron struck his skinny arm out like a whip, stopping it at once. "No, miss," he said in a panic. "Mr. Everett is downstairs now. He told me you'd already be prepared. He's going to be mighty upset if he has to wait longer."

Myfanwy puffed out a short chuckle. Sounded like someone was fighting a case of nerves.

"I'm sorry," she said. "Inform Mr. Everett there's nothing to be done. I will be down as soon as I can."

It was more than obvious that Aaron didn't like that directive one bit. Upsetting Samuel was something the enamored boy couldn't fathom. He chewed on his cheek, mulling something over in his mind while he continued to stand there.

"You *are* going to come, aren't you, miss?" he asked, spitting the words from his mouth like they were gristle. "I mean...since Miss Jennifer hasn't returned yet...Mr. Everett said there was a chance you might not want to play, and I just..." The tips of his ears matched the color in his cheeks. "It doesn't seem right being there without you. You're the reason for all of this...after all."

It wasn't lost on Myfanwy what Aaron meant by "all of this." In a crippling moment, all the shame and remorse she'd felt over the last few days coalesced inside her again, its weight almost forcing her to the floor. But Myfanwy held her ground. She wouldn't fall with Aaron watching her. She wouldn't let her guilt chain her to the spectators' seats anymore.

She'd made a mistake. In her anger, she'd lashed out at Samuel and thrown his love back in his face. But she was still here. She was still standing. And she would fix it.

But she had to get ready for the bloody match first. You

couldn't win if you didn't play. It was as simple as that.

"Of course I'm coming," Myfanwy said with a reassuring smile. "And I know it's distasteful to hear this, but it *will* take me a moment to gather my things and get dressed. Tell Mr. Everett I will be down when I can."

Aaron still didn't appreciate the order—however, he relented, backing away from the door. When he'd taken a few steps, Myfanwy called out to him. "And Aaron?" she said. "Just so you know, it wouldn't feel right doing it without you either."

⫸⫷

MYFANWY WAS ONLY halfway through her ablutions and wiping water off her face when another knock came at the door. Not as hesitant this time—it was definitely more Samuel's style.

How in the world was she supposed to get ready when everyone's impatience kept stopping her? "Please," she said. "I need more time. I'll be down soon."

Myfanwy rolled her eyes when she heard his telltale growl. "You should have been ready by now. Are you truly coming or just wasting my time?" he asked.

That is it! Myfanwy sailed to the door, whipping it open. Whatever was on the tip of her tongue was instantly lost as she regarded Samuel. She hadn't laid eyes on him in days, and he looked positively sublime in his black jacket and tight, fitted pants. It was an austere outfit and incredibly imposing. A deep longing for him to hold her spasmed in her chest.

Samuel was not having the same tongue-tied issue as her. His eyes narrowed dangerously on her dressing gown. "You haven't even changed yet?" he thundered.

Myfanwy crossed her arms defensively. "I just woke up!" she roared back. "If you'd stop interrupting me, I can finish getting ready!" Caustically, she flicked her head toward the window. "It's barely morning, Samuel. Why did you think I'd be dressed at this hour?"

He straightened away as if her question had slapped him. "*I* am. *Aaron* is. You have a match today, if you remember."

"In the afternoon!"

Samuel sniffed. "A good player is prepared. I thought that would be you. Unless..." He cast her a furtive look from under his lashes. "Unless you weren't planning on joining us?"

"Why does everyone keep saying that?" Myfanwy cried, dropping her hands to her sides with a demonstrative *thump*. "Of course I'm going. How could you think I would miss it? Do you really have such a low opinion of me?"

Samuel widened his stance, bracing himself. The man prepared for an argument. Myfanwy wondered if he was harassing her at this ungodly hour only as a way to get her to open up and fight back. Anything was better than constant avoidance, and Myfanwy had been miserably avoiding everyone.

"After the last time you deigned to speak to me, I thought it was you that had the low opinion of me."

Samuel's words dropped like a cannonball. He was hurt. *She* had hurt him. Samuel played the aloof, apathetic *man with a heart of stone* well, but he couldn't fool her. There was pain behind his eyes, tension in his shoulders. She could sense the battle raging within him. He wanted to take her in his arms too, but he was holding himself back.

"I'm sorry," Myfanwy said softly. "I was wrong to speak to you that way. You did nothing wrong."

Samuel appeared to thaw incrementally in front her. "I shouldn't have meddled," he said, sliding a hand though his hair. "You asked me not to help them exchange letters, and I should have respected your feelings."

"No," Myfanwy replied, placing a hand over his heart. He was standing too close to her, and not touching him just felt wrong. Without pause, he put his hand over hers, covering it, making sure it didn't leave. "You were right to help them. They love each other. You saw that. Perhaps you understand love better than I do."

"I'm not so sure," Samuel said quietly. He began to caress her wrist, making little circles with his thumb that caused Myfanwy to almost lose her balance. "I... I..."

Myfanwy leaned in, almost willing the words to come out of him. A twinkle of gold caught her attention, and her attention veered to the pocket watch that was half lodged inside the front pocket of his waistcoat. Samuel followed her eye line.

Staring at the piece, he inflated his lungs, painting a calmer expression on his face. "We can discuss it later. Now isn't the time."

"Oh." Myfanwy couldn't hide her disappointment. She'd hoped he would tell her that he loved her again. Would he ever?

"We do need to hurry," he said, dropping his hand from hers. "I know you think it's too early, but I want to walk the pitch, check for divots and water. We need to account for all the advantages we can."

He said the last with something resembling a smile. Myfanwy tried to mirror it, but hers felt forced. There was still so much she needed to say to him. She wanted to wrap her arms around his neck and tell him that the family they had built over the past month was more than she'd ever hoped for. That living without him seemed untenable, and she'd been so upset that day not only over losing Jennifer—she was terrified of losing *him*. The idea of him moving on and playing cricket once more in some faraway county made Myfanwy want to cry until there were no tears left. So, in some sort of defense for her heart, she'd pushed him away, leaving him before he could leave her. It was silly and childish and hopelessly dramatic, but she hadn't been able to control her hurt.

At the end of the day, cricket might very well be a game about control, a game for the sophisticated man, with all its rules. But love wasn't a game. Love was messy and dizzying and surprising. And it was made for men and women, with all their foibles and complications.

And since true love never ended, there were no winners or

losers. No givers or takers. Just two people equally invested in the happiness of the other.

Perhaps…Myfanwy *did* understand love after all.

And then and there, in the doorway of her bedroom, she made a second vow to herself. That she would spend the rest of her life showing Samuel that she understood love and would leave no doubt in his mind that she loved him.

She wouldn't lock herself away in despair as his father had, blaming the world for her troubles. She would face them head-on. And she would never stand in the way of his dreams. If Samuel wanted to keep playing cricket, then Myfanwy would find a solution that worked for the both of them. As long as they had each other, everything else would fit into place.

"Why don't you go?" Myfanwy said suddenly, backing away from him. "I don't want to cut short your pre-match routine, and I hate to make you wait for me. I'll follow soon. I promise," she added when Samuel's expression grew more concerned. "I need to prepare properly to win this match, and I can't do that with you hurrying me before I even leave the house."

"I don't know," Samuel drawled. "I'd feel better if you were with me…"

Myfanwy stopped in her tracks, headed back to him, and, without a word, rose on her tiptoes and placed an earnest, achingly faithful kiss on his lips. Samuel was stunned at first, not shifting as she lingered, but soon life sparked inside him and he curled his arms around her securely, holding her against him in a crushing embrace. The kiss was slow and sultry, relieving and incredibly intimate, and when Myfanwy eventually ended it, she could see that it had done some work to repair the damage she'd callously created.

"I always feel better when I'm with you," she replied.

Samuel's countenance was more relaxed, the inner thoughts plaguing him seemingly subdued. He rubbed his thumb against her lip, fixating on her mouth with a wistful smile. "I was afraid that wasn't going to happen anymore."

Myfanwy smiled. "Would you believe me if I told you that there's so much more to come for you? For us?"

Finally, a true grin widened on his face. "A few months ago? No. But now?" He locked his gaze with hers. "Why not?"

Chapter Twenty-Nine

AFTER PUSHING SAMUEL out of her room, Myfanwy got to business, mindfully dressing herself for the day with the kind of reverence and attention that a knight might have used before a major battle. Although she was sick of being alone, she needed this time to settle herself, to visualize how she wanted the match to go and identify the ways to make it happen. She always did this before a match. It calmed her mind and body, somehow creating a harmonious state within.

She would win today. Myfanwy knew it with complete certainty. She would win for herself and her team, for Aaron and Annabelle, for Benny and Joe, and she would win for Samuel. Because she wasn't just playing for herself and the hopes of her future cricket club. She was playing for all the people who had believed in her and helped her along in this journey. She was playing for her family.

When that last thought settled comfortably in her mind, Myfanwy finally left her room. Aaron would have been mortified—it had taken her over sixty minutes to prepare. She'd been right to send the boys on their way. The poor child might have suffered apoplexy in the drawing room.

The house was quiet as Myfanwy ran down the stairs. Sarah must have taken Annabelle for a morning walk. She hoped the little girl enjoyed the match today. The plan was for her to come to the pitch later with Aunt Abigail.

Myfanwy stood in the foyer, twirling around, looking for signs of the butler. He always made a point to see everyone off when they left. "Benjamin?" she called. But only silence answered her.

No, not silence. Footsteps.

Myfanwy turned to the noise coming from the back of the house. They were a man's footsteps, hard and forthright, and she fully expected to see the butler come into view in seconds—however, when the true figure formed in front of her, she blanched.

"Mr. Holmes? What...what are you doing here?"

The gaming hall owner's crafty eyes danced as he sauntered closer, holding his walking stick. "Miss Myfanwy," he said casually, as if he called on her home once a week. "It's lovely to see you again. When I heard Samuel had already left for the match, I was worried that I was too late. I hurried over here as quickly as I could."

He didn't seem hurried. Harry Holmes looked as dashing and clear-eyed as ever at this morning hour. But everything about his casual manner set off a warning in her head.

"Where's Benjamin?" Myfanwy asked, attempting to mimic his nonchalant affectation. Slowly, she took miniscule steps toward the door. "Did he let you in?"

Harry nodded. "Of course. He...ah...understood that I wouldn't be turned away. I needed to see you."

Myfanwy inched to the door again. "I'm sorry, Mr. Holmes, this isn't a good time. I'm running late."

"I see that," he said affably. "And I have to say, I'm in full approval."

Myfanwy frowned. "I'm sorry, but I'm going to have to ask you to leave." She reached for the door handle, but Holmes's walking stick shot out, blocking her.

He tutted, his expression wickedly convivial. "I'm afraid I

can't let you do that."

"Why not?" Myfanwy replied. "What makes you think you can come into my home and tell me what I can and cannot do?"

Harry Holmes's smile curled from ear to ear. "Money, Miss Myfanwy," he said. "A great deal of money."

MYFANWY POUNDED ON her bedroom door so hard that she nicked a gash in her knuckle. A tiny trail of blood trickled down the wood. "You can't leave me in here forever!" she cried.

The bastard answered her with a warm laugh. "Oh, don't be so dramatic," he purred. "It's only for the afternoon, a few hours at most, and then someone will find you and the others, I'm sure."

The others. Holmes hadn't come alone. He'd brought along two of his henchmen, and they'd been tasked with rounding up everyone, including Gertie, Benjamin, Sarah, and Annabelle and locking them in some other corner of the house. Myfanwy didn't know where. She only knew that much because of the snippets of conversation she caught when Holmes had picked her up and dumped her in her room.

Myfanwy punched at the door again. "You are a vile creature. Doing all this over a silly game. I thought you were above this behavior, Mr. Holmes. I heard you were rich enough."

His chuckle cut into her like shards of glass. "Only a viscount's daughter would say something so stupid. One can never be rich enough. But just so you know, I'm not *that* vile. I *was* cheering for you. I like your energy, and on any other day, I would want you to win. But there's just so much damned money to grab if you lose. Everyone's betting on you and Sam and the single ladies. Your loss will fill my pockets quite nicely."

Myfanwy huffed. "The team can win with or without me. I'm not that special."

"Oh, that's true," he agreed readily. "But then I heard from a little bird that Miss Jennifer was also out. It seems that no one knows why; however, my sources have informed me that she's recently made a little trip to Gretna Green. Scotland is lovely this time of year. I can understand the appeal."

Appeal, indeed.

Holmes went on. "Maybe you alone wouldn't make much of a difference, but with Jennifer also missing...that creates a rather sizeable loss on your team. They can still play, but the odds would definitely be against them. It's too bad, really. I thought this would be the single girls' year."

Myfanwy laid her forehead against the door. Her knuckles were red and throbbing. Punching was fruitless; she was only hurting herself.

"Just take a nap," Holmes advised. "When you wake up, this will all be over. I'll leave the key downstairs to make it easy for everyone."

How could he sound so magnanimous? Like at the end of this villainy, he was still providing a favor? "Samuel will come for you," she seethed. "He'll never let you get away with this."

"Oh, I'm no idiot, Miss Myfanwy. I'm well aware of Samuel and what he might do." It was more difficult for her to hear him; Holmes must be walking away from the door, toward the stairs. "Caution him, will you? He'll listen to you. No good will come of his vengeance. I'll be more than ready for him. Have a good day, miss."

The slimy, foul miscreant! How could Holmes do this to her? He'd seemed so pleasant when she met him before! He'd spoken so warmly about her father.

What was she thinking? Holmes was a gambler at heart, and Lord knew what else. Just because he appeared respectable, that didn't mean he was. Harry Holmes would only ever think about Harry Holmes.

"Help me!" Myfanwy cried, hitting the door with her palms. "Please, someone, help me!" But it was a lost cause. There was no one to hear her. She couldn't even scream out her window. Harry's men had nailed the sash, jamming it shut.

Myfanwy was good and locked in. Alone. Tears flooded her eyes when she thought about her team. The ladies would be so confused—so furious. She couldn't bear thinking about how abandoned they would feel, how betrayed.

She slid down the door. After a while, she didn't know how long she'd sat there. Long enough to come to the realization that it wasn't possible to run out of tears. They just kept coming, like a bottomless bucket of misery.

Her sobs were so loud and graceless, she almost didn't hear the little patter of footsteps creeping down the hall.

"Sissy?" came a small, worried voice. "Where, Sissy?"

Annabelle! The bastards hadn't locked her up with the others after all. Myfanwy's heart broke for the child; she must be so worried and anxious as she wandered the house calling for—

Sissy?

Sister.

Calling for her older sister. Calling for Myfanwy.

She scrambled to her knees. "Annabelle! Annabelle, darling. It's me. It's Sissy. I'm locked in my room. Can you hear me?"

"Sissy? Sissy!" Annabelle cried, high voice growing louder as she ran to Myfanwy's door. The handle rattled. "Sissy, open!" the little girl ordered her in a panic.

"I can't, darling," Myfanwy replied evenly, trying to allay the girl's fear. "But you can help. I need you to find something for me. A key. I don't know where it is, but I think it's downstairs. Probably in the drawing room or library. Can you do that for me? Can you find it? It will be just like the game we always play."

A pause. Then a little *thump*, and Myfanwy could picture Annabelle folding her arms and dropping to the ground on her bottom, just the same as she did whenever she was frustrated with her older sister. "Sissy not nice. No key. Not a fun game."

Myfanwy closed her eyes, praying for patience. She knew all those times she'd sent Annabelle on wild goose chases would come back to haunt her. Served her right. "No, darling, there is a key. I promise. I'm not fooling you this time. And I won't ever again." Still, she heard no rustling on the other side. "Sissy wasn't good. You're right. Sissy wasn't fun, but she will be from now on. She'll play more, and she'll be the best big sister she can be."

It was small, but something shifted on the other side. The handle rattled again as if Annabelle was using it to rise back to her feet. "Sissy isn't bad. Sissy is a good sissy," the little girl said. "I love Sissy."

"And I love you too," Myfanwy choked out, having never known how important it was to hear Annabelle say those words. "I love you so much."

Hands clapped, and Annabelle jumped up and down. "A game. A game. A game."

"Yes, a game," Myfanwy replied, smiling despite her circumstances, wiping away her tears. "Find me the key and you win."

"Do I get dessert...with cherries?"

Myfanwy's laughter turned into a hiccup. "Darling, if you win, you can have cherries every day for the rest of your life."

Chapter Thirty

"STOP STALLING, EVERETT. We either start now or you forfeit. I'm not going to wait around all day for this nonsense."

Samuel looked up to see Lord *fucking* Cremly smiling at him in that unctuous, upper-class way of his, and he wanted nothing more than to unleash his frustration on the man's smarmy face. He reached for his pocket watch instead. The match was meant to start fifteen minutes ago. Even if she'd taken her time, Myfanwy still should have arrived long before that.

He couldn't believe it. He didn't want to. Could she have been lying to him? Had she really planned to not play without Jennifer?

Samuel stared at the nine women on his team dawdling uncertainly next to him, as bewildered and astonished as he that their match had started this way.

No. Myfanwy wouldn't do this to them. She might be hurting, but she would never put her feelings before all of theirs. She was the captain, and captains rose above such petty emotions.

Something must be wrong. Samuel should have trusted his instincts earlier. He never should have left without her. Myfanwy should be by his side. In life. In the match. It didn't matter. After this dreadful day was over, he would tell her that and not allow any arguments. He was tired of playing with her. He loved her, and that was that.

But he had to find her first. He turned back to Cremly. "I need more time. I have to go home and check on something. I'll be back in fifteen minutes. If I'm not, then you start without me."

"What?" Lady Everly cried, coming after him. "You want us to start two players down, without a captain or a coach? Don't tell me you're giving up on us too?"

"For Christ's sake, Jo. I'm not giving up," Samuel exclaimed, harsher than he intended. Jo didn't bat an eye to the outburst. She was made of sterner stuff. "You're the captain until then. Joe and Benny are here. I have to check on Myfanwy. Something isn't right."

Cremly let out an exasperated groan. "No. No more waiting. You start now or you forfeit. You can leave if you want, Everett. I'm sure the girls can lose just as easily without you here to watch."

Fuck, he hated that fucking man. Samuel kept his attention on Lady Everly. He could see the battle she waged. The lady knew something about being passed aside and humiliated, and he desperately hoped she would find some faith in him.

"I promise, I'll be back," he said.

Against her better judgment, Lady Everly relented. "Fine. But I'm giving you fifteen minutes. If you're not back with Myfanwy at that time, I will make the rest of your life a living hell. Do you understand me, Mr. Everett?"

He'd thought to laugh, but her pointed features stopped him. "I do—"

"I'm here. I'm here!" a high-pitched voice called out across the field. "Don't start without me!"

Samuel's heart leaped at the sound. And it wasn't only him. It felt like the entire team released a worried breath as they turned toward the frantic woman. But as the figure came closer, Samuel's stomach began to drop.

Jennifer.

It was Jennifer racing across the dewy grass, with Sir Bramble scrambling to keep up. She skidded to a halt in front of the group. "I'm sorry I'm late," she panted, her hair scattered down her shoulders. She hastened to pin it back in her bun while Sir Bramble watched adoringly, holding her bonnet.

For the first time, Samuel knew exactly how the poor bastard felt. He would gladly carry Myfanwy's reticule, parasol, hat, and gloves, if only she were next to him.

"We should have been back hours ago," Jennifer explained, fixing her bonnet on her head. "But there was rain, and everything took longer than it was supposed to. I'm sorry, but I'm here now."

The other women were demonstrably relieved by the little speech, but Samuel had to speak up. He had to make sure everyone was aware of the particulars. "Aren't you married?" he asked, switching his gaze between Jennifer and a red-faced Sir Bramble.

A few awkward coughs escaped from the others.

Jennifer lifted her chin to Samuel. He'd never seen the sweet girl act with such confidence before. He liked it. "I am," she replied, sharing a moony look with the baron. "Two days ago."

Samuel hated himself for what he had to say. "And you know this team is only for single ladies…which you are not."

A shadow of disappointment flashed across her face. She turned her nose up and looked away from him, losing some of her verve. "I'm aware of that," she replied. "I will leave it up to the team. As I've always said, we are a very democratic club. We will vote. If they want me to play, then I will; if they wish for me to cheer on the sidelines, then I will do that."

All eyes fell on Lady Everly. "Fine," she said helplessly. "All those in favor of Jennifer playing, raise your hand."

Six hands rose, including Joe's, Benny's, and Samuel's.

"What?" Benny asked when several of the ladies gawked at him. "I'm a part of this club too. I get a vote."

"It's a tie," Aaron said, coming up from behind Samuel's back.

A few grumbles and a round of hushed tones came from the group.

"No, it's not. I haven't voted yet."

Once more the team turned toward a new voice, and Samuel almost fell to his knees.

Myfanwy!

He could tell she'd been running. Her face was blotchy and covered in sweat, but she came to them slowly, almost timidly, with little Annabelle's hand in hers, as she glued her focus to Jennifer.

"Where the hell have you been?" Samuel roared, hauling Myfanwy and Annabelle into a giant bear hug. The little one squirmed out of the embrace to skip over to Aaron.

Thankfully, Myfanwy stayed put and nuzzled into his chest, whispering, "I'll tell you later. Now isn't the time. The only thing you have to know right now is that I love you. Truly and utterly, I am hopelessly in love with you and have been for most of my life. You think you changed, but you never did. I'm always loved the same man, and that was you."

Samuel closed his eyes, arching his neck so that his face pointed to the sky. She loved him. Yes. That *was* all he needed to know. Everything else could wait.

After a moment, he ducked his head into her neck, kissing the goosebumps that formed. "I love you too," he whispered. "So much. I always have."

Myfanwy lifted her head to catch his gaze. "I know," she said, smiling mischievously. "I wouldn't have undressed *any* man playing cricket. I was undressing my future. That made it perfectly acceptable."

Samuel chuckled, kissing Myfanwy's forehead. She gave him this short moment of bliss, where it seemed destiny was not only waiting for them but was already being lived.

However, when she eventually tapped him on the shoulder, prompting him to relax his hold, Samuel begrudgingly let her go. *Later,* he told himself. *Later.*

Myfanwy left him and walked up to Jennifer. The entire group became silent as if they were watching a clash between David and Goliath but weren't sure who was playing who.

Myfanwy struck first. "Congratulations," she said, swallowing before she could get the word out.

Jennifer regarded her warily. "You aren't…you aren't angry at me?"

Myfanwy shook her head. "No. I'm delighted for you."

"Really?"

Myfanwy sighed, shooting an imploring look Samuel's way. "Well, maybe not *ecstatically* delighted, but very, very delighted."

It took a second, but Jennifer answered with a smile. Her face formed it so easily that it seemed as if she'd been doing nothing but giggling the last few days. When Myfanwy did the same, Samuel realized that her smile fit just as easily. Because she had been happy with him, so very happy.

Jennifer looked over Myfanwy to her other teammates. "It seems you have the deciding vote," she pointed out. "Do you want me to play with you?"

"You're married now," Myfanwy said, her voice sounding odd and hollow. "Are you sure you even want to play with us?"

"You know I do," Jennifer said quickly. She dabbed a tear at the corner of her eye. "I love you all. You're my friends. I don't care if I'm married. I just want to play with you."

Myfanwy's eyes also became misty. Most of the players' eyes were. Hell, Joe was blubbering like a baby at Samuel's side.

"I wouldn't want to play with anyone else." Myfanwy turned around to speak to the group. "We might have started as the Single Ladies Club, but at our heart, we're a cricket club. And if any one of you want to make that rash decision and walk down the aisle, then you won't be penalized by me."

Samuel rolled his eyes. Myfanwy would remain Myfanwy to the end.

She went on, staring at Lady Everly, "We don't push people out of our club. We're family, and we'll be that way forever."

Even Lady Everly, tightly wound as she was, dashed something from her eye as she nodded at Myfanwy.

Leave it to Lord Cremly to ruin the lovely moment. "I thought we were here to play cricket! What the hell kind of a team are you running, Everett?"

Samuel angled his head to the bastard, shooting him the kind of a look that a smarter man would heed. "I'm running a winning team," he said casually. "And since you're in such a hurry to lose, I suppose we should get started. Ready, Cremly?"

⋙⋘

DAYS—EVEN MONTHS—LATER, THOSE who watched the match that day would continue to complain.

It wasn't an even match, they'd say.

Cremly hadn't prepared the matrons properly.

The singles drank some concoction that made them compete like the devil was in them.

But none of that changed the fact that the *mostly* single women had left the field that afternoon the undeniable victors, 279-42.

Even after it was found out much later that Miss Jennifer Hallett was, in fact, *not* single at the time of the match, it still was declared that she hadn't given her team a remarkable advantage. Being married hadn't changed her into a completely different person. Her play had been exemplary (as was customary), but she'd only scored forty-seven runs. Respectable, but not game changing.

Miss Myfanwy Wright, for her part, also had a remarkable game, though she was heard muttering angrily to anyone who would listen that she was disappointed that she hadn't hit a century. She did take seven wickets, though.

No, it was agreed that the single ladies routed the matrons so profoundly because every player contributed. No one was left out of the scoring; each played like their lives depended on it.

Sport, after all, was a great equalizer, and the Single Ladies

Cricket Club—nay, the newly named London Ladies Cricket Club—perfected the art of teamwork that day, moving like a well-oiled machine, determining each other's movements and idiosyncrasies like they'd known each other for years.

A wise man once said that practice makes perfect—this was true—but familiarity and respect were also heavy factors in the desired result. And no one who was watching the match that afternoon would have seen anything other than that from the single ladies.

They played perfectly. But that was only because they played as a unit. They played as a true team. A family, if you will.

Chapter Thirty-One

One month later

THE TOWNHOUSE WAS delightfully full.

Myfanwy would have never believed it, but Samuel's home was remarkably equipped to handle the crush. Since he wasn't one for decorating, she'd always assumed the interior would seem a tad aloof and remote until she'd put some effort into it. However, that wasn't the case. It only needed more people, and more laughter.

Suddenly, surrounded by her closest friends and family, Myfanwy felt the townhouse even homier and more domestic, and any errant thought that she should continue looking for her own flew swiftly out of her mind.

Even though if there was any day to ponder it, it was today.

Samuel was throwing his first ever dinner party in honor of Myfanwy's twenty-first birthday. The very day she would gain her majority—the day she was free to lead any life that she dreamed.

Staring at Samuel across the drawing room, where he was in deep conversation with Sir Bramble, Myfanwy couldn't call up those old dreams now. So much had changed in such a short period of time, and yet everything was still the same.

The only difference was that she *felt* different. Down to the marrow of her bones, Myfanwy was content, happy, blissfully in love, and still incredibly single.

Over the past month, Samuel hadn't appeared in any hurry to broach the subject of marriage, even though—for all intents and purposes—they behaved like a married couple. Not one night went by that Myfanwy didn't share his bed, and she had no intention of halting the habit anytime soon.

She blamed herself. She was more than aware that her previous opinions about marriage had, no doubt, scared the man off the idea, and she wasn't sure how to bring the idea to the table again.

Exchanging *I love you*s had become a nightly ritual, and that seemed to be enough for Samuel. Would it be enough for her?

A pang of longing hit Myfanwy as she caught Benny Hardcastle's eye and the man lumbered over to her, a glass of punch in his hand.

"I know I already said it, Miss Myfanwy, but happy birthday. I hope you're having a good enough time this evening."

"I am, Benny, thank you," she replied, inwardly shaking off the odd sensations threatening to choke the fun out of the night.

"Samuel wanted to have the party at the tavern, but I told him that wouldn't do. You deserved a more respectable place for your special day."

The man looked so proud of himself that Myfanwy couldn't help but laugh. "Thank you. I am glad you prodded Samuel in the proper direction."

"I'd do anything for him," Benny said wistfully, raising his glass toward Samuel. "Did you hear he got me a position as one of the coaches for the Players team? I couldn't believe it when he told me. I'm actually starting to come around to the idea that I might have a future with coaching."

"Well," Myfanwy replied, "I'm certain Samuel wouldn't want anyone to yell at him but you."

Benny smiled impishly. "You know I'll do a good job of it."

"I do," she said, patting his arm as he meandered back toward the refreshments.

Myfanwy had known it would only be a matter of time before the men's teams came sniffing for Samuel, after it got out that his leg was healing. Slowly, he began playing again—a match here, a match there—and finally he settled on playing for one of the smaller clubs outside the city.

He remained a professional, still not understanding why anyone would play without getting paid. Only the people who knew him best could see how his left eye altered his game, and that he'd lost a step or two when racing between the wickets. But, surprising everyone, Samuel didn't seem to mind. He played because he loved it. He especially enjoyed working with the younger players, helping to massage their potential. Myfanwy had no doubt that he would return to coaching again sooner or later. Cricket was something that he would never want to walk away from—even if it was on his own terms.

Myfanwy's fears of Samuel leaving them all behind were unfounded. Even while playing, he was still a vital member of the London Ladies Cricket Club. He'd even donated the field next to his tavern to the club permanently so that they would always have a place to meet and play. Although privacy was something of an issue. They'd made such a splash walloping the matrons that many came to watch their practices each week. Myfanwy and the ladies didn't mind much. The cheers and claps were always welcomed.

"That's not the expression I was hoping to see," a familiar voice said, cutting off Myfanwy's thoughts.

Samuel stood in front of her, grand and imposing, a gentleman of his house. She didn't think she'd ever seen him look so proud, so comfortable, even when thousands of people were screaming his name.

"What's wrong?" he asked.

Myfanwy's smile was gentle. "Nothing at all," she said, sweeping a long gaze around the room. "I'm just happy, I suppose."

"Content?"

"Very."

He lowered his head to her. "And nothing could make you more so?"

Myfanwy laughed, shaking her head. "I don't think so."

"Hmm," Samuel said, taking her hand. "That's not good enough."

Slicing through the crowd, he took her outside the drawing room. She tugged on him when he reached the stairs. "Samuel, we can't leave now," she argued, though she could already feel heat begin to rise inside her. Whenever he guided her upstairs, one inevitable thing happened. "We can't."

Samuel regarded her oddly, one side of his mouth up in a crooked smile. "But that's where your present is."

She rolled her eyes. "I'm sure I can wait until everyone leaves to have it," she answered dryly.

"But I don't want to wait."

Myfanwy glanced from side to side. "Contain yourself, Samuel."

"No. I don't want to contain myself. If you won't go to the bedroom, then I'll just have to do it right here."

"What?" Myfanwy squawked, twisting her neck to make sure no one was in listening distance. She retreated. "What are you—"

Samuel's grin transformed his whole face. Was one of his eyes truly white? Myfanwy couldn't tell anymore. When he smiled at her like that, all she saw was love.

He reached into his jacket pocket and took out—the brown cotton sack.

The tincture? Myfanwy had plenty enough as it was. Weeks ago, when Samuel had gone to the Lucky Fish to kill Harry Holmes, the men settled matters amicably by cutting a deal to go into the tonic business. Instead of beating each other to a pulp, they devised a way to begin selling the miracle muscle-relaxing tincture to the masses. They even elected Holly to run the business. The woman didn't have to worry about coins rattling in her dress anymore. She only dealt in paper money nowadays.

Myfanwy accepted the sack from Samuel, vaguely registering that his palms were sweaty.

"Thank you?" she replied awkwardly.

"Open it," he said.

"Oh, all right." Myfanwy slipped her hand inside the sack. The smooth glass of the tiny bottle wasn't to be found. Instead, she landed on a little box. A red box that fit easily in her palm. As Myfanwy opened the lid, Samuel sank to one knee. Without a grimace of pain to be seen.

"Samuel... I—" Myfanwy's words cut off. Inside the box was a beautiful gold ring with three sapphire stones at its center.

"I adore you," Samuel said. "You know that. I've told you enough. But, my love, I want you to be my wife. I want to spend my life with you. You're the one who showed me that I still had a future, and I will always be grateful, but that future will mean nothing unless you share it with me."

Her vision clouded with tears. But Samuel was so clear to her. His expression was wonderfully sincere and open. With one hand, she reached out to cup his cheek, and he held it instantly, kissing her palm.

Myfanwy couldn't form a sentence. "I don't... I..."

Samuel smiled bashfully. He took the box from her, taking the ring out. With great intention, he slid it onto her finger. "I've waited to do this. You have no idea how many times I dreamed of doing it. But it had to be today. It had to be on the day when you were given everything—your money, your freedom." He laid a reverent kiss on the ring as if he was a knight offering his service and loyalty. "I didn't want you to decide on a life with me until you had the world at your fingertips."

Myfanwy dropped to her knees, holding Samuel's face in her hands. She drowned him in kisses and vowed to do so for the rest of her life. "It was always you," she said against his lips, "from the very beginning. I only ever wanted you. Forever."

"Are you sure?" Samuel asked. "You can do anything in your life, and I'm asking you to spend it with me. Forever is a long time."

Myfanwy snuck another glance at her exquisite ring and hugged him with all her might. "Not when you're happy."

About the Author

I'm a lifelong reader of romance novels. Some of my earliest memories are of sneaking into my mom's room at night and stealing any books I could find.

After moving around quite a bit, I've finally put down roots in New England with my two sons and husband. I've always been a writer, starting out in newspapers, but it wasn't until my sons began going to school full-time that I began working toward my dream of becoming a romance author.

I enjoy crocheting toys for my kids, hiking with my Saint Bernard, and watching Real Housewives on the couch with my very old and very fat pugs.